Acclaim for the Work of DONALD E. WESTLAKE!

"Dark and delicious."
—*New York Times*

"Donald Westlake must be one of the best craftsmen now crafting stories."
—*George F. Will*

"Westlake is a national literary treasure."
—*Booklist*

"Westlake knows precisely how to grab a reader, draw him or her into the story, and then slowly tighten his grip until escape is impossible."
—*Washington Post Book World*

"Brilliant."
—*GQ*

"A wonderful read."
—*Playboy*

"Marvelous."
—*Entertainment Weekly*

"Tantalizing."
—*Wall Street Journal*

"A brilliant invention."
—*New York Review of Books*

"A tremendously skillful, smart writer."
—*Time Out New York*

"You're a prisoner?" she kept saying. "A convict? At the penitentiary?"

"Yes," I said, and went on with my story.

It took a while to tell, and by the time I was finished I was utterly weary and in despair. "Poor baby," she said, and cuddled my head against her bosom for consolation, and shortly after that we went to bed.

I woke up and it was still dark. But what time was it? I sat bolt upright and said, "Hey!"

"Mmf?" A sleepy form moved obscurely in the darkness next to me. "What?"

I remembered everything, I knew I had told the whole thing to this woman I didn't even know. But I didn't care about that now, I had a much more urgent problem. I said, "What time is it?"

"Um. Oom." Rustling and rattling. "Twenty after five."

"Holy Christ!" I shouted, and jumped out of bed. "I've got to get back to prison...!"

HELP
I Am Being Held
PRISONER

by **Donald E. Westlake**

A HARD CASE **HARD CASE CRIME** CRIME NOVEL

A HARD CASE CRIME BOOK
(HCC-132)
First Hard Case Crime edition: February 2018

Published by

Titan Books
A division of Titan Publishing Group Ltd
144 Southwark Street
London SE1 0UP

in collaboration with Winterfall LLC

Print edition ISBN 978-1-78565-682-8
E-book ISBN 978-1-78565-683-5

Design direction by Max Phillips
www.maxphillips.net

Typeset by Swordsmith Productions

The name "Hard Case Crime" and the Hard Case Crime logo are trademarks of Winterfall LLC. Hard Case Crime books are selected and edited by Charles Ardai.

Printed in the United States of America

Visit us on the web at www.HardCaseCrime.com

for Abby — the gentle jailer

HELP I AM BEING HELD PRISONER

1

Sometimes I think I'm good and sometimes I think I'm bad. I wish I could make up my mind, so I'd know what stance to take.

The first thing Warden Gadmore said to me was, "Basically, you're not a bad person, Kunt."

"Künt," I said quickly, pronouncing it the right way, as in koont. "With an umlaut," I explained.

"A what?"

"Umlaut." I poked two fingers into the air, as though blinding an invisible man. "Two dots over the U. It's a German name."

He frowned at my records. "Says here you were born in Rye, New York."

"Yes, sir," I said. Wry, New York.

"Makes you a U.S. citizen," he said, and peered at me through his wire-framed spectacles, challenging me to deny it.

"My parents came from Germany," I said. "In nineteen thirty-seven."

"But you were born right here." He bunk-bunked a fingertip on his desktop, as though to suggest I'd been born in this office, on that desk.

"I'm not denying American citizenship," I said.

"I should think not. Wouldn't do you any good if you did."

I felt the confusion was now coming to a natural end, and that nothing I said would be useful, so I remained silent. Warden Gadmore frowned at me a few seconds longer, apparently wanting to be sure I didn't have anything else contentious to say, and then lowered his head to study my records some more.

He had a round bald spot on the top of his head, like a small pancake on a dead hedgehog. It was a very serious head.

Everything here was serious: the warden, the office, the very fact of the prison itself. I relished seriousness now, I felt it was long overdue in my life. It seemed to me that jail was going to do me a lot of good.

The warden took a long time over my records. I spent a while reading his name on the brass nameplate on his desk: *Warden Eustace B. Gadmore.* Then I spent a further while looking around this small crowded office at the black filing cabinets and the photographs of government officials on the institutional green walls and the rather disordered Venetian blinds raised over the large window behind the desk. Gazing over the warden's bald spot and through that window I could see a kind of smallish garden out there, completely enclosed by stone walls. A fat old man in prison denim was at work in the gray November air, wrapping burlap around the shrubs bordering the garden. A narrow rectangular brick path separated shrubs and grass from the inner flower bed, at this time of year full of nothing but dead stalks. Next spring, I thought, I'll see those flowers bloom. It was, all in all, a comforting idea.

Warden Gadmore lifted his head. When he peered up at me through his glasses I could no longer see his bald spot. "We don't tolerate practical jokers here," he said.

"Yes, sir," I said.

Bunk-bunk; he prodded my records. "I don't find this amusing reading," he said.

"No, sir." Wanting to reassure him, I added, "I'm cured, sir."

"Cured?" He squinted, as though to hide his eyes from me behind his cheekbones. "You mean you used to be crazy?"

Was that what I meant? "Not exactly, sir," I said.

"There wasn't any insanity plea at the trial," he said.

"No, sir. I wasn't crazy."

"I don't know *what* you were," he said. Bunk-bunk. "You injured a number of people."

"Yes, sir."

"Including three children."

"Yes, sir." And two Congressmen, though neither of us mentioned that.

He frowned at me, squinted at me, strained toward me without quite moving from his seat. In his fussy way he was on my side; he wanted to understand me, so he could understand what was wrong with me, so he could fix it.

I said, "I've learned my lesson, sir. I want to be rehabilitated."

The guard standing back by the door, the one who had walked over with me from the Orientation Center where I had spent my first night here at Stonevelt Penitentiary, shifted his weight in his big black gunboat shoes, expressing by the creak of his movements his disdain and distrust. He'd heard that line before.

Bunk-bunk. Warden Gadmore gazed past me, thinking. I gazed past him, watching the old gardener outside, who was now calmly peeing on a shrub. Finished, he zipped himself and wrapped the same shrub in burlap. A warm winter.

"Against advice from several quarters…"

Startled, I refocused on Warden Gadmore, who was frowning at me again, waiting to capture my attention. "Yes, sir," I said.

"Against, as I say," he said, "advice from several quarters, I have decided to give you a work assignment here. I don't know if you appreciate what that means."

I looked alert and appreciative.

"It means," he said, looking very solemn, "that I'm giving you a break. Very few individuals prefer to sit around their cells all day with nothing to do, but we only have work for about half our inmates. New men usually have to prove themselves before they get a work assignment."

"Yes, sir," I said. "I see. Thank you."

"I'm taking a chance on you, Kunt," he said, pronouncing it wrong again, "because you don't fit any of our normal categories of prisoner." He began to check them off on his fingers, saying, "You aren't a professional criminal. You ar—"

"No, sir," I said.

"—en't a radical. You did—"

"No, sir."

"—n't, uh." He looked slightly exasperated. "You don't have to say, 'No, sir,' every time," he said.

"No, sir," I said, and immediately bit my lower lip. He looked down at my records again, as though he'd been reading from them aloud, though he hadn't been. "Where was I?"

"I'm not a radical," I suggested.

"Exactly." Nodding seriously at me, checking the items on his fingers again, he said, "You didn't commit a crime of passion. You aren't here because of drugs. You're not an embezzler or an income tax evader. None of our standard prisoner categories fits your case. In one way of looking at things, you aren't an actual criminal at all."

Which was true enough. What, after all, had I done? I had parked a car on the shoulder of the Long Island Expressway on a Sunday afternoon in early May. That, however, was an argument which had already been rejected at my trial, so I didn't pursue it now. I merely looked eager and innocent, ready to accept whatever decision Warden Gadmore might choose to make.

"So I'm assigning you," he said, "to license plates."

Vision of self adorned with license plates, fore and aft; obviously not what he meant. "Sir?"

He understood that I didn't understand. "We manufacture license plates here," he said.

"Ah."

"I'm assigning you," he said, sneaking another quick look at my records to see where he *was* assigning me, "to the packaging shop, where the plates are enveloped and boxed."

Solitude in a cell must be worse than I'd imagined. "Thank you, sir," I said.

Another look at my records. "You're eligible for parole," he told me, "in twenty-seven months."

"Yes, sir."

"If you're sincere about rehabilitation—"

"Oh, I am, sir."

"Obey our rules," he said. "Avoid bad companions. This could prove the most beneficial two years of your life."

"I believe that, sir."

He gave me a quick suspicious look. My eagerness was perhaps a little more fervent than he was used to. He chose not to press the point, though, but merely said, "Good luck, then, Kunt." (*With an umlaut*, I thought, but didn't say.) "If you behave yourself, I won't see you in this office again until you're discharged."

"Yes, sir."

He nodded past me at the guard, saying, "All right, Stoon." Then, looking down at his desk as though I'd already left his office, he closed the file of my records and tossed it into a half-full tray on the corner of his desk.

Prison etiquette requires that the guards hold the doors for the inmates. Pretending not to know that, moving quickly while pretending to move slowly, I reached the doorknob before Guard Stoon. The chewing gum I'd been packing motionless in my left cheek I quickly palmed while turning, and pressed it to the underside of the knob as I pulled the door open. It's a brand of gum which, so long as all the flavor hasn't been chewed out of it, remains semi-moist and gooey for half an hour or more after leaving the chewer's mouth.

I had opened the door, but Stoon gruffly gestured me to precede him. I did, knowing he would only be touching the knob on the other side while closing the door, and the two of us left the office building and headed across the hard dirt prison yard toward my new home.

2

My name is Harold Albert Chester Künt. I am thirty-two years old and unmarried, though three times in my early twenties I did propose marriage to girls I'd become emotionally involved with. All three rejected me, two with embarrassments and evasions that were in a way worse than the fact of the rejection itself. Only one was honest with me saying, "I'm sorry. I do love you, Harry, but I just can't see spending the rest of my life as Mrs. Kunt."

"Koont," I said. "With an umlaut." But it was no use.

I don't blame my parents. They're German, they know their name only as an ancient Germanic variation on the noun Kunst, which means art. They came to this country in 1937, Aryan anti-Nazis who emigrated not because they loved America but because they hated what had become of Germany. So far as possible, they have remained German from that day to this, living at first in Yorkville, which is the German section of Manhattan, and later in German neighborhoods in a number of smaller upstate towns. My father eventually learned to speak English almost as well as a native, but my mother is still more German than American. Neither of them has ever seemed aware of any undercover implications in the name we all share.

Well, I have. The wisecracks started when I was four years old—at least I don't remember any from further back than that—and they haven't stopped yet. I would have loved to change my name, but how could I explain such a move to my parents? I'm an only child, coming to them rather late in their lives, and I just couldn't hurt them that way. "When they die," I'd tell myself, but they're a long-lived pair; besides, thoughts like that put me in the position of wishing for my parents' death, which only made things worse.

I came to the early conclusion that my name was nothing more than a practical joke played on me by a rather sophomoric God. There wasn't any way I could get even with Him directly, of course, but much could be done against that God's wisecracking creatures here below. Over my life, much *has* been done.

The first practical joke I myself performed was in my eighth year, the victim being my second grade teacher, a woman with a rotten disposition and no heart, who regimented the children in her charge like a Marine Sergeant with a bunch of stockade misfits to contend with. She had a habit of sucking the eraser end of a pencil while thinking up some group punishment for a minor individual misdemeanor, and one day I gouged the gray-black eraser out of an ordinary yellow Ticonderoga pencil and replaced it with a gray-black dollop of dried dog manure carefully shaped to match. It took two days to infiltrate my loaded pencil onto her desk, but the time and planning and concentration were well worth it. Her expression when at last she put that pencil into her mouth was so glorious—she looked like a rumpled photograph of herself— that it kept the entire class happy for the rest of the school year, even without the array of frogs, thumbtacks, whoopee cushions, leaking pens, limburger cheese and dribble glasses which marched in the original eraser's wake. That woman flailed away at her students day after day like a drunk with the d.t.'s but it didn't matter. I was indefatigable.

And anonymous. I've read where Chairman Mao says the guerrilla is a fish who swims in the ocean of the populace, but I was already aware of that by the age of eight. The teacher invariably gave group punishments in response to my outrages, and I knew of several of my classmates who would have been happy to turn in the 'guilty' party if they'd had the chance, so I maintained absolute security. Besides, my activities weren't limited to authority figures; my classmates, too, spent much of that school year awash in molasses, sneezing powder, chewing gum and exploding light bulbs, and would have loved an opportunity to chat en masse with the originator of all the fun. But I was never caught, and only once did discovery even come close; that was when a group of three fellow students entered the boys' room while I was stretching Saran Wrap over the toilets. But I was a bright eight-year-old, and claimed to be taking the Saran Wrap off the toilets, having discovered it there just in time to avoid a nasty accident. I was congratulated on my narrow escape, and was not suspected.

So. In the second grade, the main elements of my life were already firmly established. My name would be an object of crass humor, but I would return the insult with humor just as crass but much more decisive. And I would do so anonymously.

Until, in my thirty-second year, I would leave a carefully painted naked female mannequin sprawled leggily on the hood of a parked Chevrolet Impala on the verge of the Long Island Expressway just west of the Grand Central Parkway interchange on a sunny afternoon in early May. Returning from a neighborhood bar forty-five minutes later, I would find that one result of my prank had been a seventeen-car collision in which twenty-some people were injured, including the three children referred to by Warden Gadmore, plus two members of the Congress of the United States and the unmarried young ladies who had been sharing their car with them.

Neither the warden nor I had mentioned those Congressmen, but they were the deciding factor. Even with the injured children I might have gotten off with a suspended sentence and a warning; the Congressmen got me five to fifteen in the state pen.

3

My first cellmate, who was also the man I would be replacing in the license plate shop, was named Peter Corse, a stout wheezing old man with watery eyes and dough-white skin and the general aspect of a potato. When I met him he was a very bitter man. "My name is Künt," I said. "With an umlaut." And he said, "Who pays for my upper plate?"

I said, "What?"

He opened his mouth, showing me a lower set of tiny teeth of such porcelain-white falseness that they looked as though he'd stolen them from a doll. Above were gums that looked like a mountain range after a forest fire. Thumping these gums with his doughy thumb he said, "Oo ays uh iss?"

"I'm sorry," I said. "I don't know what you're talking about." I was beginning to believe I'd been locked in a cell with a mental case, a big overweight dough-white old man who was crazy as a loon. Wasn't that unusual punishment? I looked back through the bars at the corridor, but of course Guard Stoon was already gone.

Corse had finally taken his thumb from his mouth. "My upper plate," he said in a fading whine. "Who pays for it?"

"I really don't know," I said.

He stumped around the small cell, complaining in a querulous voice, gesturing angrily with his big soft arms, and gradually I got the story. He had been in this prison thirty-seven years, for some unstated ancient crime, and now all at once he was being paroled, before he could chew. The prison dentist had taken away his teeth, but had so far replaced only half of them. In the outside world, who would pay for his new upper plate? How would he live? How would he chew?

He truly did have a problem. He didn't have a Social Security number, so far as he knew, and had never heard of Medicare until I mentioned it; would either of those pay his dental bills? He had no family or friends on the outside, no skills other than packaging license plates, nowhere to go and nothing to do. Even *with* his teeth his prospects would have been bleak.

He insisted they were pushing him out only because the prison was overcrowded, but I believed that what had happened to him was simply some horrible misapplication of man's humanity to man. I was convinced some official somewhere was delighted with himself for rescuing Peter Corse from oblivion and sending him out into the world again with no hope, no future, no family and no upper plate.

I did sympathize with him. I offered to write a letter for his signature to his Congressman—I couldn't write mine, he being one of the two in the accident that had brought me here— protesting the situation, but he refused. He came from that last generation of Americans who would rather die than ask anybody for anything, and he was determined to keep his toothless integrity to the end. He spent much of his time muttering and grumbling dark threats about how he would get back in here one way or another, but they didn't mean much. What could a man in his age and condition do, really?

We only had a week together, but in that time we became fairly good friends. It made him feel better to have somebody he could complain to, who would neither laugh nor ignore him. He also liked playing the role of the old pro, showing the new boy the ropes. He'd developed simple cleaning and storing rituals in his cell over the years to make life easier for himself, and I adopted them, every one. On the yard he introduced me to some of the other older cons, including the gardener I'd watched through Warden Gadmore's window. Butler, his name was, Andy Butler, and up close he had masses of thin white hair, a round nose, and a simple beautiful smile; I wasn't surprised when Corse told me Butler traditionally played Santa Claus in the prison Christmas pageant.

Corse also told me which cons to stay away from. There were three groups of tough guys on the yard that I should avoid, and there were also the Joy Boys. This last bunch never caused trouble on the yard, but they had made the shower room their personal territory on Mondays and Thursdays. "Never never take a shower on Monday or Thursday," Corse told me, and rolled his eyes when he said it.

At work, too, Corse was my Virgil. It was his job I was taking, and during the week which was his last and my first he showed me how it was done. It was a simple job, but satisfying in its way. I was to sit at a wooden table, with a stack of thin paper envelopes on my left and a stack of just-painted license plates on my right. In front of me I had a rubber stamp like a supermarket price marker and a stamp pad. I would take the top two plates from the stack, check them to be sure they were both the same number and that the paint job had been properly done, and then insert them together into an envelope. I would then adjust the rubber stamp to the same letter-number sequence as the license plates, wump it onto the stamp pad, wump it onto the envelope, and toss the package of plates and envelope onto the far side of the table in front of me, where a rawboned tattooed man named Joe Wheeler would check the number off on his packing list and put the plates into a cardboard carton, ready to be sealed up and shipped out to the Motor Vehicle Bureau in Albany.

There was a strangeness about the week I shared with Peter

Corse. He had been here thirty-seven years, prison had freeze-dried the juice and the life out of him—like a cancer victim frozen after death to await a cure—and now he was leaving. And I had arrived, to take over his cell and his job and his relationships with his old cronies. I'd been looking forward to the new life I'd lead in prison, but this was maybe going too far.

Corse always kept his lower plate in a glass of water under his bunk while he slept, and the night before he left I hid it in the foot of the bed. When he found it he would think he'd left it in his mouth last night, lost it in his sleep, and that it had traveled to the other end of the bed because of his movements while asleep.

Except that he didn't find it. I can't think why not, it wasn't hidden that well. He was frantic when he got out of bed, of course, but he was poking through his blankets when I left for my license plate job and I assumed he'd have his teeth back in his head in just a few minutes.

That night, however, when I transferred to his bunk, the lower plate was still there. That made me feel bad for a while—particularly because this was the kind of thing I was trying to stop doing—but after all half a set of teeth hadn't been that useful to him. He was better off starting from scratch than trying to suit a civilian upper plate to these institutional monstrosities.

4

After three weeks my job was changed. A guard named Fylax, who disliked me in a brooding sullen way, called me out of line after breakfast and told me not to report to the license plate shop any more, but to get over to the gym at ten o'clock. "You've got a new job," he said.

"Thanks."

"Don't thank me. A whole lot of us tried to talk the warden out of giving you anything at all."

I didn't understand that attitude; I hadn't done anything to anybody since I'd been here, except for Corse's teeth and the warden's doorknob and a little business with pepper in the mess hall on two occasions. Nothing that could be traced to me. Fylax had simply chosen to dislike me, that's all. Who all those others were who had talked against me to the warden I didn't know, but I suspected they existed principally in Fylax's mind.

Though maybe not. At the gym I had to report to a trusty named Phil Giffin, and he laid eyes on me. "I don't know where you think you get off," he said, giving me an angry look from under thick black brows. "This is a goddam plush job. It isn't for new fish, and it isn't for short timers, and it isn't for cons outside our own group."

I was all three, a new fish and a short timer and a con outside Giffin's own group. Looking apologetic, I said, "I'm sorry, I didn't ask to change. It just happened."

"It just happened." He stood frowning at me, a wiry narrow leathery man with a cigarette smoldering in the corner of his mouth, and I suddenly realized I'd seen him several times out on the yard. He belonged to one of the groups Corse had warned me against.

I said, "I'll ask for my old job back. I don't want to be in the way."

I found out later he'd been trying to decide whether or not breaking my legs would be the best way to solve the problem. If I were to spend two or three months in the hospital, his group could arrange for someone they approved to take my place here. But for reasons that had nothing to do with me and everything to do with not making himself and the gym overly noticeable, he finally shrugged and said, "Okay, Kunt, we'll try you out."

"Künt," I said. "With an umlaut."

But he had turned away, heading off across the gym floor, and I moved quickly to catch up with him.

There are monetary seasons of thaw and frost in institutions dependent on government funds. During a rich thaw ten or so years ago, this gymnasium had been constructed on a site formerly outside the prison walls. A number of lower middle class homes had been condemned, purchased by the state, razed, and the gym put up in their place, tied in at one end with the original prison wall. It was a huge structure containing three full basketball courts, a warren of offices and locker rooms and shower rooms, and an extensive supply area filled with sports equipment, but with no windows anywhere except in the wall facing the rest of the prison compound. It was like being in some converted nineteenth-century armory; I half expected show horses to appear, practicing their drill routine.

None did. However, the prison football team was doing calisthenics on one basketball court, dressed in sweatsuits and helmets, and two intraprison basketball squads were playing a non-league practice game on another. Giffin led me through all this activity, and I spent the time admiring the precision and persistence with which the basketball players fouled one another, tripping and kneeing, hooking fingers in waistbands, rabbit-punching wrists, and still finding time to take an occasional shot at the basket.

The supply area was where we were headed. A doorway with a shelf-top half door blocking it was the entrance, guarded by a sleepy-looking pale giant in prison denim, leaning on the shelf and poking at his teeth with what looked like a blunt needle but turned out to be the pin from a bicycle pump. His flesh was slightly pink, as though just barely sunburned, and his hair and eyebrows were so pale a yellow that they almost disappeared. Him too I had seen with that tough-guy group out on the yard.

The giant nodded at Giffin as we arrived, and pulled the half-door open to let us through. He glanced at me with lazy curiosity, and Giffin jabbed a thumb in my direction, saying, "This is a guy named Kunt. He got assigned here, believe it or not."

The giant gave me a look of humorous disbelief. "Your name is what?" He had a thin, high voice that reminded me of Peter Corse.

"Künt," I said. "With an umlaut."

"He's *working* here," Giffin said, emphasizing the word as though he were saying more to the giant than the simple word would ordinarily allow.

Apparently the giant got the message. He frowned at Giffin and said, "Oh, yeah?" It seemed to me that various non-verbal statements went back and forth between the two of them, little eye movements, head shakings, shoulder shrugs. At the end of them, the giant said, "That's gonna be a little complicated, Phil."

"We'll talk it over later," Giffin said. "In the meantime, put him to work on something."

"Right."

Giffin gave another shrug and head-dip, conveying another message to the giant, and went away. The giant went on studying me for a few seconds, continuing to poke at his teeth, and then took the pump pin out of his mouth to say, "What was that name again?"

"Künt," I said. "With an umlaut."

"Koont," he said, bless him. "Phil must of heard it wrong."

"I guess so. My first name's Harry."

He stuck a big pink hand out. "I'm Jerry Bogentrodder," he said.

"Glad to meet you," I said, and as his big hand closed around mine I was willing to bet that no one had ever played with the possibilities of *his* name.

He turned from me, looking speculatively back into the supply area, a maze of bins, shelves, aisles and storerooms. "Let's see," he said. "The football uniforms just come back from the laundry, you could sort them out."

"Certainly," I said, demonstrating eagerness to please.

He led the way back past bins of basketballs, shelves of bowling shoes, racks of baseball bats, rooms piled with stacks of bases, hoops, pucks, pins, pads, helmets, sticks, flags, ponchos and cans of white paint, to a small gray concrete room furnished with a large library table, several wooden chairs and a white canvas laundry cart. As with every other room in this area it was windowless, lit by fluorescent ceiling lights. In a way it was much more cell-like than my actual cell, which was furnished with two single Hollywood beds, two small dressers and two wooden chairs, and which had a nice view of the main yard through the iron mesh covering its window.

Jerry Bogentrodder pointed at the laundry cart. "You sort everything by number," he said. "Fold them all, stack them up nice. When you're done, come on up front again."

"Fine," I said.

He went away, and I went to work.

All football players have numbers, of course, but here at Stonevelt the inmates already had numbers in their roles as prisoners, so the same numbers were carried over to their football function. It was a bit strange to pick up a football jersey and see 7358648 emblazoned across the chest and again across the back. The pants had the number once, across the ass. On the jock it was printed on the waistband, and on each sock it formed a kind of design around the top.

This was a job not unlike the license plate factory, and also involving numbers. The time passed pleasantly enough as I folded and sorted and stacked, and it must have been an hour or more later when a short, skinny, shifty, weasel-eyed fellow in prison denim went by the doorway, paused to look in at me with quick suspicion, and then hurried on. I thought nothing of it, went on working with the laundry, tying an occasional sock in a knot, and five minutes later another one appeared.

This one, however, didn't just walk on by. He saw me, stopped, frowned, looked down the corridor toward the front of the supply area, looked at me, looked back the way he'd come, looked at me again, stepped into the doorway, and said, "Just who the fuck are you?"

"I work here," I said.

He didn't like that at all. "Since when?" he said. He was medium height, stocky, with heavy features and black hair and an aggressive manner. The backs of his hands were covered with rocklike bumps and black fur.

I said, "I just started today."

"Oh, yeah? Does Phil Giffin know about this?"

"He's the one who brought me here," I said.

He gave me a sharp, piercing look. "You sure of that?"

"Yes, sir," I said. He was a prisoner like me, so there was no reason to say 'sir' to him, but something about his manner called forth a respectful response.

With the same sharp piercing look he said, "What's your name, Jack?"

"Künt," I said. "With an umlaut."

"We'll see about this," he said, gave me a punching kind of nod as though to say I could consider myself dealt with, and marched away.

That was curious. I sorted and folded and stacked, and thought about things, and the more I thought the more it seemed to me something was going on.

An illicit poker game? That could be it, that would explain why the people in this section of the prison were so jealous of their area, so suspicious of strangers.

Could they have smuggled a woman in somehow? I could suddenly see her, spending her days and nights in a room full of duffel bags, living on food stolen from the mess hall, servicing a select clientele beneath the fluorescent lights. The sports section; yes, indeed.

No. A poker game was likelier, that or something else along the same lines.

All at once I wanted to know. I put down 4263511's jock, walked over to the doorway, leaned out, and looked up and down the corridor in both directions. Nobody in sight. To my left, the corridor led past several storerooms and locker rooms and a large communal shower to the main area of shelves and bins, and past that to the exit. To my right, the corridor ran perhaps ten feet, and stopped at a closed door.

That's where they had come from, the two men I'd seen. With another look over my shoulder toward the front, I moved cautiously on the balls of my feet to that door. An ordinary metal door, painted naval gray, with an ordinary brass knob. I pressed my ear to the cold metal, listened, heard nothing, looked back again, and very hesitantly reached out to touch the knob.

The door opened outward. I pulled it toward me an inch at a time, constantly listening ahead and looking back. My heart was thumping so heavily I could feel it in my wrists. I seemed to be blinking without letup.

With the door halfway open, I peeked around it, and saw nothing but the dark green backs of a row of metal stand-up lockers. Seven feet high, they formed a barrier wall that made it impossible to see anything else about the room.

Well, I still wanted to know, and I still heard nothing. Holding my breath, I stepped around the door and across the threshold, then pulled the door quietly shut behind me.

The room was perhaps twenty feet wide, with the door centered. The row of lockers left an aisle about three feet wide between themselves and the wall, stretching in both directions not quite all the way to the end.

For no particular reason, I chose to go to the right. I walked down there, silent, breathing shallowly, and at the end peeked cautiously around the last locker before finally walking around it completely and surveying the empty room.

Totally empty. This row of lockers faced an identical row of lockers standing against the opposite wall, about eight feet away. Two long wooden benches were bolted to the floor in the middle space. A dozen lockers on the door side had combination padlocks on them. Otherwise, there was nothing to see, nothing to explain what either of those men had been doing in here. Nor to explain everybody's tension at my presence.

I walked down the row of lockers to the group with padlocks. I pulled one experimentally, but it was solidly locked. A nearby one without a padlock opened readily enough, but showed me an empty metal interior with the standard shelf and hooks.

What in *hell* was going on? I turned around and around, trying to figure things out, and all at once one of the lockers against the rear wall opened and a man in civilian clothes stepped out. Short, fiftyish, sharp-faced, wearing a brown leather jacket and a cloth cap, he took one look at me and yanked a small wicked pistol out of his jacket pocket.

"Oh, my God!" I said, and fainted.

5

They locked me in a room full of bases while they decided what to do with me. That was Jerry Bogentrodder, the other two cons, and the man in civilian clothing who'd been in the locker. "We can unload the body," I heard one of them say as they closed the door. "That's no problem."

"We'll see what Phil has to say," Jerry Bogentrodder said, and I heard them all troop away down the corridor.

I still didn't know what I'd stumbled into, but of one thing I was sure: Peter Corse had been absolutely right when he'd told me to stay away from this bunch. I was sure I'd seen all of them in that same group with Phil Giffin, even the man in civvies, and if I'd had any choice I would absolutely have stayed away from them forever.

I sat on a stack of bases and brooded. If only I hadn't let my curiosity get the better of me. If only I hadn't been transferred from license plates. If only those Congressmen had gone to Atlantic City instead. If only I'd been born with a different name.

I was in there perhaps two hours before it occurred to me there might still be a chance to survive. It was *my* body they'd been talking about unloading. Did I want that? Of course not. Could I fight off four or five tough cons, one of them armed with a gun? Never. Could I survive despite that, despite everything? Maybe.

My potential salvation was due simply to my being a prisoner in a penitentiary. Since I was on work assignment right now, I wouldn't be subject to any sort of headcount until dinnertime, but the instant my cell-block lined up for dinner my absence would be noted. Where was Künt the last time anybody saw him? Over in the gym. Time for a search, then.

So. All I had to do was stay alive until dinnertime and the inevitable search. Then I would be found, I would report everything I'd seen and heard to the guards, and I would be safe. Relatively.

Safer, anyway, than if my body was in the process of being unloaded.

Well, if I was going to survive until dinnertime, the best thing to do would be separate myself from the tough guys. And the simplest way to do that was to bar the door.

Meaning these bases I was sitting on. About fifteen inches square and two inches high, they were made of tough gray canvas filled with dirt or some other lumpish heavy material, and they were normally put out on the yard during baseball games. This being November, off-season for baseball, they were all in here, twenty or more of them, heavy stolid things, stacked up along the wall.

It was a chore to move them, but well worth the effort. One at a time I lugged the bases over and plopped them down against the door. Let's see them open *that*, I thought.

My barrier was about waist-high when the door opened, *outward*, and Phil Giffin stood there looking at me, poised with a base in my arms. He gave my work a jaundiced look and said, "You expecting a flood?"

"Uh," I said.

"Get this shit out of the way, will you?"

The door opened the wrong way. With the base sagging in my arms I said, "You aren't going to kill me, are you?" I don't know why, but for some reason his face looked wrong for murder; he wouldn't be so exasperated if he meant to kill me.

"That's all I need," he said, "a disappearing con. Move this crap, so we can talk."

I moved it, hurrying. He leaned in the doorway till the pile was two bases high, then stepped over it and sat on a stack I'd made just to the left of the door. He took out a cigarette and lit it, and watched me move the rest of the bases out of the way. Then he said, "Shut the door. Sit down."

I shut the door. I sat down.

He considered me, critically. "Well, you don't look it," he said.

I didn't know what I didn't look, so I just sat there. "I did a quick run on your records," he said.

That surprised me. I hadn't been at Stonevelt long enough then to know that a disguised subculture of trusties actually ran the place at the day-to-day level, just as the subculture of career sergeants actually runs the Army. Giffin had merely gone to the trusty who was Warden Gadmore's filing clerk, had put in his request, and had been handed my records faster than if the request had come direct from the warden.

I felt sudden embarrassment. I had no idea what Giffin was in jail for, but I doubted it was for being a practical joker. I felt the awkwardness of the bush leaguer who has inadvertently annoyed the old pro. I said nothing, and looked contrite.

"I guess you're one of those baby-facers," he said, still studying me as though it was hard to believe his eyes. "Anyway, you must be tougher than you look, so I'll take a chance on you."

What in the name of God was he talking about? Then the wording of the indictment came back to me, the actual crimes with which I'd been charged, and it all became clear. The authorities hadn't been able to bring me to trial charged with putting a naked mannequin on my automobile hood, nor was being a habitual practical joker a felony, though I've occasionally heard people claim that it should be. The indictment had been specific yet vague: "grievous bodily harm," "malicious intent," "assault with attempt to injure," "felonious assault." I had been convicted of synonyms which had not quite fit my case.

The result was, Phil Giffin was now prepared provisionally to accept me as an equal. Of course, this decision of his was also prompted by his need to keep things quiet and not do anything that might draw official attention, but my misleading records certainly helped. If he had learned from those records that I was an untrustworthy and possibly unbalanced inveterate practical joker, he might have decided it was safer to let his friends unload the body after all, and brazen out the search that would follow.

A sheep in wolf's clothing, I was safe for the moment.

Giffin leaned closer to me. Smoke curled up over the harsh angles of his face from the cigarette hanging out of his mouth. Squinting from the smoke, he said, "I'm gonna tell you a story, Kunt."

I did not correct his pronunciation. I nodded.

"Back when this gym was first built," he said, "maybe fourteen years ago, there was a guy in here doing a five-and-dime, and it was a cousin of his wife's was one of the subcontractors. You follow me?"

I didn't, yet, but I nodded.

"So what happened was," Giffin said, "the wife of the con bought herself a house across the street from the gym, just past where they tore all the other old houses down. Then her cousin and a couple guys, they dug a tunnel across the street from the basement of the house right into the gym construction. You follow me?"

"He escaped," I said. And I was thinking that the tunnel must still exist, and Giffin and his friends must be organizing themselves into an escape attempt of their own. I had blundered into the middle of a group of desperate men planning a prison break, and I was God *damn* lucky those records of mine had painted me as black as they had.

But Giffin shook his head. "What," he said, "are you crazy? I already told you, this guy's doing a five-and-dime. How long's he gonna be in? Three years at the most, and he's out on parole. For that he should break out, put himself on the ten most wanted list?"

"Oh," I said. A five-and-dime; five- to ten-year prison term. "Then I don't follow you," I said.

"You got the picture of the tunnel?"

"I think so."

"Right," he said. "It goes from the basement, it crosses under the street, it comes over to the gym. Now this subcontractor, he's doing the concrete block on the outer walls, so what he does, he makes an extra wall in one section, so he's got a space like three feet wide between two walls that nobody knows anything about. And he puts in concrete block steps, and they lead down to the tunnel."

"The locker," I said.

"Right," he said. "There's three lockers across there that you can't open from the outside unless you got the key. You pull on them otherwise, they act like they're stuck. You know the way them kind of lockers slide sometimes."

I nodded.

"Behind those three," he said, "is the way in to the steps that go down to the tunnel."

"That's wonderful," I said. "But if this fellow didn't want to escape, what's the use of the tunnel?"

"You don't get it?"

"No," I said. "I don't get it."

Giffin leaned forward even closer, smoke curling into his eyes, and tapped me on the knee. "He used to go home for lunch," he said.

I gaped.

"That's right," he said. "Two, three times a week, the last fifteen months of his stretch, he'd go on home maybe ten o'clock in the morning, shtup the wife, eat a little pasta, watch the reruns on TV, say hello to the kids when they got home from school, then shlep on back over here for dinner headcount."

"That's beautiful," I said.

"That's just the word, Kunt," he said.

"Call me Harry," I said.

"Beautiful is the word, Harry." Giffin winked through his cigarette smoke, and finally leaned back. Sitting on the bases, legs spread a bit, hands on his knees, he said, "So now you got the idea."

I frowned. "Wait a minute," I said. "That was fourteen years ago. That man's been out for years and years."

"Well, sure. Whadaya think, that was him pulled down on you?"

I didn't know what I thought. I said, "There's people still using the tunnel?"

"Naturally." Giffin grinned a little, the cocky grin of a man on top of the heap. "A special few of us," he said. "We get ourselves assigned to sports supply, we work out a schedule of who goes when, and we take life the way we can get it."

"You get yourselves assigned?"

Another wink. "Some of us got a certain influence," he said.

The subculture of the trusties again, though I didn't know it yet. I said, "Then I wasn't supposed to be here, was I?"

"Up till now," he said, "we managed to keep strangers out of here, but for some reason the warden's got a bug up his ass about you. Usually when the warden wants to give somebody soft duty for a reward, and he's gonna send the guy here, our friends talk him out of it. If the con's an intellectual, we get him sent to the library instead. If he's an ordinary joe, we get him made a driver or maybe a messenger. But the warden's got this thing about how you should experience teamwork or something, see how people get along together in sports. Nobody could do a thing about it."

"I'm sorry," I said.

He shrugged. "Not your fault," he said. "We figured maybe we could keep you dumb on it, at least till we found out more about you, and maybe after a week or two we could unload you somewhere."

"You mean, kill me?"

"Shit, no. What's all this stuff about killing? We'd just plant a shiv under your bed before an inspection, something like that. Get you taken off privileges."

"Oh," I said.

"But the first thing that happens," he said, sounding disgusted in retrospect, "is you go poking your nose around and walk right into Eddie coming back." He shook his head. "I can't believe such a fuck-up."

"I kept seeing these guys go past my door," I said. "And you and Jerry Bogentrodder were both so mysterious, I thought there was a poker game going on back there."

"A poker game." He shook his head again, then sighed and slapped his palms down decisively on both knees. "Well, what the fuck," he said. "You're here, you seem okay, we'll take a chance on you."

"Thank you," I said.

"You keep your mouth shut and your nose clean," he said, "after a while we'll let you go for a little walk yourself."

"I appreciate that, Mr. Giffin," I said.

"Call me Phil," he said. Getting to his feet, he stuck his hand out for me to shake. "Welcome aboard, Harry," he said.

I stood. I took his hand. "Glad to be here, Phil," I said.

6

We were standing at the shelved half-door, Phil and I, looking out at basketball players practicing their lay-ups. In the last two weeks Phil had gotten steadily more friendly and open with me, based mostly, I think, on the fact that I'd never informed the authorities about the supply area's tunnel.

Well, why should I? There was nothing to be gained by informing, and everything to lose. In addition to the promise that someday soon I too would be able to use that tunnel, there was the pleasant safety of my association with Phil and his friends. I was now myself a part of one of those groups that Peter Corse had pointed out to me on the yard, was a member of the group whenever I was in public either on the yard or at the mess hall, and the reputation of the group was now my reputation as well. I could even take a shower on a Monday or a Thursday if I so desired; no Joy Boy would dare to lay a hand on me.

Now Phil and I were chatting casually about this and that when Eddie Troyn arrived, looking as foolishly neat as ever in his pressed prison denim. A onetime Army officer, Eddie had a passion for military neatness that tended to make him look like a dressed-up mannequin in a sporting goods store. He was the fellow I'd seen in civilian clothing my first day here.

"Hi, Eddie," I said. I'd gotten to know all seven of the tunnel insiders in the last two weeks, and they had all reluctantly gotten to know and accept me, though none of the others were quite as friendly as Phil Giffin and Jerry Bogentrodder.

"Hello, Harry," he said, and added, "thanks," when I pulled the half-door open for him to come in. "Going through," he told Phil, which was the shorthand they used with one another; meaning, of course, that he was taking the tunnel.

"I'll walk back with you," Phil said. To me he said, "See you in a minute."

"Right."

They walked away, disappearing amid the bins and shelves, and I watched the basketball players do their lay-ups. Figure eight, with the basket at the center. One man looped in from the right, received the ball, drove under the basket and did his shot, while another man looped in from the left, took the rebound, and passed it to the next man looping in from the right. The man from the right then proceeded on to the end of the line coming from the left, and the man from the left...

I was going to sleep. The damn thing was hypnotic; symmetrical, regular, flowing, easy, rhythmic...

I was going to sleep again. Looking around, I saw that Phil had left his cigarettes and matches on the half-door's shelf. I took a cigarette from the pack, took one paper match, and stuffed it head last into the cigarette. I used a second match to push it well in, so that when I was finished the match head was not quite an inch from the end of the cigarette. I tossed the other match away, shook half a dozen more cigarettes from the pack, put my doctored cigarette back, returned the other cigarettes in front of it, and put the cigarettes and matches back where they'd been on the shelf.

And all the while I was idly remembering what I'd been told by Phil about the tunnel. That original day tripper, a man named Vasacapa, had been unable to keep its existence totally a one-man secret. He'd been forced to let a few of the trusties in on it, and as a result the tunnel had multiple users from the very beginning. But no one who had ever used it was interested in escaping, nor in doing something foolish that would get them all caught. Either they were short timers like Vasacapa himself, or they were so high on the trusty ladder, with so many in-prison privileges and advantages, that they didn't want to risk losing their position.

During Vasacapa's last two months in prison, he had actually held down a part-time job in a local supermarket on the outside, as an assistant produce manager. Once he was a free man, he shifted to full-time employment in the same store, and of course he kept the house at the other end of the tunnel. His former fellow inmates continued to use the tunnel, and Vasacapa con-structed a private entrance from his driveway into the basement for them, so they could travel at any time they pleased without disturbing him or his family.

Three years ago Vasacapa had died, and his widow had decided to sell the house and go live with a married daughter in San Diego. Over the years, as each tunnel insider had finished his prison term, his place had been taken by another inmate, chosen by the insiders in a democratic vote; like a fraternity. When the widow informed the current insiders of her plans, they realized they couldn't let the house be sold to a stranger, yet no one of them had the cash—or credit—to buy the place him-self. So they pooled their resources and bought the house as a group. The wife of one of them—Bob Dombey, the shifty-eyed first man I'd seen coming from the locker room—had been brought up from Troy, New York to front the combine, had bought the house in her own name, and was now living in it.

The agreement was that the group owned the house, and that a member whose term was up and who left the prison gave up his share but was paid back his investment That had origi-nally been twenty-three hundred dollars per man; so that now whenever an insider left prison, the group gave him twenty-three hundred dollars, which it then got back from the man who took his place. If an insider died, which had happened twice so far (both times of natural causes), the new man still paid the twenty-three hundred dollars, which was sent without explanation to the deceased's next of kin.

My appearance had screwed up this well-oiled operation completely. The man I'd replaced, a professional arsonist out now on parole, had been paid his twenty-three hundred dollars, but the group couldn't ask me for the money unless they were willing to let me in as an equal partner, and none of them was at all sure that was the case. I'd been more or less shoved down their throats by the warden, and most of them resented it.

So they didn't know what the hell they were going to do. Nor did I. And in the meantime my only course was to wait, keep my mouth shut, and hope for the best.

If only I knew what was best. The idea of going through that tunnel of theirs once was very pleasant, very exciting; but the idea of becoming a part of this conspiracy was terrifying.

The whole situation raised yet again my old problem: was I good, or was I bad? A hardened professional criminal would simply join in with these commuters, pay his money, and live content within the bent rules. A truly honest man, interested in perfecting society and rehabilitating himself, would have gone to the warden and told him the full story at the first opportunity. But I, stuck somewhere between the two extremes, dithered, did nothing, and waited for circumstances to sort things out without my help.

Phil was away with Eddie Troyn for about ten minutes. When he came back, the basketball players were still making their infinity sign and I was still brooding about my prospects. Phil had Max Nolan with him, and he said, "Max can take over at the door here for a minute. Come on with me."

"Right," I said. "Hello, Max."

He nodded, neither friendly nor hostile. A muscular, thick-waisted man of about thirty, Max Nolan looked more like an outside agitator living near a university campus than a professional crook. He had thick brown hair, a bit longer than prison regulations allowed, and a bushy, drooping moustache, and he was serving ten-to-twenty for various kinds of grand larceny. In fact, Max had started out as a campus radical, had seen jail the first couple of times as a result of anti-war demonstrations, had moved on from there to drug busts for possession, and then had graduated to burglary and the use of stolen credit cards.

There's a funny double progression going on in prison these days, as more and more radicals arrive, sentenced for drugs or politics. The rebels are radicalizing the criminals, which is why there've been so many prison riots and strikes recently, but at the same time the crooks are criminalizing the radicals. A college graduate who enters prison for smoking marijuana or bombing an army recruiting office comes out knowing how to jimmy apartment doors and crack safes. A few years from now the world in general may be in for an unpleasant surprise.

Anyway, Max was one of this new breed, who had been at Stonevelt three years and managed to ingratiate himself early on with both establishments: the official one headed by the warden, and the unofficial one run by the trusties. "It's just like college," he told me once. "You brown-nose the teachers and buddy-buddy your roommate."

But he told me that when he knew me better. At this point he merely nodded when I said hello, and let it go at that. So I went away with Phil, who led me back to the locker room at the rear of the building, where I found three of the others waiting for us, sitting on the benches or lounging against the lockers.

I stopped dead when I saw them. Eddie Troyn, Joe Maslocki and Billy Glinn. Joe Maslocki was a former welterweight boxer in for manslaughter, a tough guy with a battered face and chunky body; he was the second returnee I'd seen that first day, the one I'd felt impelled to call "sir." Billy Glinn was simply a monster, a being designed for no purpose other than to destroy people with his bare hands. He wasn't quite as tall nor quite as wide as Jerry Bogentrodder, but he gave an impression of much more strength and much more viciousness. He seemed *denser* than most human beings somehow, as though he'd actually been born on some larger, heavier planet. Saturn, maybe.

I knew instantly that they'd decided what to do about the problem of me, and I stared hopefully into each face, trying to read what that decision had been. But there was nothing there; Billy Glinn looked like a monster killing machine as always, Joe Maslocki looked like a welterweight boxer between rounds, and Eddie Troyn looked as military and disapproving as ever.

When Phil tapped my arm I jumped as though he'd used a live wire instead of his finger. I stared at him, and he pointed, saying, "Put those on, Harry."

I looked where he was pointing, and saw a pile of civilian clothing on the nearer bench. Suddenly smiling, suddenly feeling wonderful, I said, "I'm going through, huh?"

"That's right," Phil said, and when I looked around at the faces I now could see they were all smiling. They'd accepted me.

The civvies were rumpled tan slacks, a green plaid flannel shirt, a green V-neck sweater with gaping holes in both armpits, and a reversible cloth zippered jacket, blue on one side and brown on the other. "That's the best we could do," Phil said, while I was putting the stuff on.

"It's fine," I told him. "Fine." And it was; anything that wasn't prison blue denim pants and prison blue cotton shirt was fine and more than fine.

I was reversing the reversible jacket, thinking my ensemble

called more for the brown side than the blue, when a sudden thought struck me. What if they'd made the other decision? What if in fact they hadn't really decided to accept me, but had decided to unload me instead? What better way to unload somebody than to walk him off the prison grounds, walk him directly to the shallow grave and then shoot him, or cut his throat, or have Billy Glinn reduce him to component parts?

I looked around again at their four faces, while I fumbled with the reversible jacket. It was true they were all smiling, but were those actually smiles of friendship? Was Phil Giffin's smile comradely or smug? Was Eddie Troyn's smile so strained only because it was unmilitary, or also because it was untrustworthy? Was that smear on Billy Glinn's face a grin of friendship or a leer of anticipation?

Phil said, "You ready, Harry?"

Christ, no, I wasn't ready. But what could I do? Plead with them, promise them eternal silence if they would only let me go? I would plant a shiv in my cell myself just before inspection. I would do whatever they wanted.

I blinked, licked my lips, was about to speak when Joe Maslocki said, "Really gets to you, don't it, Harry? Getting outside the wall."

Friendship; it couldn't be anything else. They'd accepted me. "That's the way I feel, all right," I said, and slipped on the jacket.

7

Through the looking glass. Through the locker.

It was a narrow squeeze through the locker doorway, but inside there was more room. Two side partitions and the back were gone, leaving a space the width of three lockers and about four feet deep—a rectangular opening through the fake inner wall to the rough concrete block surface of the actual exterior wall.

There was light, a dim bulb screwed into a simple porcelain fixture over our heads. Phil had gone ahead, and the other three were coming along behind me. Steps led steeply down to the left, concrete block steps flanked by tight concrete block walls, leaving a space no more than two feet wide. We descended eight steps to an area with the dimensions of a telephone booth. Phil knelt and crawled away into a large circular opening at floor level, so once again I followed.

Concrete pipe, drainpipe, about three feet across. More dim bulbs were spaced along the top at long intervals, and the curving bottom of the pipe was covered with carpeting. It was easy and smooth, traveling on all fours on soft broadloom; when they'd used the word "tunnel," I hadn't thought it would be like this.

Every so often, the color and texture of the carpet would change, and I finally realized these were remnants, strips left over after wall-to-wall carpeting had been installed. The subcontractor, Vasacapa's cousin-in-law, had apparently made his customers bear the cost of this construction; the concrete pipe, too, had surely been finagled from some other site.

After what seemed a very long time, I at last emerged into a long narrow corridor, again with carpeting on the floor. I stood up and moved to one side to let Joe Maslocki through, while at the same time I looked around at this new place.

The left wall was rough concrete, and so was the short wall behind me with the drainpipe hole in it. The right-hand wall was a framework of two-by-fours, with what looked like paneling attached to it on the other side. The corridor extended about fifteen feet to a flight of stairs going up.

"We never go out more than two at a time," Phil told me, while the others crawled out of the tunnel. "We'll go first."

"Fine," I said. I was feeling claustrophobic; first the tunnel and now this narrow corridor, filling up with tough and dangerous men.

Had they accepted me? Why should they; I wasn't one of their breed, any more than I was of honest men's breed. I was some sort of misfit, stuck forever in the middle. Or maybe not forever, not if I was in the process of delivering myself to some isolated place to be unloaded.

Once again paranoia touched me, and I peered at the faces crowded around mine. But it didn't do any good to stare; I could look at a man and he would seem amiable and friendly, and the next time I looked the exact same expression would seem tough and menacing. How can you ever know what's going on in people's heads?

"Come on," Phil said.

No choice. I followed him along the corridor and up the stairs. An ordinary wooden door on the left led out to the most beautiful mundanity: a gravel driveway, with weeds growing between the ruts. It was about two in the afternoon, a crisp, cloudy, late November day in upper New York State. The air was cold and clear, the pale gray cloud cover was low but not oppressive, with no suggestion of rain.

Phil and I walked down the driveway to the sidewalk. Ahead

of us, across the street, reared the anonymous high gray wall of the penitentiary. It looked like a sculptured impression of the clouded sky. I live behind that wall, I thought, and for once the idea of my forced retirement didn't please me.

At the sidewalk, Phil turned right and I went with him. The houses on this side, facing that heavy wall, were small single-family units, with tiny front yards and barely room for a driveway between houses. A working-class block, shabby but respectable blue-collar.

At the corner Phil and I turned again, away from the prison. Looking back, I saw Joe Maslocki and Billy Glinn coming out the driveway and going down the sidewalk in the opposite direction. I said to Phil, "Where we headed?"

"We'll just take a walk," Phil said.

We walked three blocks through the same kind of residential neighborhood before we reached a business street. For all that time, Phil seemed content to just stroll along and breathe the free air, and I did the same. When we got to the business street, we stopped in a luncheonette, Phil got us two coffees in a booth, and then he said, "Well, Harry, whadaya think?"

"I think it's beautiful," I said.

"You want in?"

Later I would have more than one occasion to give that question deep thought, but at the moment it was asked I considered none of the implications; such as, for instance, the criminal nature both of the act and of my new companions. I was outside the wall, it was as simple as that. "I want in," I said.

"There's maybe more to it than you know right now," he said. "I got to tell you that."

The tiniest of warning lights went on at the end of some cul-de-sac of my head, but I was looking the other way. "I don't care," I said. "Besides, what's the alternative?"

"You get yourself transferred out of the gym," he said. "Easy as that."

I managed a not-entirely-honest grin. "You mean you wouldn't unload me?"

He knew what I meant, and grinned back, "Nah," he said. "We talked it over, and you're okay. You'd keep your mouth shut."

My grin still shaky, I said, "I thought maybe you were bringing me out right now to unload me."

"What, on the street?" He shook his head, and his own smile turned hard. "No disappearances around that gym," he said. "No searches, no mysteries. If we figured we had to bump you, we'd do it right in the prison, a long way from the gym."

My throat was dry. "How?" I said, and swallowed. He shrugged. "You could fall off one of those upper tiers in the cell-block," he said. "You could get mixed up in somebody else's knife-fight out on the yard. We could get you transferred to a place with big machines."

That last one made me close my eyes. "All right," I said. "I get the idea."

When I opened my eyes again, he was giving me a quizzical grin. "You're a funny bird, Harry," he said. "Anyway, now's when you say whether or not you want to come in."

"I want to come in."

"Even though there's stuff I can't tell you in front." That was the second time he'd mentioned that. But what stuff could there be? Maybe I had to promise that if anybody else discovered the tunnel I would join in with the murdering. It was a promise I would definitely make and definitely not keep. What else could there be? I said, "It doesn't matter. I've been outside now, and I want to do it again. I'm with you."

His grin this time seemed to show relief; maybe his assurances about not unloading me if I'd chosen the other way hadn't been one hundred percent accurate. Maybe if I'd decided to transfer away from the gym I would have found myself working amid big machines.

The grin, though, whatever it meant, didn't last long; it was followed by a serious look, meaning that now we were going to get down to business. He said, "You got somebody holds your stash on the outside?"

All my money was held for me by my mother, which didn't seem the best thing to tell him, so I just said, "Sure."

He reached into a pocket and slid a dime across the table toward me. "There's a phone booth over there," he said. "Call your contact, collect. Tell him to send a check for twenty-three hundred bucks to Alice Dombey at two-twenty-nine Fair Harbor Street, Stonevelt, New York."

I repeated the name and address, and went to the phone booth.

My mother was home, and utterly bewildered. In her heavy German accent she said, "Horreld, you're out from prison?"

"Not exactly, Mama. What I'm doing is kind of a secret."

"You escaped from prison?"

"No, Mama. I'm still in prison. For another two or three years. Mama. Listen, Mama, can you keep a secret?"

"You doing another joke, Horreld?"

"Absolutely not, Mama. This is very serious. It is absolutely not a joke, and if you don't keep this secret I could wind up getting killed. I mean it, Mama, this time I'm dead on the level." I was immediately sorry I'd used that last phrase.

But apparently my sincerity had made an effect on my mother, because in a more normal tone she said, "You know I wouldn't tell a secret on you, Horreld."

"That's good, Mama, that's fine. Now listen—"

I told her what to do, to take the money out of our joint savings account and make up a money order and where to send it. She copied everything down, saying, "Ya, ya," the whole time, and when I was finished with my instructions she said, "Horreld, tell me the truth. Are you lying?"

This was the formula of truth between us, and had been since I was a little boy. Whenever she said, "Horreld, tell me the truth. Are you lying?" I then told her the absolute truth. She had never used the power lightly, and I had always taken it seriously. When two people are as close as mother and son, they have to find some method by which they can live together within one another's foibles, and this was the way we had chosen to permit us to live together inside the network of secrecy, fraud and double-dealing which is the natural dwelling place of the confirmed practical joker. So now I said, "I'm telling you the truth, Mama. I need the money for a secret reason that I can't tell you about. I'm still in prison, and if you tell anybody, even Papa, about my calling you or about you sending the money, I'll be in a lot of trouble with the law and also in a lot of trouble with some very tough people in the prison. I could get killed, Mama, and that's the truth."

"Okay, Horreld," she said. "I'll send the money."

"Thanks, Mama," I said, and went on to ask after Papa's health and how were things at the used-car lot which had been my last place of employment before my trial. She said, "A man came in and said there was sand in his gas tank, and Mr. Frizzell wants to know was that you."

"I'm afraid it was, Mama," I said, and on that note we ended the conversation.

Phil was waiting patiently in the booth. I gave him his dime back and said, "The money's on its way."

"Good." He gestured at my coffee. "You done?"

"Sure."

We left the luncheonette, strolled two blocks past clothing stores and appliance stores and five-and-tens, and then Phil pointed across the street and said, "I got to go to the bank."

"The bank?"

"I got an account there."

He said it as though it were the most natural thing in the world for a convict to have an account in a local bank. But of course it was, wasn't it? For this particular convict it was, anyway.

And for me, too. I felt as though my brain had been injected with Novocaine, which was slowly wearing off. Feeling, sensation, understanding were gradually coming to me. I was *outside the wall.*

And I was crossing the street, I saw, toward not one bank but two. On the right was a hulking gray stone Greek temple, with pillars and complicated cornices and all. Gold lettering on the windows said *Western National Bank.* On the left was a perfect study in contrasts, a four-story building that couldn't have been more than ten years old. The upper floors showed mostly wide office windows interspersed with red or green plastic panels, and the first floor contained a Woolworth's on one side and a bank on the other, both with large windows fronting on the street. The bank, called *Fiduciary Federal Trust* on its windows, was cheek by jowl with Western National and couldn't have been more different. Western National was as grim and tight as the prison I'd just come from, while Fiduciary Federal was wide open; through its big windows I could clearly see the open, airy, brightly lighted interior, with lines of customers and a sense of casual bustle.

Phil and I crossed the street and promptly bumped into one another as I angled toward Fiduciary Federal to find him angling toward Western National. "Oops," I said.

He pointed to the Greek temple. "That one," he said.

"Oh. I just took it for granted, uh…" I gestured toward the cheerful openness of Fiduciary Federal. It hadn't occurred to me Phil might choose the bank that looked like a prison.

"A couple of the other guys use that one," Phil said, as though that were some sort of explanation.

We went on into the bank. The inside was austere, echoing and high-ceilinged; more a Buddhist temple than a Greek, somehow. Phil took a check from his wallet, filled it out, and cashed it with a smiling girl teller who apparently knew him. They exchanged hellos and comments on the weather. Then he gestured to me, saying, "Here's a friend of mine, Harry Kent."

I almost corrected him. Then, in a blinding flash, what he had done blossomed in front of me. He had given me an alias! For the first time in my life, with utter justification, I could be somebody other than Harry Künt. With an umlaut.

She gave me a smile, saying, "How are you?"

I gave her a huge smile right back. "I'm just fine," I said. Oh, let my prison term never end, I was thinking. What did I care what they called me inside those walls; in this wonderful world outside I was Harry Kent. What a beautiful name, what a noble name! It sounded like something out of Shakespeare. *Harry of Kent awaits without, milord. Without what, varlet? Without his fucking umlaut, milord.*

When we left the bank, Phil said, "Had enough for one day, Harry?"

"No," I said.

He grinned at me. "Yeah, I know how you feel. You'd be surprised, after a while you get used to it. You get a turn to go out, you don't even do it."

"Never," I said.

"I used to say that. You'll see."

You never needed an alias as much as me, I thought, but I didn't argue the point.

8

When we got back, a committee of five was waiting for us in the room where I'd been folding the football uniforms my first day. Jerry Bogentrodder was there, looking big and pink and friendly, but with a black circle around his right eye. Billy Glinn was there, looking big and gray and deadly. Eddie Troyn the military man was there, and Bob Dombey, still with the same suspicious weasel expression as when I'd first seen him hurry past this doorway, and Joe Maslocki, the battered ex-welterweight. I assumed Max Nolan was still on duty out by the half-door, and with Phil and me that was the full complement of eight.

The five of them were sitting around the big wooden table in the middle of the room, and none of them seemed to have any expression at all on their faces. Phil, pulling another chair out to join them, said to Jerry, "What's the black stuff around your eye?"

"The goddamnedest thing," Jerry said. "I found a thing like a kid's telescope, and when I looked through it there was like this black paint or something on it. I can't get it off."

Phil had settled into a chair, and I had followed suit. It was amazing how nobody was looking directly at me.

"That's too bad, Jerry," Phil said. Then he jabbed a thumb toward me and said, casually, "Well, he's in." Suddenly everybody was grinning and shaking my hand, everybody was cheerful, everybody was telling me how glad they were to have me one of the crowd. The relief was patent on every face, even

Billy Glinn's. Yep, I would have been seeing those big machines all right.

The welcoming ceremonies finally wore themselves out, and Phil turned to Joe Maslocki and said, "Okay, Joe. Tell him about the robbery."

9

"Eep," I said. Then, when everybody looked at me, I said, "Frog in my throat," and pretended to cough. Billy Glinn whumped me on the back a little more than necessary.

Joe Maslocki waited impatiently for me to return to health. His bashed-in boxer's face looked earnest and impassioned, and when I finally got Billy to stop whumping me so I could give my attention elsewhere, Joe leaned across the table and said in a low voice throbbing with intensity, "You know what we got, Harry? We got the greatest alibi in the world!"

I looked at him.

He waved a tattooed arm to include our surroundings. "How could we commit no crime? We're in the big house."

"That's right," I said.

"Now, look," he said, and bunk-bunked his finger on the tabletop just the way Warden Gadmore had done to my records, except that the warden had done it while thinking things over, and Joe did it to make a point. "We're all gonna get outa here someday," he said. "When's the best time to pull a really big score, set ourselves up for life? Right now!"

"That's right," Jerry said, and there was a general murmur of assent.

"We been doing these little stings," Joe said, "but that ain't—"

I said, "Stings?"

"You know," Joe said, throwing it away, "little burglaries, nothings."

"Small scores," Phil explained to me, "to cover our expenses."

"Expenses," I said.

"The electric bill for the tunnel," Phil said. "Civilian clothes, things like that."

"And don't forget," Jerry told him, "Fylax and Muttgood."

"Right," Phil said. "We got two screws on the payroll."

So that was why Fylax had so patently disliked me. I said, "They know about the tunnel?"

"What, you crazy?" Phil shook his head and said, "They know we got action, that's all. They don't ask, we don't tell. We give them their salary and they mind their own business."

"Enough," Joe Maslocki said. "Harry can figure it out for himself. You got an operation like this, you're gonna have expenses."

"Well, sure," I said. I'm in a madhouse, I thought.

"So we cover the expenses," Joe said. "Naturally."

"Naturally," I said.

"But that's not what I'm talking about," he said. "Forget about copping TV sets and knocking over gas stations."

"Okay," I said. I was happy to.

"What I'm talking about," Joe said, "is a major score. I figure somewhere around a hundred, maybe a hundred fifty grand." He looked at Phil. "Am I right?"

"That's what we figure," Phil said.

They were all so calm, so businesslike. There was nothing to do but sit there and be just as calm. That, or run screaming from the room.

Joe said to Phil, "Did you show him the banks?"

"Just to look at. I didn't tell him anything."

"Okay." Still intense, plugging away like the welterweight infighter he used to be, Joe told me, "What we got out there is a couple banks you could knock over with a softball."

"Uh huh," I said.

"Maybe not quite that easy," Jerry said, grinning.

"It's a goddam easy couple of banks," Joe insisted. "And they're goddam full of money."

"You see," Phil told me, "this is a twice-a-month town."

Should I pretend that made sense? I smiled blankly.

"Most towns," Phil went on, "the people get paid once a week."

"On Friday," Joe Maslocki said.

Phil nodded. "But this town," he said, "only has two big employers, the prison and the Army base, and they both pay twice a month."

"The fifteenth," Joe said, "and the thirtieth."

"So that means twice as much folding money," Phil said, "every time somebody cashes their paycheck."

Joe, leaning passionately toward me, said, "You see the picture?"

"I think I do," I said.

"Just before the fifteenth," Phil said, "and just before the end of the month, the local banks get in a whole bunch of cash from out of town."

"Ah hah," I said.

He said, "At first we thought maybe we'd hit an armored car coming in. Eddie had a nice little scheme worked out for that."

"An ambush," Eddie Troyn said; the military man. "Counter-insurgent tactics," he said, and now I saw what his natural smile looked like. It was a simple baring of teeth, a curling back of the lips and widening of the mouth, and on a fully fleshed man it would have looked perfectly all right. But Eddie Troyn had no spare flesh at all, and the smile turned his normally bony face into a death's head. It suddenly occurred to me to wonder what this ex-military man had done to get himself reassigned to a penitentiary.

But Joe Maslocki wanted my attention. "That was small change," he said, pushing the idea away. "We want the whole thing. The whole thing."

"There's only four banks in town," Jerry told me. With a little grin he added, "Joe wanted to hit all four."

"We still could," Joe said, as taut and intense as ever. "We blow up City Hall for a diversion, knock out all four banks at once. There's eight of us, we could do it easy."

Eight of us. Including me.

"Logistically," Eddie Troyn said, "it's quite a challenge. But not impossible, no, not impossible." And he did his smile again.

Phil said, "But we'll settle for two. You're lucky, Harry, you got here just in time to climb on the gravy train."

"Yeah," I said. I smiled or something.

He said, "You can see why I couldn't tell you before you were definitely in."

"Oh, sure," I said. "Certainly."

"We've got three weeks," Joe said.

I said, "Three weeks?" Fortunately, one of the things a practical joker learns early in life is how to hide his reactions. I don't believe I jumped more than half an inch off the chair, and I covered that movement by pretending to shift to a new position.

Joe was explaining the timetable. "We got Christmas coming," he said. "That's when people spend money. We not only got paychecks getting cashed, we also got Christmas clubs, and we got people taking money out of savings accounts."

Phil said, "There'll be more cash than ever, the middle of December."

"So that's when we do it," Joe said.

Phil gave me a big grin. "Some Christmas present, huh, Harry?"

10

The next night, I went out by myself to do a little sting.

I had thought it would only be possible to get out during the daytime, but it seemed I was wrong. The gym was open every evening, for basketball and calisthenics and so on, which meant one or more prisoners had to be on duty during that time in the supply area. Activities in the gym, particularly inter-block league basketball games, frequently ran as late as ten-thirty or eleven o'clock, and some early member of the tunnel brigade had talked the prison authorities into believing it could take two hours or more to finish the clean-up after everyone else had left. So bunks were put into the supply area, and the night-workers were simply locked into the gym after everybody else had left.

It all meshed very well. Since men on work assignment were only subject to two headcounts a day, at breakfast and at dinner, this meant we tunnel people could spend all day or all night on the outside. It would be possible to leave around nine in the morning and return by five-thirty, or to leave at about eight in the evening and not come back until six-thirty the next morning. The only limitations were that somebody had to be in the gym at all times to mind the store, but other than that the prison could be more or less reduced to a diner at which one ate two meals a day.

All of which was lovely. But items like stings and bank rob-beries were less nice. So it was with mixed emotions that I went crawling out through the tunnel alone at eleven that night, to do my first sting.

They'd all given me advice. "Don't hit anything too close to the prison," Bob Dombey had told me; but it was his wife Alice who lived in the house at the end of the tunnel, so I believe he was thinking more in terms of his neighborhood than the prison. Joe Maslocki said, "Swipe a car, use it to pull your job, then leave it right back where you got it. These hicks won't even know it was gone." "Don't hit the Shell station out by the highway entrance," Max Nolan told me. "The night guy there's a cowboy. He packs a gun, he's just crazy enough to blow your head off."

I thanked everybody, assured Max I wouldn't hit the Shell station, and went crawling slowly away through the tunnel. There was a great temptation just to lie down on the carpeting midway and not worry about anything anymore, but I kept moving ahead, and eventually emerged in the dim light of the Dombey basement. Bob was spending the night at home tonight, and I could hear the sound of television from upstairs; Bob and Alice, spending a cozy evening before the tube.

I left the house and walked aimlessly away, following the same route I'd taken with Phil yesterday, strolling along, trying to figure out what to do. I had so many problems I couldn't make up my mind which one to think about first.

There was the robbery, of course, coming up in less than three weeks; Tuesday, December 14th was the target date. And there was the more immediate problem of this alleged sting I was on.

I was going to have to show something for my night's work; but what? I owed Phil four dollars, Jerry seven, and Max three-fifty. I didn't have a penny to my name, and no way to get anything. And I certainly wouldn't actually commit any robberies, no matter what cute slang names they went by.

The problem with money was that the prison authorities didn't permit anybody to have cash. If a friend or relative sent a few dollars to an inmate, that money was impounded and the inmate was given an equivalent credit at the small store in Cell-block D which was the only legitimate place where money could be spent. Stationery and stamps, razor blades, chewing gum, paperback books, things like that. The idea of running things that way was to cut down on thievery inside the prison and also to cut down on contraband (drugs, homemade alcohol, pornographic pictures) by keeping the prisoners too stony broke to be able to buy anything on the banned list. There was some cash around the place, of course, despite the injunction against it, but I hadn't as yet found a way to get hold of any of it.

My own money, about three thousand dollars in savings now that I'd paid the twenty-three hundred for my share of the Dombey house, was all in a bank in Rye. There was no way on earth to get at it now, at eleven o'clock at night, five hundred miles to the south. And even if there were a way for my mother to get hold of it, how could she send it to me? Send it to the prison and it would be impounded, and I had no address on the outside. Letters sent to General Delivery can only be claimed by people showing proper identification, and that was something else I didn't have.

Besides which, come to think of it, I couldn't call my mother in the first place. True I could make the call collect, but first I'd have to have a dime so I could reach the operator.

My wandering had taken me to the business street where I'd been yesterday with Phil. A few cars drove by, but I saw no pedestrians. Looking around, trudging along in the cold air, I saw again those two banks next door to one another across the street. "A couple banks you could knock over with a softball," Joe had called them. The gray stone Greek temple facade of Western National looked more solid and forbidding than ever at night, particularly with the pair of gold-colored metal doors ten feet high filling the space between the two middle pillars where the main entrance was by day. It didn't look like a building you could hurt very much with a softball.

Fiduciary Federal next door was a different story. Although closed and empty, it was as bright as day inside. Through the wide windows the canary yellow walls could be seen in the glare of huge fluorescent ceiling fixtures. From across the street I could make out the pens chained to the desks. A softball might conceivably get us into that place, but it would be like breaking into a goldfish bowl.

The whole idea was impossible, that was obvious on the face of it. Breaking into either of those banks was absurd; breaking into them both simultaneously was lunatic.

The question was, whether or not my new comrades would go ahead and try it anyway. And if they did, would I be with them when they were caught.

A virus, I thought. I'll catch a virus two days before the robbery, I'll be bedridden but noble. "That's all right," I'll say. "Go on without me. Split up my share among the rest of you, I don't mind."

Did I see me getting away with that? I did not.

As I stood there looking at the two banks, a car pulled up over there, a maroon Chevrolet, and a man in a gray overcoat got out. He was carrying something soft and black in his hand, a small black bag. He went up to the front of Western National, just to the left of the door, then walked back to his car without the bag, got in, and drove away.

Hm.

Watching the car depart, I saw that a block or so away a movie theater was letting out after the final show of the evening. Perhaps thirty people were emptying out onto the sidewalk, turning their coat collars up, talking together, spreading out and away in various directions. Looking at them, I suddenly realized I was cold. I was still in the borrowed civilian clothing, with only the reversible jacket, and up till now I'd been too worried and distracted to think about the fact that it was colder out now than yesterday afternoon, and that this jacket was nowhere near enough protection.

God *damn*, I was cold! I didn't even have a coat collar to turn up, like those people walking in my direction.

I had a sudden frightening thought. I'm a suspicious character, I thought, visualizing myself as I must look to those people coming toward me: a loner, shabbily dressed, scuffling around in the middle of the night with no apparent destination in mind. And in a town dominated by a state penitentiary. They'll think I'm an escaped prisoner, I thought. (It was only later it occurred to me that technically I *was* an escaped prisoner.)

There were perhaps a dozen people coming my way along the sidewalk. I dithered, trying to decide whether to walk boldly toward them or to turn tail and run, and in the end did neither. The people approached, mostly couples, mostly young, and all at once I knew how to keep them from thinking I was an escapee; I would disguise myself as a bum.

The first couple approached. I shambled up to them, my head down, my hands in my jacket pockets. "Buddy," I mumbled, "you got a dime for a cuppa coffee?"

He already had a quarter in his hand. He was embarrassed at being tapped in the presence of his girlfriend, and he already had the quarter in his hand, the quicker to get rid of me. "Here," he said, brusque but falsetto, shoved the quarter into the palm I hastily pulled from my pocket, and hurried on, his arm around his girl's shoulders.

I was astounded. He'd already had the quarter in his hand! He'd known I was a panhandler before I did!

The next couple ignored me. An older couple gave me a dime. A pair of middle-aged ladies hurried past. A fortyish man in a leather jacket grumblingly told me to go fuck myself. The next couple gave me a quarter. The final couple, mid-twenties, full of high good spirits, stopped to chat. "You want to be careful in this neighborhood," the male said, reaching into his pocket. "The cops can get tough around here."

What a thought; first time out on my own and get picked up for begging. "Thanks," I said. "I'll move on."

The girl, sympathetic but too cheerful in her own life to really give much of a damn, said, "You ought to go to the Salvation Army or somewhere. Ask people to help you."

Advice, Ambrose Bierce said, *is the smallest current coin.* "I'll do that," I said. "Thanks a lot."

The man had finally come up with some coins, which he pressed into my hand as though they were a message to be taken through the lines. "Good luck, fella," he said.

I was beginning to hate them. My misfortune was merely capping their perfect day. ("And," I could hear them telling one another later, in bed, after a perfect copulation, "we helped a bum.") "Thanks," I said, for the third time, and after they walked on I opened my hand to look at a dime and two nickels. I'd been given a lot of valuable advice, and twenty cents.

Which meant a total of eighty cents. I was both elated and depressed, as I walked off with the coins jingling in my jacket pocket. Half a minute ago I'd had nothing, and now I had enough to call my mother *and* have a cup of coffee *and* have a pastry or something with it. On the other hand, eighty cents was still a far cry from the kind of money the boys back in the gym were expecting to see. (It was also depressing that my bum imitation had been so thoroughly effective.)

As I walked along, it seemed to me the advice I'd been given had probably been worthwhile. Business streets would tend to be more thoroughly patrolled by the police after dark, and loitering strangers in such areas would be more likely to be picked up for questioning. Since I couldn't think of a single question I could possibly be asked that I would be willing or able to answer, I made a right turn at the next intersection, and moved away into a residential area again.

But this wasn't doing me any good. I was cold and moneyless, and I wanted to solve both problems, rapidly, without getting into worse trouble than I already had.

Not too many years ago I could have solved both problems by sending a telegram to my mother asking her to wire me some money, and I could have waited in the warm all-night Western Union office for the couple of hours until the money arrived. But that was back in the days when there was such a thing as a telegram. I know there's still a company around called Western Union, but God knows how they make their money these days—not with telegraphy.

I walked two blocks in semi-darkness, traveling from street-light to streetlight, looking at the small houses on either side. It was a weeknight, and most of the windows were dark, the good citizens already in bed, resting mind and body for the honest labor of tomorrow. I could have been like them, asleep now in a conjugal bed in Rye, next to a practical and faithful yet extremely attractive wife. With a sense of wistful envy I looked at the lawns, the driveways, the slanted roofs, the curtained windows. On the open porches were toys, chairs, milk boxes, bicycles. I might steal a bicycle; I could travel faster, and the pedaling would warm me. But I wasn't a thief, I had never stolen anything in my life.

At the second intersection, I saw some sort of open business establishment at some distance down to my left. Walking that way, I finally saw that it was a diner on a corner, with three cars parked out front. I started to enter, then noticed that one of the three was a police prowl car. I hesitated, almost left, and decided the hell with it. I could enter, couldn't I? I had money, didn't I?

Two uniformed cops were sitting at the counter chatting with a heavyset blonde waitress. At the other end of the counter a man in a shabby brown suit was eating a full meal; a salesman, probably, passing through. A young couple in a booth were having an intense, impassioned, embittered, nearly silent argument; whispering and muttering at one another, making constricted hand gestures, eyes blazing as each one tried to hammer a point across.

I took a booth far from the cops and the quarrelers, picked up the menu from between the sugar and the napkin dispenser, and looked to see what my eighty cents would buy me. And abruptly into my mind came the memory of a newspaper report I'd read years ago, a stunt a fellow had pulled that I had approved of completely. It had been very much in the practical joker line, but since it had been done for money I had never tried the same thing myself. Could I make it work? Was it already too late at night?

The waitress came over: huge-busted, dressed in white. She had been chipper and carefree with the cops, but was noncommittal with me. "You ready to order?"

"Oh. Ah…" Another quick look at the menu, a typewritten sheet of paper in a clear plastic holder. "Coffee," I said. "And the clam chowder."

"Manhattan or New England?"

"Uh…New England."

"Cup or bowl?"

All these decisions. I looked at the menu again, at the comparative prices for a cup or bowl of chowder, and the cost decided me. "Cup," I said. That would leave me with fifteen cents; I might even have a doughnut for dessert.

She was about to leave. I said, "Would you have a felt-tip pen I could borrow?"

"A what?"

"You know; the kind of pen with the soft tip."

"Oh, those damn things," she said. "They don't go through the carbon paper."

"That's right."

"Yeah, I think there's one in the cash register."

"Thanks."

She went away, came back with my coffee and a black felt-tip pen, and went away again. The table had already been set for two, facing one another, so I reached across to the other setting, pushed the silverware out of the way, and took the paper place mat. I folded it in half with the diner name inside, and carefully lettered my sign on the white back:

CLOSED

FOR REPAIRS

USE BOX

Below that I drew an arrow pointing straight down. I made the letters as thick and even and official-looking as possible, and drew the arrow blunt and solid, for that no-nonsense effect.

The waitress brought my clam chowder while I was still printing. She pursed her lips when she saw what had been done to the other place mat, and wordlessly gathered up the extra silverware before I did something terrible to *that*. She marched it away to safety, and when she came back a third time, with a plate of crackers, I gave her the pen and once more tonight said, "Thank you."

"Any time," she said, though without much conviction, and went off to be chummy with the cops again.

Hot food. It was delicious. While I ate I thought about this scheme and tried to decide what I would do if it didn't work, which it probably wouldn't. I had planned on calling my mother, but what did I have to say to her? I still had no way for her to send me money, and even if I did it wasn't a solution to the problem of tonight.

The salesman walked slowly by, burping, popping Tums into his mouth. He paid the waitress and I heard him say to the cops, "What's the weather up north?"

"Cold," one of them said.

The salesman expressed gratitude for that news, and left.

When I finished eating I carefully reversed the contents of the sugar canister and salt shaker. Then, just as carefully, I rolled my homemade note to keep it from creasing, and put it in my shirt pocket, where it stuck up almost as high as my collar. I kept it in place by zipping up my jacket, took my eighty cents out of my pocket, and left the excess fifteen cents as a tip, mostly because of the place mat. Then I walked down to the group at the other end of the counter, gave the sixty-five cents to the waitress under the incurious glances of the two cops, and left.

It was a brisk walk back, retracing my steps through the residential area. Half a block from the business street I tiptoed silently up onto a front porch, opened the milk box there, and took out the four empties I found inside. Then I carried the box away with me, and hurried on downtown.

The banks were two blocks to the left, on the other side. There was no traffic at all now, which for my purposes was both good and bad. I wanted privacy, but I also needed customers, who might not be forthcoming at eleven-thirty at night in a small town in the middle of the week.

I considered both banks, and the gray stone monolith of Western National seemed somehow better suited architecturally to my milk box, which was a steel-colored metal cube with a lidded top plus thick sides for insulation. I put it on the side-walk under the night deposit slot, took the note from my pocket, unrolled it, and tried to find some way to attach it to the building. I should have asked the waitress for some Scotch tape.

Then the simple solution came to me: I opened the night deposit slot, slid the back half of the place mat into it, and closed the slot again with the note hanging out. Stepping back near the curb, I surveyed my handiwork and decided it wouldn't fool anybody.

But it was all I had; and in any case I shouldn't hang around here, admiring my work. Checking both ways, still seeing no traffic and no pedestrians. I hurried off, and had gone nearly a block before I began wondering where I was going.

Nowhere. With no more money, I couldn't go back to the diner. The air was getting steadily colder, so I couldn't stay out-side. There was nobody around for me to try with my panhandler imitation. I did see an open bar up ahead, but I was afraid to go in there with no cash to spend.

So I went back to the Dombey house. The lights were out, so Bob and Alice had gone to bed. Vaguely, to distract myself, I tried to work up some prurient thoughts about that, an inmate outside the prison and in bed with a woman, but it was impos-sible. I hadn't met Alice Dombey, but I'd met her husband, the first man I'd seen passing the laundry-room door, the hunch-shouldered skinny one with the shifty weasel expression, and there was just no way to fantasize him married to a sex symbol.

I went through the side door and downstairs to the corridor Vasacapa had constructed. The twenty-five watt bulb burned dimly in the ceiling. There was no radiator in here, but some heat did seep through from the rest of the house. I sat down on the carpeting, leaned my head against the paneled wall, and gave myself over to brooding thoughts.

And sleep. I don't quite know how it happened, but the next thing I knew I was lying on my side, all curled up, and I'd been sound asleep. Cold had awakened me, and when I moved I was as stiff as a motel towel. I creaked and cracked, moaned and groaned, and slowly made it to my feet, where I hopped up and down and flapped my arms around in an effort to get warm.

Christ, but it was cold; the Dombeys must be the thrifty type who turn the heat down during the night. I'd been in prison a month and a half and this was the worst night I'd ever spent anywhere, and I was *outside* the goddam jail.

Well, there was no point in it. A warm bunk awaited me in the gym, so I might as well get to it. Awkwardly I lowered myself to my knees again and entered the tunnel.

I was about halfway back when I remembered the note and the milk box, and realized I ought to go back and see if I'd caught anything.

I really didn't want to. There wouldn't be anything in the milk box, I was sure of it, and I was cold enough already without another long useless walk. I also wanted to go back to sleep.

But I had to check, didn't I? Facing Phil and Joe and the others tomorrow with no money to show them—no, not if there was any alternative at all. So I had to go back.

Did you ever try to turn around in a three-foot-wide concrete pipe? Don't. At one point I was wedged in so completely, with my head between my knees and my shoulders stacked up together somewhere behind me, that I was convinced I'd never be able to move again; I could see Phil, tomorrow afternoon, sending Billy Glinn down to dismantle me in order to clear the blockage.

Finally, though, I did get myself facing the other way, and by then the exercise had made me warmer, more limber and very nearly awake. Except for a splitting headache and a total sense of despair I was in pretty good shape as I crawled back through the tunnel and hurried through the still-dark streets toward the bank. A clock in a barbershop window told me it was twenty minutes to four.

There was a gray canvas bag in the milk box. I stared at it, refusing to believe it, then stared suspiciously all around, expecting a trick. Practical jokers, of course, always have to believe that someone else is going to return the favor in kind.

There was no one in sight. The parked cars in the general vicinity all seemed to be empty. When I hesitantly reached into the milk box and prodded the gray canvas bag, no alarm bells jangled, no spotlights flashed on. But I did hear the clink of coins.

Well I'll be damned, I thought.

I took the bag out of the milk box. I could feel coins in there, and wads of paper.

Son of a *bitch*, I thought.

I stuffed the bag inside my jacket, grabbed my note from the night deposit slot and jammed it into a pocket, and walked briskly away, leaving the milk box as mute testimony to the gullibility of man.

I had just committed my first true felony. We have all read the statements of prison reformers claiming that jail creates more criminals than it rehabilitates, and by golly it turns out to be true!

11

The damn bag didn't want to open. I stood in the Vasacapa corridor in the Dombey basement, wrestling with the gray canvas bag full of money, and gradually my new self-image as a master criminal crumbled into ashes at my feet. Some crook; I couldn't steal my way into a canvas bag.

In my defense, I must say it was a tough bag to crack. Made of heavy canvas, it had a reinforced mouth that closed with a zipper, which in turn was attached by a small gleaming metal lock that would only open with a key. I fussed and fidgeted with the damn thing, listening to the coins clinking and the paper rustling in there, until finally I noticed a nail tip jutting through the side wall of the corridor, where Vasacapa had put up his paneling. Since this side of the wall hadn't been finished, it was the back of the paneling I was looking at. Something had been fastened to the wall over there, with a nail that poked all the way through, extending a full inch into the corridor.

So I gashed the bag to death. I kept scraping it against the nail until I'd gnawed a hole in it, and then forced and pried and gouged until the hole was big enough for me to shake the contents out onto the carpet.

Coins came tumbling out first, quarters and dimes and nickels bounding around like playful fish on the silent carpet, and then a thick wad of paper held together with a red rubber band.

The paper was money: bills, half a dozen checks, and a deposit slip. The checks were made out to Turk's Bar & Grill, and it was likely that Turk, or his representative, had been treating himself to a few on the house tonight, which was why he'd fallen for my sign-and-milk-box routine. Although as I remembered it, that fellow I'd read about in the paper several years ago had caught all sorts of citizens when he'd done the same thing. A businessman late at night, tired, impatient to be home, distracted by the events of his day, sees a note and something that looks vaguely like a strongbox, and just drops in the day's receipts. In fact, the only reason that former practitioner of this dodge had gotten himself arrested was because he'd kept doing it too often. A mistake I wouldn't repeat; this had been my first felony, and would be my last.

It *is* bad companions, by God; our mothers were right.

The deposit slip told me how much I'd collected in cash. One hundred thirty-two dollars in bills, eighteen dollars and forty cents in change. One hundred fifty dollars and forty cents.

Yes, sir.

The cash all went into my pockets, except for a dime that Max Nolan found in the carpet two weeks later. The checks and deposit slip went back into the canvas bag, and I went back into the cold to unload them.

I walked a block, found a garbage can next to somebody's house, and stuffed the bag in amid the corn flakes boxes. Then, jingling pleasantly, warm despite the cold, I marched back to prison.

12

I had been out getting a Post Office box, and when I got back Joe Maslocki told me, "You better get over to the warden's office. Stoon was around looking for you."

"Stoon?" He was the guard who had accompanied me to the warden's office my first day here. I said, "What's the problem?"

He shrugged. "Who knows? I told him you were out looking for a box of stolen jockstraps."

"Okay," I said, and left the gym, and hurried across the yard toward the building housing the warden's office.

This was two days after my successful milk box routine. That hundred and fifty dollars had finished the job of cementing my membership in the tunnel club, particularly when I'd related how I'd hidden near the bank and had leaped out to assault a businessman with a brick, relieving him of his night deposit cash. But I had no intention of stealing any more money, with either brick or milk box, so that's why I'd been out getting a Post Office box. I'd phoned my mother and asked her to send me a thousand dollars in a check made out to Harry Kent, and she had promised she would. With that money I would open a checking account, and from now on whenever the boys believed I was out making a sting I would simply return with money I'd withdrawn from the account.

I could see that life was going to get a bit complex in the months ahead. Talk about wheels within wheels. To the prison authorities I was an inmate. To seven of the inmates I was a tunnel insider, involved in robberies and assaults. To postal clerks and bank tellers and possibly other people on the outside,

I would soon become an ordinary local citizen named Harry Kent. And only I—if things went well—would know the whole truth.

I hadn't asked for this, I really hadn't. I'd been reasonably content in the license plate shop. But the ball had started rolling, and so far I hadn't found any way to make it stop.

Now, approaching the warden's office, I suddenly remembered the last thing he'd said to me on our first meeting: "If you behave yourself, I won't see you in this office again until you're discharged."

I wasn't about to be discharged, not six weeks into my sentence. I had obviously not been behaving myself, but if the warden knew about the tunnel wouldn't he want to see all eight of us, not just me?

Something's gone wrong, I thought. I didn't know what it was, I didn't know yet how bad it was going to be, but one thing I knew for sure: something had gone wrong.

Guard Stoon was coming out of the building as I was going in. He looked at me and said, "Oh, there you are. Warden Gadmore wants to see you."

"They just told me," I said.

"Come on, then."

I followed him inside, and down the squeaky-floored hall. Glancing back at me, he said, "You find the jocks?"

I had no idea what he was talking about. "What?"

"The jocks," he repeated.

Oh, of course: Joe Maslocki and his stolen jockstraps. Why had he given an insane excuse like that? "Yeah," I said. "I found them."

"Where were they?"

"One of the Joy Boys had them," I said.

"Figures," he said.

We went into the warden's anteroom, and I waited fifteen minutes before Stoon came back out and said, "Okay, Kunt."

"Künt," I said. "With an umlaut."

Stoon's reaction to everything was to express weariness. Expressing weariness, he said, "Warden Gadmore wants to see you now."

I went into the office and stood in front of the desk. Warden Gadmore was looking at documents on his desktop, showing me his bald spot. He lifted his head finally, gave me a critical look, and extended a smallish piece of paper toward me. I went on looking at him, and he jiggled the paper slightly, saying, "Go on, take it."

I took it. I was now holding a torn-off piece of ordinary white typing paper, about four inches square. Written on it in large, uneven printing, using a black felt-tip pen, were the words HELP I AM BEING HELD PRISONER.

The warden said, "Well, Kunt, what do you have to say for yourself?"

"Künt," I said. "With an umlaut."

He gestured impatiently at the piece of paper in my hand. "That looks like perfectly good English to me," he said. Behind me, over by the door, Stoon shifted his weight from one foot to the other.

"Yes, sir," I said. I had no idea what was going on. The warden said, "You think that's funny, Kunt?" He left out the umlaut.

I didn't correct him; I'd suddenly understood what this was all about. I said, "Warden, *I* didn't write this."

"Oh, no? Let me tell you something, Kunt. When that package of license plates was opened down there in Albany, and that girl Motor Vehicle clerk saw that message in with the license plates, she didn't think it was funny at all. Do you know what she did, Kunt?"

"Künt, sir," I pleaded. "With an umlaut."

"She fainted!"

"I'm sorry to hear that, sir, but I—"

"Kunt," he said, more in sorrow than in anger, and more in mispronunciation than in either, "I thought we understood one another the last time you were in here."

"Oh, yes, sir. I wouldn't—"

"We don't have much of a sense of humor around here, Kunt," he said.

Oh, to be outside. Oh, to have somebody call me Mr. Kent.

"Sir," I said, "I just didn't do it."

"You were assigned to license plates," he said. "Were you not?"

"Yes, sir, but—"

"You have a record of this sort of thing," he said. "Have you not?"

"Well, I suppose I—not exactly *this* sort of—"

"You have the only mind that *I* know of in this institution," he said, "that gets a twisted pleasure from this sort of prank."

"I'll take a lie detector test. I'll swear on a stack of—"

"That's enough," he said, and made a sweeping palm-down gesture to cut off my protestations.

I stopped. A million words quivered in my throat, but I said none of them.

He frowned up at me. I was still holding the message in my hands, and I didn't want to, I hated the association with it. On the other hand, it might not be psychologically sound to put it down on the desk with him staring at me like that.

Behind me, Stoon shifted his weight.

The warden took a deep breath. He lowered his head, opened a folder that presumably contained my records, and scanned various pieces of paper.

Movement attracted my eye. I looked over the warden's bald spot, out through his window at the small enclosed garden out there, and saw the stout old gardener, Andy Butler, pottering around again, just as he'd been doing the last time I was in this room. I didn't see him pee on any bushes this time, but as I watched him packing mulch or something around the base of some plants, he lifted his head and our eyes met. I knew him slightly now, having been introduced to him by my toothless friend Peter Corse, and it pleased and heartened me when he smiled in recognition, giving a brief nod of the head. More than ever he looked like Santa Claus out of uniform.

I didn't dare nod my own head, not with Stoon behind me and Warden Gadmore in front of me, but I did risk a quick smile and a friendly lifting of the eyebrows. Then I lowered my gaze to the warden's bald spot again, just as his finger began bunk-bunking on my dossier.

Should I argue with him, plead with him? Should I repeat my denials? In plain fact I *hadn't* sent that message; wasn't there some way to convince him of that?

I wasn't used to being innocent. I knew perfectly well how to pretend innocence, but when saddled with the real thing I was at a loss. All right; so what would I do to display innocence if I were in fact guilty? I would stand here silent, in order to avoid being accused of protesting too much. So that's what I did.

Innocent, I pretended to be guilty in order to remember how to pretend to be innocent. There ought to be a simpler way to get through life.

Warden Gadmore lifted his head. He brooded at me. I met his gaze steadfastly, with all the false innocence I could muster, and at last he sighed and said, "All right, Kunt."

I did not correct him.

"I don't say I believe you or disbelieve you," he said, clearly disbelieving me. "I'll tell you this: any man can make a mistake. Any man can take a little while to adapt to the changed circumstances here."

I wanted to scream that I hadn't done it, I was *really* and *truly* innocent, this time I wasn't kidding. I stood there, silent.

He said, "So we won't say any more about this. And we'll assume, Kunt, that it won't happen again."

"Thank you, sir," I said. And I was thinking. Don't pull anything in this office. Don't do it. I thought of a stunt involving the wastebasket, and I pushed it from my mind. Don't do it.

"Because if it does happen again," he said, "it won't go so easy on you."

"No, sir," I said. Calmly, not protesting too much, I added, "But, sir, I honestly and truly—"

"That's all, Kunt," he said.

I swallowed. Do nothing, I told myself. "Yes, sir," I said.

Stoon and I left the warden's office together. I did nothing, for which I was profoundly grateful.

Stoon accompanied me down the corridor, our shoes squeaking companionably together on the floor. He shook his head and said, "You really are a killer, Kunt."

"I didn't do it, you know," I said. "This time, I'm really innocent."

"Everybody here is innocent," he said. That old wheeze. "Go on out and talk to the boys," he suggested. "There isn't a guilty man in this pen."

What was the use of talking?

Stoon and I separated at the exit, and as I crossed the yard two thoughts suddenly dropped on my head like a barbell out of an upstairs window.

THOUGHT A: If I had managed to be more offensively guilty in the warden's office, he would have taken me off privileges, and I would have ceased to be a member of the tunnel club, and I would no longer have a bank robbery looming up in my future.

THOUGHT B: Joe Maslocki and the others would want to know what the warden had wanted to talk to me about. The truth would necessarily bring out my past history as a practical joker. It wouldn't take long after that for the boys to realize who they had to thank for the succession of dribble glasses, sticky door knobs and exploding cigarettes they'd been experiencing over the last few weeks. What they would do to me then I wanted even less than I wanted to become a bank robber.

As to Thought A, I felt a great ambivalence about my involvement with that tunnel. I loved being able to get out of prison, I loved being able to enter a world in which I was known as Harry Kent, and I loved the freedom from Joy Boys and other internal prison menaces. On the other hand, there was that goddam bank robbery looming up. If I had a good solid chance to get away from the gym and the tunnel—as I'd almost just had, if I'd thought of it in time—would I take it to avoid the robbery, or avoid it to take the advantages? I really didn't know, and the question was giving me a headache.

As to Thought B, I had no ambivalence at all. As soon as I thought of a convincing lie about my meeting with the warden, I would tell it to everybody I saw. And I would redouble my efforts to stop all this booby-trapping. I'd been looking forward to prison curing me of that bad habit, but so far it hadn't helped much. I *had* managed to avoid doing anything in the warden's office just now, but that had been pretty much of an extreme case. But hopeful, just the same. And I would lie.

In fact, here came the opportunity. Jerry Bogentrodder and Max Nolan were strolling across the yard toward me, and Jerry called, "Hey, Harry, you know the warden wants to see you?"

"I just came from there," I said.

The three of us strolled together. Jerry said, "Any problem?"

"No," I said. I wondered what I would say next, and listened hopefully. "It was about my blood type," I said. I thought, What the hell does that mean?

Max Nolan looked puzzled. Even his droopy moustache looked puzzled. He said, "Blood type?"

I'd had to start off by lying to a college graduate. "There was some question in my records," I said. I'm insane, I thought. Beavering on, I said, "If I was some special kind of negative, they wanted to know if I'd volunteer."

"Oh," Max said.

"I'm a different type," I said.

The three of us strolled. Gazing back at the conversation just past, it seemed to me there was a certain believability about it. The damn thing had come out somewhere after all. I was both relieved and quite proud of myself.

As a result of some long-ago architectural rearrangement within the prison, there was now in the yard a flight of steps that went nowhere. Five wide steps went up to a blank concrete wall. The tunnel group had established those steps as their own territory, which all other cons kept away from. Jerry and Max and I strolled over there through a thin to moderate traffic of milling inmates, and took seats. None of the rest of the group was around. Jerry and Max sat on the top step, and I settled two steps below them.

With only half the prison population involved in work assignments, the yard was pretty much occupied all day long. Inmates walked around, chatted with one another, shot craps illicitly in corners, made assignations to meet later in the showers, got into fist-fights and less frequently knife-fights, discussed escape plans, described their civilian sex lives to one another, and generally worked off excess energy. Now, while Jerry and Max talked,

I sat in the cold sunshine and watched the cons move back and forth. I thought my own thoughts, tied Jerry and Max's shoelaces together, and thanked my lucky stars the warden hadn't made a bigger thing about that message in the license plates.

No! Clenching my teeth, cursing myself under my breath I untied those damn shoelaces again. I thought, I have to stop that. I really do.

13

I was letting a tiny bit of air out of every basketball when Eddie Troyn came over and said, "Let's organize our rendezvous."

I looked up at him. His face was as clean and bony as a cow-skull in the desert. The crease in his prison denims was so sharp it made me squint. I said, "What?"

"We have surveillance detail this afternoon," he said.

I knew he talked that way—rendezvous, surveillance—but that didn't mean I knew what he was talking *about*. I said, "What surveillance? What rendezvous?"

He expressed displeased surprise. His eyebrows had some difficulty riding on that bony forehead. "Didn't Phil tell you?"

"Nobody told me anything," I said. I'd been planning to spend this afternoon opening my local bank account, since the check had come from my mother yesterday.

"Breakdown in communication," he said severely.

I tossed the basketball from my lap back into the bin and got to my feet. "What am I supposed to do?" I asked him.

"Bank surveillance," he said. "We all take shifts." My stomach contracted. Bank surveillance. This had to have something to do with the robbery. Trying for an unconcerned facade, I said, "Sure, Eddie. When do you want me? Now?"

"No, not till they close, at three."

Oh, that was all right, then. Not all *right*, but at least I could still open my checking account today. "Fine," I said. "You want to meet at the bank?"

"You know the luncheonette across the street? I'll be in a front booth there at three."

"Right," I said.

He shot a starched work-shirt cuff and frowned at his watch. "I read," he said slowly, gazing at the watch, "eleven-twenty-three." Then he looked at me.

He wanted to synchronize watches! "Oh," I said, and looked at my watch, and I read eleven-nineteen. "Right," I said. "I mean, check."

"See you at three," he said, and marched off.

I looked at the bin of basketballs, but I didn't feel like fouling up any more of them, so I went on and did productive things until lunch, and then went out and took care of business at the bank.

I had, of course, my choice between two banks: Western National and Fiduciary Federal. I wasn't sure which of them I would go to as I walked downtown, and in fact I was leaning toward Western National since I'd been in there once with Phil, but when I got to the banks I remembered it was also Western National where I had pulled my milk box stunt. That bank had been the victim of my first—and so far only—felony, and I felt a certain embarrassment in its presence. So I opened my account at Fiduciary Federal, where they gave me a book of temporary checks and told me my check on the Rye bank should clear in three days.

Returning to the street, I found myself smiling around at the downtown scene with an air almost proprietary. In some damn way, this was becoming my home town. I was a local boy now, with a Post Office box and a bank account of my very own.

And my own civilian clothing, at least partly. I was still wearing the borrowed shirt and pants, but out of my ill-gotten gains I'd bought myself a good wool sweater and a heavy leather jacket. Winter was settling in for a long visit in upstate New York, and I meant to be ready for it.

If only I could be ready for everything else that was going to happen around here. Spending the next hour browsing through the local stores, easing along with the ebb and flow of Christmas shoppers, stopping to look at model railroad displays, I couldn't stop brooding about the upcoming bank robberies. What was I going to do? What *could* I do?

Nothing. Wait and see. Ride with events, and hope for the best.

God.

14

At three o'clock I met Eddie Troyn in the luncheonette, at a front booth by a window facing the street. He looked at his watch as I slid into the seat opposite him, and said, "Four minutes after."

I looked at my own watch, which read three on the button. "Check," I said.

Looking out the window, he said, "You understand the mission?"

"No, I don't."

He gave me a quick pursed-lip glance, then looked out the window again. The whole world was run too sloppily for his taste. "Communication in this outfit is hopeless," he said.

"Nobody told me anything," I agreed.

"We watch Fiduciary Federal," he said. "We mark everybody who goes in or out between closing time and the departure of the last employee."

I looked over at Fiduciary Federal. Through the big windows I could see there were still several customers inside. A guard was standing just inside the mostly glass doors, letting each customer out when they were finished. "Right," I said.

"Not counting those customers," he said.

"Oh."

He glanced away from the bank long enough to push a notebook and ballpoint pen toward me. "You'll write down what I tell you," he said. "Every fifteen minutes we'll reverse assignments."

"Right," I said.

I opened the notebook and poised the pen, and nothing happened. I watched Eddie, and Eddie watched the bank, and nothing at all happened. After a while my fingers began to cramp and I put the pen down. After another while my eyes began to water and I looked away from Eddie—out the window, in fact, in the general direction of the bank.

After about ten minutes a waiter came to take our orders. He was a high school boy with an after-school job, and he did not have his entire heart and soul in this activity. It took him a long while to understand that we wanted two cups of coffee, and when he wandered away I was fully convinced we'd never see him again. With or without coffee.

As a place to have a quick snack, this luncheonette wasn't maybe the best in the world. As a place in which to establish a stakeout without drawing any attention to ourselves, it was ideal. We couldn't have drawn that boy's attention if we'd set ourselves on fire.

At three-fifteen I said, "My turn." Since I was already looking at the bank, that simple statement was all I had to do in order to take over the watch.

Peripheral vision told me that Eddie had taken back the notebook and ballpoint pen.

This was very boring. Partly for something to do, and partly because I was morbidly interested in the details of the felony I'd been committed to, I asked after a while, "How are we going to do this thing anyway? Those banks look pretty solid."

"You haven't been told the plan?"

"As you pointed out," I said, while still watching nothing happen at the bank across the street, "communication is not this outfit's strong suit."

I could hear the doubt in his voice, as he said, "We operate pretty much on a need-to-know basis."

I looked at him. "I'm a member of this gang, aren't I?"

"Watch the bank," he said.

I watched the bank. The last customer had departed ten minutes ago, and nothing else had happened since. Nevertheless, I watched the bank. I said, "I'm a member of this gang, aren't I?"

"Of course," he said. "We're all on the same team."

"Then I need to know," I said.

"You're probably right," he said. I could hear him coming to a fast yet solid decision. "Very well," he said. "We'll begin with an unauthorized entry into Fiduciary Federal following the close of the business day."

"How do we do that?"

"This observation of routine is helping to establish that question," he said.

Sometimes it took a few seconds to get through Eddie's words to what he was saying. The military prism through which he viewed the world made him at times a bewildering conversationalist. But very neat. Working my way through this one, I came to the kernel of thought at the center, and suddenly realized the gang didn't yet know how they were going to get into that bank.

Hope blossomed in me, out of season.

Eddie said, "Having gained access to the interior, we will then require the personnel remaining in the bank to telephone their homes and explain to their next of kin that an unexpected state audit of the bank's records will necessitate their working late, possibly through the night."

I nodded. Nobody went in or out of the bank. Inside there, clerks moved back and forth, involved with the closing activities of the day.

Eddie said, "We will then induce the senior officer present to open the vault."

That word 'induce.' I didn't like that word 'induce.' Eddie said, "You can't watch the bank with your eyes closed."

I opened my eyes. "Just blinking," I said. "Your eyes get tired when you keep looking like this."

"Four minutes left to your tour," he said.

"Right," I said. "What about the other bank?"

"Just watch Fiduciary Federal," he said.

"No, I meant the robbery. How do we get into Western National?"

"Ah," he said. "That's the brilliance of the scheme. Joe Maslocki deserves the citation for that."

"Fine," I said. I thought dark thoughts about Joe Maslocki.

"When the Fiduciary Federal building was put up, seven years ago," Eddie said, "it was necessary to short-circuit a part of the alarm system used in the Western National vault."

I frowned, and remembered not to look away from the bank. "How do you know a thing like that?"

"Our team," he said, "has friends in the local building trades. Remember, that's how the tunnel was constructed in the first place."

"Oh. Right."

"Radio silence," he said.

I couldn't help it; I looked away from the bank. I stared in bewilderment at Eddie and said, "Huh?"

He gave me a meaningful head nod. I looked to my left, and damn if the high school boy wasn't back, with our coffees. He put them down without looking at either of us, stood frowning at them for a few seconds, and then drifted aimlessly away, like a paper boat in a puddle.

I looked back at the bank.

Eddie said, "The Western National vault is wired against tunneling from every side, except where it is conjunctive with the

Fiduciary Federal vault. In effect, the two vaults share a common wall and a common alarm system excluding that wall."

"Oh," I said. I could see it coming.

"Once we have breached the Fiduciary Federal vault," Eddie said, "we will in a way be behind the lines of the Western National vault. We will tunnel through the wall from vault to vault."

"Ah," I said. But it seemed to me that bank vaults, with or without alarm systems, did tend to have very thick and very solid walls. I said, "How long does this tunnel take to dig?"

"Perhaps three hours."

I glanced at him, glanced away, and he said, "You are relieved." I glanced at him again, and he was watching the bank, having pushed the notebook and pen back over toward me.

I picked up the pen, had nothing to write, and put it back down. I said, "Three hours? I thought it would take a lot longer than that."

"Not with the laser," he said.

I looked at him. "Laser?"

"The one we'll take from Camp Quattatunk," he said.

I said, "Camp Quattatunk."

"The Army base," he said, as though that explained everything.

I remembered having heard there was an Army base around here somewhere, but this was the first time I'd heard its name. Or that we would be getting a laser from it. I said, "A laser. That's one of those burning ray machines, isn't it?"

"Of course."

"And we're going to get one at this Army base."

"Yes."

"How?"

"Steal it," he said.

Of course. I said, "We're going to pull a robbery at an Army base so we can pull a robbery at two banks."

"Positive," he said.

Positive. I said, "When do we do this Army base robbery?"

"The night before the banks."

Monday, December thirteenth. Two and a half weeks from now. I picked up the coffee and sipped it and it tasted like my future: cold, bleak, thin and not very sweet.

"Two female employees exiting," he said, "at three thirty-seven."

I looked at my watch. Three thirty-three. "Check," I said, and wrote in the notebook "2 fem emp X 3:37." Then I looked out the window and saw two girls, bulky in their overcoats, walking away from Fiduciary Federal Trust, as the guard locked the door again behind them.

If only it looked harder to get into. Or easier.

I didn't want to think about the Army camp at all.

15

In the midst of madness we are in apparent normalcy. Nine days after my stakeout duty with Eddie Troyn I had a Saturday night date. With a telephone repairman named Mary Edna Sweeney.

It was actually a double date, set up by Max Nolan, involving him and another local girl, named Dotty Fleisch. Max had broached the subject of finding me a date earlier in the week, and I had expressed immediate interest. "I'm not talking about great stuff," he had cautioned me. "All the good gash goes out of town to college. In the summer around here you can write your own ticket, but this time of year you take what you can get."

"I'll take it," I had said.

There was nothing wrong with Mary Edna Sweeney. On the other hand, there was nothing right with her either. She was twenty-five, deeply involved in her telephone company job, and she'd apparently had three boyfriends in a row who'd joined the Army, been shipped to unlikely places, and promptly married girls they'd found in the foreign clime.

All of these departures had made Mary Edna just a bit nervous; she tended to look startled at sounds like doors closing or car engines starting. Otherwise, however, she was a placid girl, a bit heftier than my usual tastes, with large, sweet, dark eyes and masses of black hair. "I have to keep my hair tied up when I'm working," she told me, "but boy, as soon as I get home I let it fly."

"I never met a lady telephone repairman before," I said.

"The telephone company is an equal opportunity employer,"

she said, with that primness which unimaginative people reserve for nobler thoughts they've memorized. "They're experimenting with male operators," she said. "And I'm an experiment the other way."

"A repairlady."

"A repair*person*," she said.

I said, "You do all that repairperson stuff? Climb the poles and everything?"

"Sure," she said. "Of course, I can't wear a skirt." And she blushed. Girls in small towns still blush.

This conversation took place in the Riviera Restaurant & Cocktail Lounge after the movie. We had had an absolutely traditional first date; Max and I had crawled through the tunnel at just after seven o'clock, had met the girls in front of the Strand Theater, there had been introductions, and we had gone at once into the darkness to sit next to one another without touching while we watched a double feature. A double feature. Unfortunately the first picture was a caper movie about a bank robbery, full of hardened criminals and violent action—including the pursuit, beating and painful death of a squealer—and it left me a little limp. It took the entire second feature, a comedy about a giraffe that swallowed an experimental formula and became a super-genius, to bring me out of my doldrums and make it possible for me to exchange dialogue with Mary Edna Sweeney at the Riviera, to which we had repaired for cheeseburgers and a pitcher of beer.

Mary Edna was a friendly enough girl, but she wasn't someone I would have crossed a crowded room for. Nor an empty room either. But she did have one absolutely first-rate quality which put her above every other girl I'd ever gone out with: she thought my name was Harry Kent.

Dotty Fleisch was more of the same, without being quite an

exact carbon copy. Paler, plumper, more given to bursts of speech or outbreaks of giggle, she was definable from Mary Edna without being any more or less desirable. Max had apparently been dating her off and on for several months, having told her he was a civilian employee out at Camp Quattatunk who lived in quarters on the base; I was now given the same background, and in the course of the conversation I learned for the first time that Camp Quattatunk wasn't an Army base in the usual sense of the word but was an arsenal, a storage depot for military equipment. Thus, no doubt, the laser.

Which led to thoughts of robbery. Certain scenes from the caper movie came vividly back into my imagination, in perfect color. I flung myself into conversation, trying not to look over my shoulder.

At one point, in the men's room, I discovered that the paper-towel dispenser could be rigged so as to bring the entire load of paper towels out when the first one was tugged, but other than that it was just impossible to think about anything except the robbery. The caper movie had made it all much more real and much more desperate.

Finally we all left the Riviera and separated, Max and his Dotty going off in one direction arm in arm, Mary Edna and I trailing away in the other, walking side by side but not touching. The streets we walked along were tree-lined, but at this time of year the trees were leafless, bony grasping things reaching out from the streetlights, branches clutching together over my head like medieval punishments.

The specter of the bank robbery followed me along the sidewalk, making the already cold air even colder. Scenarios of disaster ran in repertory through my head: the robbery would occur and degenerate into gunplay and I would be shot to death; we would be caught and I'd stand trial for robbery and jailbreak and possibly even murder and be sent up forever; we would get away with it and I'd spend the rest of my life waiting for the axe to fall as inevitably it would; we would get away with it and the gang would insist on more robberies and one of the preceding scenarios would inexorably follow; in the course of the bank robbery I'd be called upon to shoot somebody and would refuse and be shot by my own people; or I'd do it and become a murderer as well as a bank robber; I would attempt some desperate ploy to prevent the robbery from taking place and would be found out by my co-conspirators and would be unloaded; or I'd be found out by the authorities and would be charged with jailbreak and attempted robbery; or... The variants were endless, it seemed, and not a happy one in the lot.

Meanwhile, Mary Edna spoke at length on the subject of telephone company training films. No topic was likely to capture much of my interest right now, so telephone company training films were about as useful as anything else to fill in the spaces. I managed an occasional appropriate comment, Mary Edna pointed out occasional poles she had climbed for one purpose or another, and eventually we reached the smallish two-family house in which she lived on the second floor with her widowed mother and two younger sisters.

It was so hard for me to remain aware of Mary Edna's presence. It wasn't her fault, it was that damned robbery. I was dimly aware of a slight sense of awkwardness when I said good night to her on her porch and politely waited till she had unlocked the door and gone inside, but it wasn't until Max asked me the next day how I'd made out that I realized Mary Edna had been anticipating some sort of overture from me. A kiss, at the very least, possibly some groping. Who knew what she might not have had in mind? The next night, lying in my solitary bunk in my cell, the sounds and sighs of sleeping men in their other cells all around me, I thought of how almost any of them—enforced celibates all—would have behaved the preceding night on Mary Edna's front porch, and my own behavior, or lack of behavior, struck me as very strange.

But on that first date night, spurred on by the caper movie, I just couldn't think about anything except the robbery. It was scheduled for ten days from now, Tuesday the fourteenth of December. I had first heard about it over two weeks ago, the time was rushing by, and I wasn't getting anywhere. My only forlorn hope was that the gang, who seemed to have everything else thoroughly planned, would never find a way to make that initial entry into Fiduciary Federal Trust, no matter how much surveillance was done. If we couldn't get into the bank in the first place we couldn't rob it, could we?

I walked with my fingers crossed.

16

The following Tuesday, at four-thirty in the afternoon, one week to the day before the scheduled robbery, I myself showed the boys how to get into the bank.

I was on surveillance duty with Billy Glinn this time, the two of us sitting in the usual luncheonette, drinking the usual rotten coffee brought by the usual sleepwalking high school boy, watching nothing happen across the street. I was doing the watching and Billy was telling me a story about a time when he'd found a fellow having intercourse with a girlfriend of Billy's in the back seat of a car out behind a country roadhouse. "He run off into the woods," Billy was saying, "but I didn't take out after him right off."

"You didn't?"

"First," he said, "I figured to settle that little girl down a bit, so I pick her up and whump her on the side of the chest. Under the arm, you know, I don't want to hurt her titties, just bust a couple ribs to slow her down. I figure if she's in the hospital I'll *know* where she is. Then I went after the fella's car, I pulled off the doors and the fenders and pulled the steering wheel out and messed up the engine a little bit and took and threw the hood up in a tree. Then I went off after the fella himself out through the woods. So when I caught up with him it turn out he took off so fast he left his pants behind—he's bare-ass naked out there in the woods. Well, I was almighty angry at that fella, so—"

"Uh!" I said. "Typewriter repairman going in."

"What say?"

"Typewriter repairman," I repeated; and immediately could have bit my tongue. I'd made the announcement without thinking, partly because it was so rare for anything at all to happen over there at the bank, but mostly because I really didn't *want* to know what Billy had done to the naked man in the woods. I was identifying too completely.

"Typewriter repairman," he said, finally understanding, and when I glanced at him he was laboriously printing the information in the notebook in his large childlike hand, misspelling magnificently and concentrating on every curve and every straight line. A pink tongue-tip protruded from a corner of his mouth, like a flower on a slag-heap.

It was too late. I knew at once the typewriter repairman was our route into the bank, and I also knew there was no way now to stop the information from getting back to Joe Maslocki and the rest. If only I'd kept my mouth shut Billy, absorbed in the story he was telling, would never have noticed the typewriter repairman at all. But I'd told him about it, and he was writing it down, and in the fullness of time the rest of the group would also know. My last hope was gone, and I'd done it to myself.

If only he wouldn't think to write down the name of the company.

He said, "What's the name on the fella's truck?" Shit fuck. I looked at the Ford Econoline van out in front of the bank, reading the company name emblazoned there. Did I dare lie? No, I did not dare lie. "Twin Cities Typewriter," I said.

"Twin," he said, and wrote it with all the grace and speed of someone etching his initials on cast iron with a rock. "Ci—" he said. "—tieeeees," he said.

While he was working his way through *typewriter*, the last nail was hammered into my coffin. "Here he comes out," I said, despairing, all hope gone. "He's carrying a typewriter."

"Hee hee," Billy said. Even he knew what it meant. "Wait till the boys hear about this."

I was willing to wait forever. I watched the repairman put the typewriter away in the back of his truck, then get behind the wheel and drive away. Billy kept hee-heeing.

I felt so miserable that I forgot and took a sip of the coffee.

17

There was a certain morbid fascination in watching the gang put the pieces of the robbery together. Like, no doubt, the condemned man gazing out his cell window as the scaffold is being built.

I lived the next several days in a combined state of dulled terror and fatalistic interest. The caper movies I'd seen over the years had led me to understand that a major robbery was a complicated affair, and yet the movies had somehow glided over those complications; if a gang needed a truck, or a centrifuge, or a Warsaw telephone directory, they simply got one between scenes, when no one was looking. The truth I was living turned out to be equally complicated, but much more difficult.

There were so many elements to the thing. Either some way had to be found to borrow a truck from Twin Cities Typewriter on the afternoon of the robbery, or some other Ford Econoline van would have to be stolen and stored and repainted with Twin Cities' name and colors. A uniform had to be found for Eddie Troyn to match the uniforms worn by the bank guards. The names and addresses and home phone numbers of the late-staying bank employees had to be learned, to cut down the possibility of a double-cross—a teller, for instance, phoning police headquarters rather than his wife. A typewriter had to be picked up somewhere for delivery to the bank, and it had to be the same color and make as all the other typewriters used there.

Then there was the laser. That was another entire robbery in itself, as major in its own way as the bank job. And, in fact, even more frightening; forcing entry into a bank began to seem like kid stuff in comparison with breaking into an Army storage depot patrolled by rifle-toting soldiers. So Camp Quattatunk had to be cased, more uniforms had to be obtained, the specific location of the laser had to be determined, a getaway vehicle had to be provided for, and a complete game plan had to be organized.

It turned out that Phil Giffin, Joe Maslocki, Billy Glinn, and Jerry Bogentrodder all had experience in this line of work—were in fact professionals at it. Phil and Billy were both in Stonevelt because of capers that hadn't quite worked out—another cheerful thought—while Joe and Jerry had been sent up for activities outside their professional careers: manslaughter during a barroom argument on Joe's part, check-kiting during a slack robbery season for Jerry. Max Nolan's professional qualifications were more along the line of burglary and credit card thievery, Bob Dombey it turned out was a forger by trade, and Eddie Troyn never quite got around to mentioning what it was that had brought him here. As for me, the role I was called on to play was that of general thug, a utility hoodlum with more of a social and educational veneer than most. All of the members of the group subscribed to the theory that the toughest guys are the ones who brag about it the least, which I suppose made me the toughest tough guy any of them had ever met in their lives. I did no bragging at all.

But I did play an ongoing role in the robbery preparations. I followed the bank manager's secretary home one evening to get her address, then hung around and got the family's last name from the mailbox. I was not present when Max Nolan bought the Minox camera with the stolen MasterCharge card, but I was exceedingly present when Phil Giffin used it to make an interminable photographic essay of the interior of the bank. I was along to shield him from curious eyes that time, though he did complain later that I tended to spend most of my time shielding him from the things he was trying to take pictures of. There were three or four pretty good pictures of me when we got them all developed, but Phil didn't offer them to me and I didn't feel I should ask, so I never did get them.

I was also present to stand chickee when Max Nolan burgled the appliance store late one night to steal a beige Smith-Corona electric typewriter, and he felt I was so assured and helpful on that little sting that he chose me to be his partner two nights later when he broke into the Army-Navy store for military uniforms. Standing out on the sidewalk both those nights, watching the flashlight flicker here and there in the depths of the store, cowering as the occasional late automobile drove by, I shivered and my teeth chattered and it was not at all from the cold.

During this same time, my efforts to rehabilitate myself as a practical joker and booby-trap setter went into total decline. Gimmicks and snaffles poured from me like some sort of nervous tic, bedeviling my fellow prisoners like a sudden outgrowth of poison ivy. Coffee cups when lifted turned out to have no bottom, or the sugar put in them was salt. Ankle-high cords mined the hallways. I learned that the hot and cold water lines to the main shower room could be reversed and did so on Thursday morning, just in time for the Joy Boys. Benches in the mess hall turned out to have loose screws holding them together, so that when ten men sat down the bench would drop with a clatter and a chorus of startled cries. Sink faucets were plugged so that water didn't run down into the sink but shot straight out onto the belt of the man turning the tap on. Floors were greased, doorknobs were soaped, milk pitchers in the mess hall were buttered; I've seen a half-full milk pitcher spurt from the hand of the man trying to hold it, sail up and out into the air, arch over the flinching man on the other side, and land in a bowl of green beans on the next table.

Of course there were occasional fights, loud recriminations, every once in a while some angry soul dripping water or ketchup or egg yolk yelling that the joint was infested with a practical joker, but the place was just too large for my activities to become generally noticeable. The prison population was nearly six thousand, and even in a good week I couldn't expect to drench, draw or drop more than a hundred of them—usually less than half that number. And not every one of my victims realized he'd been deliberately attacked; a man trying in vain to open a greased doorknob, for instance, was more likely to curse the stupidity or dirtiness of the person preceding him than to think this gook had been put on here on purpose.

I also left my fellow bank robbers strictly alone. I'd done a few things to them in the beginning, but my terror of the robbery had spilled over into a general fear of the men planning to commit it. I decided to be discreet for once, and did none of my little tricks anywhere around the gym. All I needed was for Phil Giffin, say, to start looking for a practical joker, and to talk to some trusty from the warden's office who might know the truth about me, and I wouldn't have to worry about bank robbery or anything else ever again.

On the following Saturday, three days before the robbery, Max and I double dated again, this time with another pair of girls, whose names were not Mary Edna or Dotty. I have no idea who they were, what they looked like, what they did for a living, or anything else about them. I was in a kind of immobile frenzy, unable to think about anything other than the steps leading to the robbery or my string of little land mines. After the inevitable double feature—I retained no memory of either movie—we went to the Riviera for the inevitable hamburgers and beer, and all at once I began, in a loud and cheerful and obnoxious voice, to tell dirty jokes. I never tell dirty jokes, and I was amazed at how many of them it turned out I knew. The

girls and Max—and probably everybody else in the place, too—
seemed stunned by me, but I just went on recounting my stories,
whether I was rewarded with hollow laughter or not. I had no
idea what I was doing, but I'd lost control a long time ago so I
just sat there and let it happen.

Finally I got to take the girl home. Remembering Mary Edna,
I ordered myself to kiss her, because I didn't want her to feel
slighted or insulted. But when the time came, she repulsed me
with something like real panic, and fled into her house without
even giving me the ritual line about having had a real good
time. My dirty jokes, I decided, must have convinced her I was
a mad sex fiend rapist. I wanted to feel bad about that, but
walking back to the Dombey house all I could think about was
that three days from now I was going to become a bank robber.

The next day, when Max asked me how I'd made out, he
informed me that his date had become sexually inflamed by my
stories and that they had had intercourse first in a parked car
on the way to her place and then again on the living-room sofa
once he got her home. So you never know.

18

As if I didn't have troubles enough, I happen to be a forty-two long. So on Monday afternoon, two days after my double date with Max and one day before the scheduled bank robbery, I was the one who put on the other uniform Max had stolen from the Army-Navy store and joined Eddie Troyn to be the inside men in the great laser caper.

Eddie had been spending a lot of time out at the camp this past week. Partly of course it was to get the lay of the land, but I think also it was partly nostalgia; Eddie liked Camp Quattatunk, he liked walking around an Army base with a Captain's uniform on, he liked giving and receiving salutes, he liked dropping into the Officer's Club and having a Jack Daniel's on the rocks and signing the bill 'Captain Robinson.' ("There isn't an Army base in the country," he explained to me, "that doesn't have at least one Captain Robinson assigned to it.")

I, on the other hand, was not happy at all. I was in the uniform of a First Lieutenant, but my own Army experience a dozen years ago as a draftee had been strictly limited to the life of the enlisted man and I didn't feel at all comfortable in the role of officer. I was positive I would make a social or military gaffe, some immediate blunder that would tell any *real* officer I was a fake and an impostor and probably a Russian spy.

Max had provided us with identification, in what I had to admit was a clever way. Eddie and I, applying at the bank where we had our checking accounts, first obtained credit cards bearing our photographs. Then Max, who considered himself an expert in altering and adapting credit cards, altered these, with heat and colored ink and the assistance of Bob Dombey to do the tricky lettering, into Army ID cards that Eddie decreed were "certainly good enough." They didn't look good enough to me, but Eddie insisted no one would look closely. The card, he pointed out, would stay inside one of the scratchy plasticene pockets in my wallet, and all I'd ever have to do would be flash it at someone disposed already to believe in it. "The color is close enough," he said, "the size is right, the photograph is accurate, the general appearance is appropriate. That's all we need."

Maybe. But all I could think was, I wouldn't be shot on Tuesday as a bank robber, I'd be shot on Monday as a spy.

There was a free Army bus only for Camp Quattatunk personnel that went out to the base from downtown Stonevelt every hour on the hour, seven A.M. till midnight. We boarded the bus at five in the afternoon, Eddie matter-of-factly and me with terror in my heart, and the driver barely glanced at our identification. We shared a seat away from the other passengers, and all too soon the bus pulled away from the curb and joined the ebb of rush-hour traffic.

I seemed to be blinking a lot. I kept looking out the window at the happy Christmas shoppers strolling along the sidewalks. None of them were penitentiary prisoners, none of them were escapees, none of them were impostors in Army uniforms, none of them were on the verge of becoming bank robbers, none of them were compulsive practical jokers, and none of them were named Harry Künt with *or* without an umlaut. To be any one of those things would be disheartening, and I was all of them.

The bus very soon left the town of Stonevelt and its rush hour behind and we traveled for a while on a small curving road through open countryside, mostly either apple orchards or uncleared forest, like alternating groups of neat and unruly children. There was an occasional farmhouse, an occasional roadhouse, an occasional grubby mobile home mounted on concrete blocks. There was little traffic once we were clear of town, all of it faster than the bus, a big-shouldered hulking lumbering thing in Army brown, looking like an ancient school-bus that had been drafted by mistake.

Nevertheless, slow or not, inevitably it did reach Camp Quattatunk. My first indication of our arrival was the sudden high metal fence topped by barbed wire that appeared on the right side of the road, cutting us off from thick pine woods. Through the screen of pine needles I glimpsed an occasional building in tan or light green, set well back from the road. At one point I seemed also to see a row of dark-colored tanks, all with their snouts pointing my way. Much more clearly I could see the red-and-white signs on the fence itself, warning the civilian world that the strands of barbed wire were electrified.

I felt they didn't want me there. I felt it was a mistake of me to intrude.

The bus slowed at the entrance gate, but didn't stop. We had already showed our identification to the driver, and so wouldn't have to show it to anyone else to gain entry to the camp. It had been Eddie's contention that the bus driver, since he was phys-ically removed from the camp at the time of seeing our identifi-cation, would be psychologically inclined to be more lax about ID cards than the MPs manning the gate, and he had turned out to be right. Now if only he was also right about everything else connected with this base there was just a chance we would get away with tonight's burglary.

Though not tomorrow's robbery. Was I going to go through with it? Would I actually walk into that bank tomorrow after-noon with these desperate criminals? If I ran away I would have to run away from the prison as well and become a hunted escapee, a role I doubted I was suited to. I would never again be able to use my rightful name, which in my case wasn't an entirely unmixed curse, but I just couldn't see myself as a successful fugitive. The question came down to a choice between fugitive and bank robber, and just which of those roles would I be the least ridiculous in. So far, I hadn't found a satisfactory answer.

And I was, in any event, about to commit my second felony, assuming the milk box trick to have been the first. But this was much more serious than any stunt with milk box and note; this was the United States Army.

Camp Quattatunk. The bus, waved through the main gate by a white-helmeted MP, had entered a neat but unreal community, looking like some science fiction parody of the Norman Rockwell type of small town. There were well-tended black-top streets, concrete sidewalks, neat lawns, shapely small trees, ordinary lampposts and stop signs. But the buildings were all large dull rectangles, one or two stories high, all clapboard, all with the same kind of windows, all painted either tan or light green. Walks were lined with whitewashed rocks, there was no litter anywhere, and the occasional pedestrian—mostly neatly uniformed military men, plus a few neatly dressed civilians—seemed more like wind-up toys than human beings. It was a model train layout, a miniature of itself. Only the automobiles, the few of them moving on the streets and the batches of them tucked away in parking lots that I caught glimpses of between buildings, hinted at reality. Bulging or beetled, shiny or rust-pocked, they showed more variety and liveliness than everything else in the place combined. I never thought I'd be anywhere that an automobile would look more natural than a tree, but the Army had managed it; Stonevelt Penitentiary was a sprawling, teeming human beehive by comparison.

The bus drove three blocks through this bloodless complex and stopped before a larger building than any of the others: *three* stories high, light green clapboard, same windows, whitewashed rocks flanking the path, one plane tree centered on each side of the crewcut lawn, large wooden sign out by the sidewalk telling us this was Headquarters of the 2137 NorBomComDak, Ninth Army, General Lester B. Winterhilf, Commandant.

We joined the other debusing passengers, and on the sidewalk Eddie looked around and said, "We might as well wait in the Officer's Club."

Fine. If I was about to be shot as a spy, I wanted my last meal to be a martini.

We walked two blocks through this architect's rendering, me carefully avoiding the eyes of everybody we passed, certain that some colonel, some master sergeant, even some raw new recruit, would suddenly stop, stare, point at me and yell, "*You're* no Lieutenant!" I was only here because this damned uniform was my size, yet it seemed badly fitted; the blouse collar was too big and sleeves too short, the shirt was too small, the trouser legs too long. I couldn't decide if my garrison cap felt too large or too small, but I was sure I was wearing it wrong—tilted too far forward, or possibly too far back.

The Officer's Club was the basic building in tan. We went up the wide outside wooden steps to the entrance, and as we did so I was suddenly flung back in memory to basic training when I was nineteen years old. Mail call. Only in basic was there an actual mail call, with a postal clerk who would stand on wooden steps like this and shout out last names to the trainees massed before him. For weeks my voice was raised forlornly: "Künt! With an umlaut! Sir!" And vainly. I merely called attention to myself, as though the name didn't do that sufficiently all by itself. People who had only heard me pronounce my name but had never seen it written down would turn to me with comic curiosity, gleams beginning to sparkle in the corners of their eyes, and they would say, "*How* do you spell your name?" "With an umlaut," I would say, in useless hope. "Kunt!" the mail clerk would cry.

It had been years since I'd thought of all that but the memory could still make me wince. Bring on that drink, I thought.

Inside the Officer's Club some attempt had been made to disguise the raw functionalism of the structure, but to no avail. The curtains on the windows, the artificial potted plants scattered about, the Japanese screens used as room dividers, all managed to make the place look merely like an impoverished touring company of *Teahouse of the August Moon*. A goodly number of officers, most of them young and moustached and looking almost exactly like Max Nolan, sat at the bar or at formica-top tables across the way. A dining room was beyond this area, impossible to see through a labyrinth of Japanese screens.

And now, inside the Officer's Club, Eddie Troyn all at once blossomed into a completely new man. The silent, rigid, humorless military pastiche I was used to altered into what he had surely been before his fall from grace; a benign authority figure, crisp and assured, almost graceful. It was amazing to watch.

Eddie had been coming to this base no more than a week, but half a dozen of the younger officers at the bar hailed him as an old-time comrade. "It's Captain Robinson!" one of them called out, in respectful delight, and they all made room for him at the bar.

"Afternoon, boys," Eddie said, reserved but genial. "This is Lieutenant Smith."

"Call me Harry," I said, because I knew if I was called Lieutenant Smith I'd never think to answer.

The bartender, a big, heavy man with meaty shoulders, had come over at once to lean toward Eddie and listen respectfully to his order. "My usual, Jack," Eddie told him. "And the same for Lieutenant Smith."

"Yessir, Captain."

One of the officers said, "How's the count coming, sir?"

"So far," Eddie answered, with mock sternness, "you boys seem to have lost three tanks and a quonset hut."

They were delighted. As our drinks were brought—Eddie's 'usual' turned out to be bourbon and water—the officers tried to top one another with suggestions about what had been done with the missing tanks and hut. One said the tanks had been stolen by gypsies, painted different colors, and used as wagons. One said the hut had been sent to New York City where it had become a four-story apartment building. Another said no, it was the *tanks* that had been sent to New York City and converted into five-room apartments, while the hut had been floated across the Atlantic to Africa where it was about to become an independent nation. Another said, "Right. They're calling it Pattonagonia," and everybody groaned.

We spent an hour at the bar with the young officers, in a general aura of coltish hilarity. Most of the chatter came from the young men, who in an easygoing way were vying with one another for Eddie's attention and approval, but Eddie too had his occasional small quips, most of them of a mildly right-wing nature. The young officers hung on his every word, whooping with laughter and clapping one another on the back at his little punch lines, while he stood swirling his drink, the small smile of the accomplished raconteur tugging gently at his lips.

Eddie was so good at this easygoing paternalism, this enjoying of an informal chat with the boys after duty hours, that I could see he was absolutely wasted in prison. I still don't know what crime he'd been sentenced for, but surely society was losing too much in refusing to permit him to be himself.

As for me, I kept quiet, smiled when everybody else laughed, pulled steadily at my bourbon and water, and kept listening for clues as to just who the hell Eddie and I were supposed to be. The general impression Eddie had apparently given was that he was here on some sort of accounting or inventory mission outside the normal sequence of such events, possibly from the Inspector General's office, or maybe even from Army Intelligence. The story seemed to be concrete enough to satisfy idle curiosity, vague enough so he couldn't be pinned down or contradicted on details, and broad enough to justify his turning up almost anywhere he wanted on the base.

My own role was dealt with in a sentence: "Lieutenant Smith is here from DomBac to help finish up," Eddie said, and of course the natural response to that was for the young men to fasten on the phrase 'finish up,' and to ask just how soon their friend Captain Robinson would be leaving, thus ending curiosity about me for good and all.

"Possibly by the end of the week," Eddie told them, "or, with Lieutenant Smith here, it could be even sooner."

One of them, grinning, said, "You'll be giving us a clean bill of health, Captain?"

"Considering the number of WAC uniform skirts that are missing," Eddie answered, "not to mention female unmentionables, I'm not entirely sure every one of you boys could be considered completely healthy." How they laughed over that, punching and poking one another. There's nothing like a joke about homosexuality to make men rub each other's shoulders.

Promptly at six-thirty Eddie consulted his watch and announced, "I believe it's mess call, gentlemen. If you'll excuse
me?"

A chorus of courses followed that, and the bartender promptly
presented his bill. With a restrained flourish Eddie wrote across
its face *'Captain Robinson,'* smacked the pen down on top of it,
and pushed it back across the bar. "Thank you, Captain," the
bartender said. "Evening now."

"Evening, Jack," Eddie said.

We zigzagged through the Japanese screens to the dining
room, which was less than half full. The management had dealt
with the decorating problem in here by turning all the lights off
and making do with candles on the tables; it was too dark to see
what the place looked like.

We took a table along the side wall, where I discovered that
the walls were fronted by dark brown draperies, and Eddie
said, "A fine group of young men, that. May they never have to
face the guns of the enemy."

By God, he was Mister Chips!

A waiter brought us menus and we ordered; Eddie had the
sole meunière and I chose the veal parmigiana. In the waiter's
hearing, Eddie said, "Perhaps a half bottle of white, Lieutenant?"
When I agreed, he ordered soave. The waiter departed and
Eddie, glancing around in proprietary satisfaction, said, "Well,
Lieutenant, what do you think of our little club?"

It didn't seem to me there were any occupied tables close
enough for us to be overheard, but if Eddie wanted to maintain
tight security that was fine with me. Particularly since, with all
the bourbon I'd put away over the last hour and a promise of
white wine to come, I was probably going to wind up as tight
as the security. So I said, "It's fine, sir. I particularly enjoyed
meeting your young friends."

"Fine men," he agreed. "They'll make their country proud some day. They remind me of a Lieutenant Eberschwartz I once knew. Motor Pool officer. Fine ingenious young man. Someone had been siphoning fuel out of the two-by-sixes at night, and Lieutenant Eberschwartz set himself to catch the fellow. But the thief was clever; he would never come around on a night when Lieutenant Eberschwartz had posted himself there. So finally he came up with a solution. He rigged a camera with a flashbulb inside an office window, and ran wires connecting it to one of the trucks' gasoline caps. When the cap was turned, the fellow's picture would be taken."

"Very clever," I said. "Did it work?"

"Beyond his wildest expectations. The thief already had several open cans of gasoline about himself when he turned that particular cap. The camera went off, but the electronic impulse of the flashbulb ignited the gasoline fumes in the air, and the explosion demolished the thief, seven vehicles and the Motor Pool office."

"Um," I said.

"Absolutely put a stop to pilfering on that base," he said, and nodded with remembered satisfaction.

"I can see where it would," I said.

"There was nothing left of the thief, of course," he said. "We had to find him by a process of elimination, scanning the Morning Reports for missing men until we'd narrowed it down to just one possibility. Then we got some sheep parts from the mess hall, put them in a plastic bag, and shipped them home to the fellow's parents. Said he died falling out of a jeep."

"Uh huh," I said.

"That's the standard explanation, of course, for all noncombatant Army deaths. Died falling out of a jeep."

"That's right," I said. "I've seen that in newspaper reports."

"The odd thing is," he said, "I once knew a fellow who *did* die from falling out of a jeep."

"Oh?"

"He was having intercourse with a nurse at the time," he said. "At a given moment she lunged upward so vigorously she flipped him completely out of the jeep."

"Was it moving?"

"Hm? Oh, the jeep. No, he landed on a mine."

"Um," I said.

"Speaking of landing on mines," he said, "that reminds me of another funny story." And he proceeded to tell it. Soon our food came, and so did the wine, but Eddie kept on telling me his reminiscences. Friends of his had fallen under tanks, walked into airplane propellers, inadvertently bumped their elbows against the firing mechanism of thousand-pound bombs and walked backwards off the flight deck on an aircraft carrier while backing up to take a group photograph. Other friends had misread the control directions on a robot tank and driven it through a Pennsylvania town's two-hundredth anniversary celebration square dance, had fired a bazooka while it was facing the wrong way, had massacred a USO Gilbert and Sullivan troupe rehearsing *The Mikado* under the mistaken impression they were peaceful Vietnamese villagers, and had ordered a nearby enlisted man to look in that mortar and see why the shell hadn't come out.

It began after a while to seem as though Eddie's military career had been an endless red-black vista of explosions, fires and crumpling destruction, all intermixed with hoarse cries, anonymous thuds and terminal screams. Eddie recounted these disasters in his normal bloodless style, with touches of that dry avuncular humor he'd displayed during our hour at the bar. I managed to eat very little of my veal parmigiana—it kept looking like a body fragment—but became increasingly sober nonetheless. A brandy later with coffee, accompanied by a Korean War story about a friend of Eddie's trapped in a box canyon for nine days by a combination of a blizzard and a North Korean offensive, who kept himself alive by sawing off his own wounded leg and eating steaks from it, but who later died in Honolulu from gangrene of the stomach, didn't help much.

Or maybe it did, in a way. By the time we left the Officer's Club, shortly before nine o'clock, I was numb with horror, but the subject of my numbness had been transferred from the laser larceny to Eddie's memoirs. I suppose I was in the best possible frame of mind for the events to follow: cold sober, and actively anxious to be distracted, even if that distraction had to be the commission of a felony.

The streets of the camp were well illuminated, but there was very little traffic. Eddie and I strolled along, he pausing at last in his recital to puff a cigar in the crisp night air and to take an obvious sensual pleasure from his surroundings; he was like the captain of a great steamship out for a promenade around the deck. This was his environment, well-understood and well-loved. All it lacked to make it really homey for him, I thought, was a few burned bodies and the distant rattle of machine-gun fire.

After three or four blocks we moved out of the housing and administrative area clustered in the vicinity of the main gate. From here on sprawled the storage section, starting with great hulking curved quonset huts, looking like headless armadillos. The ordinary streetlights were replaced here by floodlights at the corners of the buildings, and sentries stood guard at many of the doorways.

Judiciously Eddie said, "Wouldn't like an explosion around this area."

I looked at him, apprehensive. "Why's that?"

He motioned to the quonset huts around us. "Some cyanide compounds," he said. "Other poison gases, some defoliants, a few sterilizing agents. Enough chemical weaponry right here to strip the Earth naked."

"Oh," I said, and for a while after that I found it very difficult not to walk on tiptoe.

19

The building we wanted was just beyond the cylinders full of plague germs. "There it is," Eddie said. "The structure on the right."

"Uh huh," I said, and stopped scratching to look. Ever since he'd told me about the plague germs, I'd been itching all over. Also my lungs felt wrinkled.

The structure on the right was a one-story version of the basic building, with fewer windows than normal. A rifle-bearing sentry marched back and forth in front of the entry door. That is, he marched back and forth the instant he saw the two of us, a Captain and a Lieutenant, approaching his post; before then he'd been more mooching than marching. And now, as we neared him, he came smartly to a halt, did a right face toward us, snappily converted from right shoulder arms to port arms, and announced in a very young voice, "Who goes there?"

"Captain Robinson," Eddie told him. "At ease, soldier."

The sentry's body slackened a bit, but the rifle remained more or less at port arms while Eddie fished out the documents Bob Dombey had forged for him. I spent the time studying the sentry; did they really let a boy like this have bullets for that gun?

"Here you are, soldier."

The boy wouldn't take the papers. He stuck his head forward over his clutched rifle and read them as Eddie held them up in front of him. "Yes, sir," he said. "Very good, sir. You want to enter?"

"That's right."

"I don't have a key," he said doubtfully.

"I have," Eddie assured him. A week ago Eddie had returned from the base with various wax impressions, and Phil had arranged to have keys made for him in the prison machine shop. Now, Eddie took out a ring of keys, selected one, and used it with casual confidence to open the door. "Return to your post, soldier," he said, not harshly, and the two of us entered the building, pausing only for Eddie to hit the light switch beside the door, turning on a double row of fluorescent lights extending all the way down to the other end of the building.

There were no interior partitions. It was almost exactly like my old basic training barracks, a long rectangular room with square wooden pillars at intervals to support the roof. The only difference was that my barracks had been lined with windows all the way around, while this structure only sported a pair of windows flanking the main entrance and three more windows spaced along each side. No windows, so far as I could see, were in the rear wall.

There was no furniture in the building, just cartons stacked up so as to make aisles. Most of the stacks were no more than waist-high, but here and there one loomed as high as my head. Reading the stencilled notations on various cartons I learned that I was standing among machine guns, mortar shells, night sights, hand grenades…

"Ah," Eddie said. "Here they are. Find an empty carton, Lieutenant, there ought to be one around here somewhere."

That was the second time he'd done that. The first, back in the Officer's Club dining room, I'd put down to excess caution. But who could overhear us this time? Looking toward the front windows I saw the sentry marching smartly back and forth out there, with the door closed between us and him; surely there was no way he could hear anything being said in here.

Or was Eddie afraid these storage buildings were bugged? It was possible, after all; put the sound-activated microphones in, have a central listening location, and know at once if anybody was planning anything he shouldn't.

Smart, Eddie, I thought, and aloud I said, "Yes, sir," and went off looking for empty cartons.

There was a bunch of them at the very rear, all neatly stacked inside one another. They were a hell of a job to separate, and when I finally went back to where Eddie had ripped open some of the full cartons, I found he had assembled several things other than the laser. There were four Colt .45 automatics, shining wickedly black in the fluorescent lighting, plus a dozen extra clips full of bullets. There were five hand grenades. And finally there was a box about fifteen inches long and six inches square, stencilled in black with all that indecipherable lettering and numbering the military likes so much, but with one word showing absolutely plain: LASER.

I said, "What's all the rest of this?"

"Useful materiel," he said. "Is that the empty carton? Fine."

He took the carton from me and carefully packed it, wedging all the items in together so that nothing would bounce around loose. Considering what the items were, it was a precaution worth taking.

"All right, Lieutenant," he said, when he was finished. "If you'll carry that, we can be off now."

"Right, sir," I said. I picked up the carton, which weighed a ton, and followed him back down the central aisle to the front door. He opened it, stepped to one side to let me precede him out, and the sentry took one look at the carton in my arms, halted, switched his rifle to port arms, and said, "I'm sorry, sir, I won't be able to let you take that."

Eddie had been on the verge of switching off the interior lights and shutting the door. Now he paused, glancing in quick annoyance at the sentry, and said, "What was that, soldier?"

"I can't let you take any supplies from this building, sir, without a special requisition order from Major Macauley."

"But I have one," Eddie said. "I showed it to you." The sentry and I both looked at him in bewilderment. He had one? That was news to me.

And to the sentry, who said, "I don't remember seeing it, sir, I'm sorry."

"No problem," Eddie said. "I prefer to see alert young men, on the job—" While saying which, he was reaching inside his uniform blouse, to suddenly pull out the small pistol he'd pointed at me that very first day in the gym. "Just take it easy, soldier," he said. "No reason to get yourself shot. Lieutenant—" that was me "—relieve the young man of his rifle."

"Aa-uh," I said. I was standing holding a carton of explosives in my arms, between one man with a rifle and one man with a pistol. But the sentry hadn't moved, was still at port arms as though frozen in that position, so maybe there wouldn't be any gunfire after all. Hastily putting down the carton I approached the sentry, noticing just how white were the whites of his eyes, and how equally white were the knuckles of his hands gripping the rifle; it was a bit heartening to know he was every bit as scared as me. Maybe more so, since he had no idea what was going on.

"I'll take that," I said, and put my hand on the rifle. It trembled like a puppy beneath my hand. The sentry was staring, wide-eyed. I was blinking like a shipboard semaphore.

"You can't—" he started to say, and then stopped, swallowed, and started all over again. Whispering this time, he said, "I can't let go."

"Yes, you can," I assured him, and tugged slightly on the rifle. His knuckles really were white.

Behind me, Eddie said, "Step to one side. Lieutenant. If he won't give up his weapon voluntarily, I'll have to fire."

The sentry's hands snapped open, and I just barely kept the rifle from falling to the ground. But I did keep hold of it, got it into two hands, and backed away with it.

"All right, soldier," Eddie said. "Into the building, on the double."

We're right in the glare of floodlights, I thought. We're in the middle of an Army base, in the glare of floodlights, disarming a sentry. How did I get involved in this?

I realized I was holding the rifle at port arms. I wanted to shift to some other positon, but I couldn't think of one, so I stayed the way I was.

Meantime, the sentry was scooting into the building. Eddie and I followed him, and I immediately put the rifle on top of a stack of cartons, well out of the way.

Eddie said to the sentry, "Let me see your orders of the day."

"Yes, sir." The sentry too, I noticed, couldn't get past the idea of treating Eddie like a superior officer. He reached into his breast pocket, took out a folded piece of rough paper, and handed it across.

"Good." Opening it, Eddie said, "What's your name, soldier?"

"Bunfelder, sir. Private First Class Emil Bunfelder."

"At ease, Bunfelder."

Bunfelder's hands went behind his back, his feet moved to a position twelve inches apart. By God if he wasn't standing at parade rest!

Military men receive their assignments in orders of the day, typewriter-paper-size sheets with perhaps a dozen different names and assignments, all in military abbreviations. This was what Eddie was reading, and when he found what he wanted he looked up and said, "You'll be relieved at twenty-four-hundred hours."

"Yes, sir," said the sentry.

Eddie checked his watch. "Two hours forty-seven minutes from now. It won't be a difficult wait, Bunfelder."

Doubtfully, not sure what was meant, Bunfelder said, "No, sir."

Now Eddie issued both of us orders, calmly but briskly, and we followed them with dispatch. The sentry sat down on the floor with his back against a support post. He removed his belt, and I used it to tie his wrists behind the post. I then used his necktie to gag him and his shoelaces to tie his ankles together. When I was finished, Bunfelder wasn't going anywhere before his relief arrived at twenty-four-hundred hours.

"Good work, Lieutenant," Eddie said. "Now it's time for us to go."

"Right," I said.

Outside again, Eddie carefully locked the door while I picked up the carton. Then we set off down the street.

As we walked along, certain inconsistencies in Eddie's manner began to bother me, and finally I said, "Eddie, do you think that building we were in might have been bugged?"

He frowned at me. "What say?"

"Do you think there was a microphone in it, anybody listening to us?"

"Of course not," he snapped. "Don't be paranoid."

"Oh," I said. The carton was getting heavy; I shifted it to a new position.

"Come along Lieutenant," Eddie said. "We don't want to be late for the rendezvous."

"Right," I said.

"Eh?"

"Yes, sir," I said.

20

It took nearly an hour to walk to the west gate, and in that time I saw more methods of destruction than most sane people see all their lives. After the quonset hut full of chemicals and the second ring of supply buildings full of miscellaneous materiel came endless tall rows of stacked shells, parking lots lined with stripped-down jeeps and medieval-looking armored cars and big-tired trucks of various sizes, low concrete block structures full of ammunition and explosives, row upon row of self-propelled artillery, and a veritable invasion force of massed tanks, all with some sort of white cap over their out-thrust turret guns, as though they were being treated for a venereal disease.

Sentries marched back and forth at their posts, and though we passed very close to some of them, not a one asked us who we were or where we were going or what we had in the carton. Every once in a while a jeep with two or three white-helmeted MPs in it would drive slowly by, but they too accepted our uniforms at face value and went on without questioning us or wondering why we were roaming around out here after dark with an anonymous carton. Given my present circumstances I was happy for their attitude, but given the tools of mayhem available all over the place, I found myself wishing some of these people were a little more suspicious, a little more alert.

Eddie spent most of the walk pointing to this or that engine of death and telling me its nomenclature and particular qualities, plus whatever anecdotes it had put him in mind of. He also called me 'lieutenant' from time to time. Dante had it good; he only went through Hell.

We were supposed to rendezvous at the west gate with Phil and Jerry at ten-thirty. We arrived ten minutes early and sat down in the unused guard shack to rest while we waited. The carton had become very heavy after a while, so I did a lot of flexing of my arm muscles, trying to get rid of the aches I'd developed. Looking back the way we had come, at the tanks and guns and armored cars and all the rest of the armament hulking there beneath the floodlights, it began to look to me like a true battle scene, frozen in time, with white flares glaring overhead and all the panoply of destruction poised beneath, ready to kill anything that moved.

This gate and its blacktop road were not in normal use by any of the Camp Quattatunk personnel. The main gate, where Eddie and I had come in, was the only one generally open. This one here, and several other supplementary entrances around the perimeter of the huge compound, was used exclusively for movement of stored materiel in and out of the base. Those tanks over there, for instance; if one of Eddie's friends decided to use them to level Cleveland, they would exit through here rather than plunge through all the other weaponry to get to the main gate. Otherwise this entrance was kept locked. And, as the signs facing outward warned us, it was also kept electrified.

At precisely ten-thirty Eddie stepped outside the guard shack and peered into the darkness on the other side of the gate, looking in vain for Jerry and Phil. "They're late," he announced.

"They'll be here," I said, trying not to sound as fatalistic as I felt.

"That's not like Phil," Eddie said, and snapped his cuff back to look at his watch. The radium dial glinted in the darkness. Then he came back into the guard shack, a small square clapboard structure with windows on all four sides and room enough within for a chest-high desk, a couple of stools and a wooden bench. I was perched on a stool, gazing alternately at the petrified battle scene and the darkness beyond the fence, but Eddie preferred to stand, taut and serious, gazing steadfastly out the window toward our non-present gang. Once again he reminded me of a ship's captain, this time on the bridge, gazing out at the expected sou'wester.

By twenty of eleven, I was beginning to hope that maybe somebody had been caught leaving the prison, or there was trouble about the stolen car. Maybe something really serious and time-consuming had taken place and we wouldn't be able to steal the goddam laser after all. And if we couldn't steal the laser we wouldn't be able to pull the bank robbery.

That was something to look forward to.

On the other hand, if Phil and Jerry didn't show up, we could be in big trouble. There was no way for us to get through that electrified gate, since Phil was the expert in that department, who would be bringing the bypass wires and the rubber gloves and all the other things needed to de-electrify the gate without alerting the MPs back at their headquarters. Which meant the main gate was our only exit, and the last bus left the base for town at eleven o'clock. That was twenty minutes from now, and my calculations had us a good hour's walking time from the bus stop. Could we stroll out the main gate on foot at midnight and hope the MPs there wouldn't do more than glance at our ID cards? I somehow doubted it.

I said, "What time is it?"

Radium dial glistened greenly in the dark. Eddie said, "Twenty-two forty-five hours."

I translated that, and it came out quarter to eleven. I said, "Eddie, I don't think they're coming."

"Of course they are," he said.

"We've only got fifteen minutes to catch that bus."

There was enough illumination from the distant floodlights so I could see him scowl at me. "What bus?"

"The last bus back to town. Eddie, we can't just walk out that main gate in the middle of the night without—"

"Paragraph one," Eddie said. "Our transportation will be coming, I have every confidence in Jerry and Phil. Paragraph two: we could not take the bus even if we were close enough to reach it, which we aren't, because we would not be able to board it with that carton of materiel."

"We'll have to leave it," I said.

"Abort the mission? You can't be serious."

"Eddie, we don't have any choice."

"Lieutenant," he said, and his voice was icy, strong, controlled, "we will have no more defeatist talk."

"Eddie, I—"

"*Captain*, if you please!"

"Uuuuuhhhhhhhhhhhhhhhhhhhhhhhhhh," I said, and turned to look out the window toward the gate. Beyond it I saw no headlights approaching. Parking lights; they wouldn't use headlights. Well, I didn't see any of them approaching either.

"Did you hear me, Lieutenant?"

There are three rules one should live by, if one intends to make it successfully through life: Don't carry a sofa upstairs by yourself. Don't get involved with a Scorpio unless you mean it. And don't argue with crazy people. "Yes, sir," I said.

21

At eleven-thirty, one hour exactly after Phil and Jerry were supposed to have been here, Eddie roused himself from his parade rest stance in front of the gate-facing window and said, "Very well. We'll have to improvise."

Improvise. The bus was gone. There was no way off the base but the main gate, and our identification just wasn't going to be good enough to get us through that main gate with this damn carton full of death and injury. In thirty minutes the relief sentry would arrive to take the place of the one we had tied up, and the alarm would then be sounded for fair, and this entire camp would be searched with a fine-tooth comb. And not just with a fine-tooth comb, either; there would also be floodlights mounted on jeeps, and men armed with rifles and machine guns, and tracker dogs, and maybe even helicopters. We were going to be caught, my insane friend and I, absolutely no later than one hour from right now. And when we were caught, we would *really* be caught. Our very presence on this base was an even more serious offense than our absence from the penitentiary. Then there were the uniforms that we weren't authorized to wear, and the fake ID, and the grand larceny of all this shit in the carton, and the assault on the sentry…

A persistent image kept entering my brain. One summer vacation when I was a teenager my parents and I took a cottage by a lake in Maine. It rained all week, of course, but that isn't the point. The point is, there was a fireplace, and we kept a fire going in it for a little warmth and dryness, and one time after my father tossed a flat piece of old board on the fire I noticed there was an ant on it. The piece of board was about four inches wide, making a kind of highway through the flames, and the ant just kept running back and forth on that highway, trying to find some way the hell out of there. Improvise. We were now, like that ant, going to improvise.

I said, hopelessly, "I suppose the only thing to do is try the main gate. Maybe, if we go through without the carton, just maybe they won't look too closely at—"

"We will not abort," Eddie told me sternly. "Put that out of your mind once and for all, Lieutenant."

"Yes, sir," I said. When it doesn't matter what you do, you might as well do what comes easiest, and right now the easiest thing to do was to go along with Eddie's delusions. His delusion that he was a Captain, for instance, and that I was a Lieutenant. Not to mention his delusion that there was some way off this board and out of the fire.

He said, "Where's the carton?"

"Right here," I said, and patted it where I had placed it on the chest-high desk in the guard shack. "Do you think maybe we could toss the laser over the fence and then come back tomorrow and—"

But he wasn't listening to me. He was opening the carton, and then he was fishing around inside it. "Fine," he said, and took something out. "Carry the carton outside, Lieutenant," he told me.

"What are we doing?" I felt very mistrustful all of a sudden. What had he taken out of there?

"We are altering our plan of withdrawal," he said, and marched out of the guard shack. "Come along. Bring the carton."

I went along. I brought the carton.

Outside, he pointed to the side of the shack facing the battle tableau. "Put the carton down there, against the base of the building. Sit down next to it, with your back against the wall."

"Eddie, what are you going to do?"

"Move, Lieutenant. We don't have much time."

"I really want to know, Eddie," I said.

In a very soft voice, he said, "That's twice you have failed to address me in the proper manner. Is this a mutiny, Lieutenant?"

There was no way I was going to answer that question *yes*. Not when Eddie had his gun on him. "No," I said. "No mutiny."

"What was that?"

"No, *sir*," I said.

"Get on with it, Lieutenant," he said.

Reminding myself that I had no future anyway, so that it hardly mattered what lunacy Eddie had in mind, I turned away from him, carried the carton around to the back of the guard shack, put it down, sat down next to it, leaned my back against the wall, and gazed at the *tableau mordant* in front of me with bitterness and despair.

Eddie came in sight around the corner of the shack, with something in his hands. "In position, Lieutenant? Good."

I looked at him, and saw that it was a hand grenade he was holding just as he pulled the pin. "Jesus *Christ*!" I yelled, and jumped to my feet as he tossed the grenade underhand toward the gate. Then he stepped forward, casually stiff-armed me so that I lost my balance and went over onto the ground again, sat down next to me, and said, quietly, "Eight, nine—" The explosion made the ground jump, as though surprised. Red-yellow glare beamed through the guard shack windows, which didn't break; though in counterpoint to the *whump* of the grenade going off I did hear the tinkle of broken glass from the other side.

I was still trying to unscramble my brains when Eddie was already back on his feet, looking around the corner of the guard shack toward the gate. "Good," he said, with satisfaction.

It *was* a way. It was crazy, but by God it was a true way

through that gate. If we went through now, ran like hell, hid in the woods whenever we saw anybody coming, we just might make it. (We wouldn't, but on the other hand we might.)

I climbed up the guard shack to my feet and ran around the corner to look at the gate. There was a smoking hole where it had been. Live wires fizzed and spuckled on both sides, creating short-lived tiny fires in dead leaves. Twisted remnants of gate hung from sprung hinges. "You did it, Eddie!" I cried, feeling a sudden surge of ridiculous optimism. Then I corrected myself: "Captain, you did it!" I turned to him, and found him rooting in the carton again. "I'll carry that," I said. "Let's get out of here!"

Calmly he reached up, handing me one of the .45 automatics. Taking it—obedience was becoming second nature to me by now—I said, "Captain, we don't have much time. They'll be here any minute."

"Don't fire that at anybody," he said briskly. "It isn't loaded." Then he got to his feet, holding a .45 of his own, and faced back toward the camp. "Here they come," he said, still calm, still quiet, still brisk.

I looked. Here they came, all right, a jeep bouncing hell for leather through the aisles of tanks, with another one maybe fifty yards behind it. They weaved and darted and ran through the tanks as though they were under bombardment and taking evasive action. In the middle of the petrified battle scene, one element had come into furious life.

I screamed, *Eddie! Captain! We've gotta get* OUT *of here!*"

"Follow my lead," he said quietly, and stood next to the guard shack, facing the oncoming jeeps, the automatic held down at his side.

Follow his lead? Stand off two jeeploads of MPs with an empty gun? I stood there twitching, my mouth moving without words, trying to phrase the sentences that would get through to him that what we were doing was *not sensible*. "It's not *sensible*!" I wailed, and the first jeep slued to a stop at our feet.

Three MPs, white-helmeted, white-eyed. The driver yelled at us, "Captain, what's going on here?"

Eddie took a step closer to him. The other jeep was skidding up, brakes squealing. The smell of burnt rubber mixed with the acrid stink of the explosion. Eddie said, "Radicals. Weathermen, I think. Lieutenant Smith and I chased them this far. They dropped that carton when they blew the gate."

Two MPs had clattered out of the other jeep and come running over to hear the story. One of them yelled, "Captain Robinson! What happened?"

So. Not for nothing had Eddie spent a week at this base. Not only had he familiarized himself with Camp Quattatunk, he had also familiarized Camp Quattatunk with Captain Robinson.

The driver of the first jeep was getting more wide-eyed by the second. He said, "You mean, they were *inside*?"

"They've done something to the sentry of building FJ-832," Eddie told him. "You got a radio in there, Corporal?"

"Yes, sir!"

"Call in. Have that building searched. If they've killed that man—" He shook the fist with the automatic in it, then turned to the MPs standing beside him. "I'll have to requisition your jeep, Sergeant," he said. "You and your man stand guard on this gate, in case they come back." Turning again to the driver of the first jeep, he said, "Get back to building FJ-832. If they've left a bomb in there, this whole compound could go up."

"Great Jesus!" the driver said. He threw the jeep in gear, stomped the accelerator, made one of the tightest U-turns in the history of vehicular travel, and roared off again into the sea of tanks.

"Lieutenant!"

"Yes, sir!"

"You'll drive," Eddie said, and vaulted into the passenger seat of the remaining jeep.

"Yes, sir!"

"Grab that carton of evidence!"

"Yes, sir!"

I grabbed the carton of evidence and threw it on the back seat, then pushed myself in behind the wheel like a woman pushing hair under a bathing cap. There was no room for my knees, but I put them in there anyway. The engine was running, the clutch was over there, the gear lever was floor-mounted. Left foot down, right hand forward, left hand clutching wheel, left foot up, right foot down hard. Tires screamed like stuck chorus girls behind me; the jeep lunged forward, leaped down into the grenade crater, cracked my spine in seven places when it landed, bounced forward, scrabbled up the rubble, made the blacktop, and off we roared down a hollow tube between lines of pine trees.

It was a mile to the turnoff. It couldn't have taken long to get there because I held my breath the whole time. Then, when we arrived, I had the greatest difficulty forcing my foot to come away from the accelerator. It was a sharp left turn I would have to make, and I was coming at it way too fast.

So was the car coming the other way. All at once the intersection was full of a large black Buick, twisting into this road with its front wheels locked and its rear wheels skidding sideways, and there was absolutely nothing I could do but leave the road, jump the drainage ditch, and run head-on into the back of the sign that said *dead end government property no trespassing*.

The rough turf and the wooden sign stopped us more than my frantic pounding on the brake, and the coup de grace was the ditch beside the main road, which ate our front wheels and left us angled steeply downward with our headlights glaring at the weedy opposite slope a scant three inches away.

I appeared to be wearing the steering wheel on my chest. Removing it, I looked around and discovered I was still inhabiting the planet Earth. So it was likely I was still alive.

"Nicely done, Harry," Eddie said.

I gaped at him. He had tossed his officer's cap away into the ditch and was giving me his flinty smile. He was also in the process of disentangling himself from the jeep. "Time to move out," he said.

Move out. Could I move at all? I hunched up and back, pushing against the windshield frame and the back of the seat until I could catch my heels on the seat itself. Sitting briefly atop the seatback, woozy and dazed, I looked around some more and saw the black Buick roaring backwards toward the intersection from the side road. Eddie was out of the jeep by now and climbing out of the ditch, leaving clothing in his wake. Uniform blouse off, tie now sailing away behind him. And also words: "Bring the carton, Harry!"

He was calling me Harry. Was the craziness over? The Buick, braking sharply to a stop just shy of the intersection, suddenly disgorged Phil, who popped out on the passenger side and yelled, "Come on! Come on!"

I went on. I finished separating myself from the jeep's loving embrace, then picked up the carton and went staggering off across the uneven ground toward the Buick. Eddie was already there, sliding into the back seat.

I followed, pushing the carton ahead of me. Phil climbed back in, we slammed all the doors, and Jerry, at the wheel, backed up in a smart half-circle out onto the main road, shifted, and we tore off toward town.

There was civilian clothing for both of us in the back seat and we both hurriedly began to change. Phil, half-turned so he could talk to us, said, "How'd you get out?"

"Eddie blew up the gate," I said. "It was terrific. I thought we were doomed, I thought we were goddam doomed, and he just blew up the gate and commandeered a jeep and son of a *bitch*!" Relief was making me giddy; it was only with the greatest effort that I managed to stop talking.

Phil said, bitterly, "We had a surprise shakedown, the whole fucking prison. Thank God we had Muttgood in the gym, he helped us cover for you two. I gave him the idea you were off screwing each other on some roof."

"Fast thinking," Eddie said. My own comment I left unvoiced.

"But we couldn't get away for fucking *hours*," Phil said. "I really thought you people had bought the farm."

"So did I," I said. "Eddie, you're a genius."

"The first principle of military endeavor," he said. "Always keep the mission in mind. If you know *what* you want to do, you'll know how to do it."

"Anything you say," I told him, and put on my civilian pants.

Phil said, "How'd you blow up the gate?"

"With a hand grenade," Eddie told him. "I took several, thinking they might be useful."

"Hand grenades?" Phil seemed startled, almost frightened. "In this car here?"

"They're perfectly safe," Eddie said, and patted the carton.

"The hell they are," Phil said. "We don't want them. Throw them the fuck out."

Eddie cocked his head to one side. "Are you sure, Phil?"

"The laser's all we need," Phil told him. "We start cocking around with hand grenades, all we'll do is blow our own asses off. Throw them out."

Eddie shrugged. "You're the team leader," he said, opened the carton, and took one of the grenades out. He rolled the side window down, pulled the pin, and tossed the grenade out into the weeds beside the road.

"Not like *that*!" Phil yelled, and when Jerry slammed on the brakes Phil screamed at him, "Don't *stop*, for Christ's sake!" So Jerry accelerated again, and a piece of black night behind us went *boom*.

Jerry ducked his head down into his heavy shoulders. "What the hell was that?"

"Just drive," Phil told him, and said to Eddie, "Throw them out nice. Don't blow things up."

Eddie had the other grenades in his hands, holding them casually, like a juggler just before doing his act. "I didn't want a child to find one and hurt himself," he said.

Jerry said, over his shoulder, "There's a bridge up ahead. Throw them in the river."

"Fine," Phil said. "But don't pull any pins."

"Right," Eddie said.

We rode along then in silence. Eddie kept playing with the grenades, tossing them from hand to hand. We couldn't get to that river too soon for me.

22

The lying awake was bad enough, but the nightmares were worse. I spent the rest of that night in the gym, on a cot in a room also occupied by Eddie and Phil and Jerry, and every time terror drove me up out of dreams into consciousness I could only stare in wonder at those three, sleeping soggily— and in Jerry's case noisily—through all the bombs and fires of my imagination. In sleep I was chased by long-nosed tanks with lives and minds of their own, I was captured by soldiers who turned into policemen who turned into Joy Boys on some black roof somewhere, I was shot, blown up, set fire to, set on by dogs, set every way but loose.

At seven I was up, completely unrefreshed; I'd never been so exhausted in my life. I went through breakfast like a mule who's been hit on the back of the head with a rock, and then staggered away to my own sweet cell, far from the gym, far from the cares of the world, and there slept until one in the afternoon, deep, dreamless sleep from which I emerged in sudden brand-new terror, thinking, We rob the bank *today*!

Today; good God. We had the laser. Max Nolan and Joe Maslocki had found the spot right out on the street where the Twin Cities Typewriter man parked his truck every day, never later than five minutes past five, and they now had a key to fit its ignition. The typewriter had been obtained, a guard uniform for Eddie Troyn was on tap, there were more than enough guns for the whole gang, and the names and addresses and home phone numbers of the principal bank employees were all written down in a notebook in Phil's hip pocket. A surprise prison inspection, or "shake-down" as they called it, would definitely not happen today to throw a crimp in the plans, not right after one had been performed last night. There was nothing at all to stop the robbery from happening. Today.

At five-thirty this afternoon. Four and a half hours from now. I jittered out of bed, shaking and quaking, and scurried off to the gym.

Bob Dombey was there. He and Max would be staying in the gym, minding the store as it were, while the rest of us went out to commit our double felony. If I could somehow have wangled that assignment for myself I maybe wouldn't have minded it all as much. It was the thought of actually being in the bank, a gun in my hand, terrified customers cowering before me, that turned my knees to jelly. And my stomach to jelly. And my brains to jelly.

Bob, looking as shifty-eyed and weaselish as ever, was actually in a pretty good mood. "You haven't met my wife yet, have you?" he said.

"Eh?" In my condition, I could hardly remember that he was married. "Oh. Wife. No."

"She'd like to meet you," he said. "You two ought to get along, Alice is a real reader."

My image around the prison, I think I may have mentioned, was that of educated hood. To the illiterate, all readers share a bond, a commonness that assures they will 'get along' with one another, regardless of the particular thing they happen to read. It's similar to the belief among some whites that all black people know each other. To Bob's statement, therefore, I merely said something along the lines of, "That's nice." While the major portion of my brain continued desperately to chew its nails.

"We've been thinking of having a little get-together around

Christmas," Bob told me. "Alice loves to cook for a gang, and she doesn't have much chance since she moved up here."

"Uh huh," I said.

"I'll let you know pretty soon." Then he grinned, in his hunted-weasel way, ducking his head and looking up at me as though peering out of a hole, and added, "Maybe a celebration dinner after today, huh?"

"Aaa," I said, wildly trying to remember how to smile. "Mmm," I said, while my lips twitched this way and that around my head. "Well, I've got to—" I said, and wandered away in search of some grave to fling myself into.

Ten minutes later I was in the room where the baseball equipment was stored off-season, putting a good big dollop of Vaseline inside every glove, when salvation hit me like a paper bag full of water dropped from an upstairs window. "Ah!" I said, and lifted my head to stare in sudden wonder at the light that had appeared at the end of the tunnel. Could I? I could! Delighted, I slapped my palm to my forehead and thereby covered my face with Vaseline.

Drat. After I washed the stuff off—which takes *forever*—I went back to chat with Bob Dombey again, and to say after a minute, very casually, "Well, I guess I'll go on through now. See you later."

"Good luck," he said.

"Thanks."

It wasn't yet two o'clock when I crawled through the tunnel and emerged once more in the free world. Still, there was a lot to do before the bank closed, and I left the Dombey residence at the fastest possible walk, heading downtown.

I had two stores to stop at, a pharmacy and a five-and-ten. Then I closed myself in a gas station men's room for a while to do the assembly. I was fumble-fingered and hasty, and not absolutely sure what I was doing. How could such a thing be timed with the necessary accuracy? If it happened too soon, it probably wouldn't help. If it happened too late—I didn't even want to think about that.

Finally I left the men's room, with my two small packages in my jacket pockets. I walked to the bank, wrote a check for twenty-five dollars, walked around the bank a bit looking it over, cashed the check, and went out to the street. It was ten minutes to three. I proceeded to the bar called Turk's and gave the owner back some of the money I'd taken from him with the milk box.

23

Avoiding the temptation to get drunk, I left Turk's at four and walked back to the bank, where nothing unusual was happening. Discouraged but not despairing, I walked across the street to the luncheonette, where I found Phil and Jerry and Billy already seated at our regular table by the window. I joined them and Phil gave me his hard grin and said, "Well, today's the big day."

Smile, I told myself. "Sure is," I said.

They were talking about football. Jerry had played it in high school and the Army, generally as a tackle, Billy had hung around at one time with some former professional football players running a strike-breaker service in the Tennessee–Kentucky–Carolina area, and Phil ran a lively book in the prison on the pro games. Phil was at the moment discussing percentage points in the upcoming Jets–Oiler game, Jerry was describing things that could be done on the playing field to an opponent who had become annoying, and Billy was telling cheerful mountain tales of broken arms, backs, and heads.

I seemed to be blinking again. While the other three talked, I brooded out the window at the bank, where nothing continued to happen. Whenever I did glance at my tablemates, my blinking got a lot worse, yet through it I could still see them, all too plainly. I was sitting next to Billy, and his near arm looked to be the size and density of a caveman's club. His head was a boulder partially sculpted into what might with charity be called a face. His shoulders looked like football pads, but they weren't; they were shoulders.

Opposite me were Jerry and Phil. Jerry was another monster, in size if not in appearance. In fact, there was something almost baby-faced about Jerry, despite the great bulk of him, and his flesh appeared to be no harder or colder than normal human flesh. Still, his football field tales of snapping ankles and ripping nostrils made it clear he could be decisive if aroused. As to Phil, he didn't have the mass of the other two, but there was a quick, mean intelligence about him and a wiry strength that was in its own way even more intimidating. Jerry and Billy might be able to dismember me more completely, but Phil was the likeliest to realize I *ought* to be dismembered.

Around four-thirty the anthropomorphic high school boy floated by like a bottle with a note in it, was given an order for four coffees, and disappeared forever. I gazed at the bank past Billy's rocky profile, and now my left cheek was twitching. Nothing was happening over there. Nothing.

Phil said, "Getting a little nervous, Harry?"

Startled, I thrashed about, facing him. If that fool of a boy had brought coffee I would have dumped it on myself. "Nervous?" I said, blinking, twitching, scratching my left elbow with my right hand. "Me? No. Not a bit. Not at all."

Grinning, he said, "I know lots of guys nerved up ahead of time, and not a one of them ever admits it."

"Is that right?" I said. By keeping one eye closed, I could control a bit the twitching in the other.

"I knew a guy," Jerry said, "solid as a rock before a job, he'd always throw up right afterwards."

"Sure," Phil said. "It hits different guys different ways."

"Can you imagine?" Jerry said. "You stop a getaway car so a guy can throw up."

Phil laughed at that, responded with a remembrance of his

own, and I was safely out of the conversation again. I looked some more at the bank. Why wouldn't anything happen?

And why was I so nervous? In setting up my own little tricks, where there was almost always some chance of getting caught, I was invariably calm, almost casual. So why this time was I fidgeting and blinking and twitching and scratching and swallowing and feeling a sudden pulse pound in the side of my throat? Why, in short, was I becoming a nervous wreck?

Because this was different, that's why. Because in the first place it wasn't one of *my* little tricks, it wasn't my kind of thing at all. And because in the second place this was serious and maybe even deadly, a movement in which I was trying to put something over on society *and* these tough guys all at the same time, and all completely over my head. And because, goddamit, nothing was happening over there in the goddam *bank*!

Whenever I could manage to refocus my eyes from Billy Glinn's awesome profile, I could see directly across the street and through the big windows of Fiduciary Federal Trust right into the brightly lighted yellow interior, where absolutely nothing was taking place. Most of the employees had gone home by now, leaving the uniformed guard standing by the door, and possibly three people moving around behind the teller's counter, finishing the bookkeeping for the day. Everything normal. Damn. Damn. Damn.

Ten to five.

Five to five.

Five.

Five oh five.

I saw it when it started, and I froze at once—all except the twitch in my cheek—trying not to give it away that I'd noticed anything. But the guard just inside that glass door had suddenly jerked, as though he were a puppet operated by strings and somebody had just jostled his operator's elbow. I watched him turn, look, peer this way and that through the interior of the bank, then suddenly dash over to one side and bend over by the desk where I had filled out my twenty-five dollar check.

I knew what he was doing. I also understood why the bank official in the dark gray suit suddenly came dashing out from behind the counter, waving his arms and obviously shouting angrily in the general direction of the guard, who had now straightened up again, holding a wastebasket.

Phil and Jerry and Billy continued to chat together, about football and robbery and the mangling of bodies. I tried to remain very quiet, to appear to be looking at nothing in particular. The longer I could stall their discovery of what was happening, the more comfortable I would feel.

Let me get away with it, God. You let me pull all those minor ones where it didn't matter, now let me get away with this one. Please.

The guard was running toward the door, holding the wastebasket out to one side away from his body. He was just about to unlock the door when the official shouted again, apparently stopping him. The guard turned back, seemingly now doing some shouting of his own, and a brief spirited exchange took place, at the end of which the guard suddenly faced the door again, and this time stared out suspiciously at the sidewalk dotted with pedestrians.

I could imagine what the official had said. Something along the lines of, "This could be a trick, to get us to open the door." Right; suspicion, that's what I wanted, suspicion and paranoia and outright fear. Come on, I thought, let's get on with it.

A woman employee had now come out from the rear part of the bank, and was standing there waving her hands in front of her face as though brushing away gnats or mosquitoes. The male official turned to her, gave an order of some kind, and she hurried away again.

Good. Fine.

The guard was still standing near the door, holding the waste-basket out away from himself. He seemed to be asking the official what he should do with it, and from the stances and expressions of the two men the answer he got was more colorful than satis-factory. Insubordination of some sort seemed about to take place over there, when all at once they both turned to look at something else, something new, over by the side wall to the right. The guard dropped the wastebasket, and he and the official both ran over to this new thing. The woman also came hurrying back into view, apparently with some sort of report.

Yes. Yes.

Then the damn boy showed up with our coffee, breaking the thread of conversation among the other three, and while he was putting the cups down Jerry glanced casually out the window, paused, frowned, and said, "What the hell?"

"Hm?" Phil looked at him, followed his gaze out the window, and did some frowning of his own. "Now what?" he said.

It was quarter after five, much later than I'd hoped for. The commotion was in no way big enough over there, but we still did have fifteen minutes before Joe Maslocki and Eddie Troyn would be showing up in the typewriter truck. The worst pos-sible thing that could happen would be for them to arrive just before hell really broke loose, not realize anything was wrong, and actually stop the truck, get out, approach the bank. I didn't want that, didn't even want to think about it.

Come *on*!

The boy had departed, back into the mists of Lethe. Billy, who had now also been attracted to the activity going on across the street, said, "What's happening over there?"

"They're running around with wastebaskets," Jerry said.

Indeed they were. The woman had come forward and picked up the wastebasket by the door, and the guard had now picked up a second one from over on the right. There was a certain amount of milling about, all three of them talking at once over there, and then they were augmented by a fourth person, another official in a dark suit, who apparently drowned all the rest of them out by insisting on being told what was going on. Explanations, displays of wastebaskets, finger pointings in various directions, everybody talking at once.

Phil said, "What the fuck?"

Come on come on come on.

General expressions of disgust over there, more arm wavings as though brushing away flies. The guard and the woman hurried toward the rear, carrying the wastebaskets. The new arrival moved to something on a side wall and fiddled with it—probably a thermostat, turning on air-conditioning or something like that.

No. No no no, don't deal with it that simply. Make *trouble*, make a lot of noise and ruckus, call the—

A siren. A blessed siren, from the distance. Five twenty-two by the luncheonette clock, five twenty-one by the clock high on the rear wall of Fiduciary Federal Trust, and here at last came the police. The woman *did* go call them, as I'd hoped. As I'd hoped.

"There's something wrong," Phil said. "Goddam it, there's something wrong."

Billy said, "Phil, I hear a siren. I think maybe we oughta get out of here."

"It's not us," Phil told him. "Sit tight, don't draw attention to yourself. It's some other damn thing. I don't know what it is, but it isn't us."

The police car arrived, not traveling very fast at all. Not in comparison with the driving I had seen—and done—last night. The siren switched off but the revolving red light stayed on, and the police car stopped next to a fire hydrant in front of the bank. The two cops got slowly out, hitching their gunbelts, adjusting their hair under their hats, and walked across the sidewalk to the bank.

Now there was some sort of delay. The first official gestured and shouted through the glass door, but didn't open it, and the two cops could be seen to not enjoy that treatment at all. They stood with their hands on their hips and their heads cocked to one side, expressing dangerous irritation.

The guard came trotting back, and it turned out he was the one with the key who could unlock the door. He did so, and the cops started in. Almost at once they recoiled, as though they'd walked into cobwebs. They made brushing gestures in front of their faces. Reluctantly they entered the bank, and even more reluctantly they permitted the door to be closed again behind them.

Five twenty-four.

Five twenty-five.

The police car with its circling red light attracted shoppers and homeward-bound workers, who began to mill on the sidewalk, some looking at the empty police car but most looking in the windows at the bank. It became increasingly difficult to see what was happening inside there, but then the door opened again and one of the cops stood there, just outside the doorway, leaving the door open. He appeared to be answering the eager questions of the crowd.

Phil said, "Jerry, go take a walk over there. Find out what's going on."

"Right."

Five twenty-seven. I watched Jerry cross the street and mill with the other pedestrians.

I should say something, I should make a comment. It wasn't natural to be silent, not when everybody else had made a remark. My throat kept wanting to close, but I forced it and my mouth both open, and said, "Sure must be *something*, huh?"

"It's gonna screw us up," Phil said bitterly, "I can feel it. Unless those cops take off away from there we're shit out of luck."

Take off? No no, they couldn't do that. It was five twenty-nine, all they had to do was stay one minute more and it would be all over. Joe and Eddie would arrive, they'd see the police car and the crowd and the commotion, and they'd drive right on by. They'd have to, there wouldn't be any choice.

Five thirty. No typewriter truck drove by.

Five thirty-one. Still no typewriter truck. Jerry came strolling back across the street.

Five thirty-two. Red truck, where are you? Jerry entered the luncheonette and sat down. The second cop came out of the bank, went to the police car, got in, spoke on his radio.

Phil said to Jerry, "So what's the story?"

"Stink bombs," Jerry said.

Phil gave him such a look of disgust it was almost as though he could smell the things from here. He said, "*Stink* bombs!"

"That's right," Jerry said. "Some clown put these chemicals in plastic cups, with lids on them, and put them in the wastebaskets over there. The chemicals ate through the plastic and pow. You wouldn't believe the smell that's coming out of that door."

"Stink bombs," Phil said. "Even if we *do* get in there, we'll have to smell the fucking things."

No. We can't get in there, we can't. Red truck, red truck, hurry up.

Jerry said, "How do you feature a jerk like that?"

"I'd like to get my hands on him," Phil said. "Those cops gonna hang around long?"

"I don't think so," Jerry said. "I think that one's calling in now, find out what they should do. They don't *want* to be there, I'll tell you that."

Five thirty-five. The cop in the police car finished talking and got out. I tried to judge from his walk, from the set of his shoulders, from the angle of his head, what the decision had been. He walked in his slow stately cop tread around the front of the police car and across the sidewalk toward his partner.

God *damn* it, red truck!

"Practical jokers," Jerry said. "They oughta be against the law."

The red truck; I almost fainted with relief. It drove slowly past, and I could see Joe and Eddie in the cab, gawking toward all the commotion in front of the bank. That's right, Joe, that's right, Eddie, it's all loused up. You can't do it, give it up, put the truck back. By God by God by *God*, we're not going to rob that bank!

"There they go," Phil said. "That tears it."

"Son of a bitch," Jerry said.

"God damn," I said.

Billy said, "There was one time, I was with a drilling crew down in Venezuela, we had one of those practical jokers. Liked to hang a bucket of water up over a door so it'd drop on you when you come through."

"I hate those fucking people," Phil said.

"We caught up with this one, after a while," Billy said. "Funny thing, you never would of guessed he was the one. Last guy you'd think of." He grinned at all of us when he said that. He seemed to grin for a long time at me.

Jerry said, "What did you do with him?"

"Hung *him* up over a door," Billy said. He nodded. "Pretty well took care of the problem," he said.

24

We met in the trophy room, all eight of us, to talk things over.

The trophy room was next to the supply area, just off the basketball courts, a large paneled rectangle with glass-fronted cabinets containing the trophies our teams had won from one another or in league competition with amateur groups from outside the prison. Also on the walls, protected in glass frames, were the uniform shirts with the numbers that had been retired in honor of outstanding athletic performance; there was 2952646, a baseball pitcher with a 27–5 win–loss record in the 1948 season, and next to him the unforgettable star quarterback 5598317, and across the way Stonevelt's only four-minute miler, 4611502.

Most of the floor space in the trophy room was taken up by a long library table or conference table, surrounded by a dozen all-wood captain's chairs. Teams generally were given their pre-game pep talks and post-game lectures in this room, with these visual indications of past excellence surrounding them to spur them on. What we were having now was something like a post-game lecture, following a game that had been very badly lost, except that no one was lecturing. Everybody was simply griping, and I had to keep reminding myself to do my share.

Joe Maslocki said, "When I saw that fucking police car in front of that fucking bank I couldn't fucking believe it."

"When I saw your faces," Bob Dombey said, "when you all came back, I knew right away something went wrong."

Billy Glinn cracked his knuckles. Billy never talked much at meetings, but he cracked his knuckles a lot, and I didn't like the sound of it. I wished he'd stop it.

"Stink bombs," Phil said. He said it every ten minutes or so, and every time he said it he sounded even more disgusted than the time before.

"We had practical jokers in the army," Eddie said severely. "The men knew what to do with them."

I didn't want to hear what the men did with them. I said, "It's a goddam shame, that's what it is. All that work, all that setting up, for nothing."

"Not for nothing," Max said. "We can still do it, Harry."

I said, "What? But everybody gets paid tomorrow. All that extra money in the bank, all that Christmas money, it'll all be gone."

Max said, "There'll be more."

"That's right," Jerry said. "The end of the month, same thing. Two weeks' worth of paychecks."

I said, "But without all the Christmas Club money and everything."

Billy cracked his knuckles.

Joe said, "There'll still be plenty. There won't be as much, but there'll be enough."

I was going to have to go through all this all over again? "That's wonderful," I said, and Billy cracked his knuckles.

"We've got the laser," Max said. "We've got the typewriter and Eddie's uniform and the key to the truck. We've got the guns. We've got everything we need."

"We just stash it all," Joe said, "and give it another shot two weeks from now."

"That's great," I said.

Eddie said, "There's nothing wrong with the concept of the

operation. It isn't the first time in history an incursion had to be delayed because of unforeseen circumstances."

Billy cracked his knuckles.

"Some unforeseen circumstances," Jerry said ruefully, and shook his head.

"Stink bombs," Phil said. There was so much disgust in his voice this time I half expected him to throw up on the table.

"There's nothing worse than a practical joker," Bob Dombey said.

Joe said, "You can say that again."

"One time in New York City," Bob said, "I was walking south on Madison Avenue, and a perfectly respectable looking man in suit and tie stopped me and asked me if I'd mind helping him a minute. I said of course not. He had a length of string, and he said he was an architectural engineer charged with redesigning the facade of the store on the corner. He asked me if I'd just hold one end of the string against the storefront for a minute while he measured the distance across the front and down the side. He said there was a time element involved and his partner must have been stuck in crosstown traffic, and that was the only reason he was asking. So I said yes."

Joe said, "I would have told him to fuck off."

"He was very persuasive," Bob said. "I held the string, and he backed around the corner, paying string out as he went. This was at lunch hour, crowds of people going by, I never expected a thing."

Jerry said, "What happened?" He looked fascinated.

"I must have stood there five minutes," Bob said. "That's a long time when you're just standing on the sidewalk holding a piece of string, with people bumping into you. I began to feel like a fool. So finally I followed the string around the corner, and there I found a perfect stranger holding the other end of it. A man with a briefcase."

Max said, "Who was he? The partner?"

"It turned out," Bob said, "he was another victim, just like me. We became a bit short-tempered with one another before we found that out, though. We did some yelling at one another. A whole crowd of people was standing around us."

It was hard to imagine scared-weasel Bob Dombey yelling at a man with a briefcase, but it must have happened; Bob's face was getting red with indignation just thinking about it. He was almost squaring his shoulders.

Jerry said, "I don't get it. What happened?"

"This fellow," Bob said, "did the same thing to both of us."

"Which fellow?" Jerry's face was as crumpled up as a throw rug in his effort to understand. "The one with the briefcase?"

Bob shook his head. "No, the first one. He approached *me* with his story, and then he went around the corner and told the same story to the man with the briefcase. Once he had two victims holding the two ends of his string, he simply left."

Jerry shook his head. "I still don't get it," he said. "What's the point? Where's his profit?"

I felt I could safely enter the conversation at this juncture. "Practical jokers aren't out to make a profit," I said. "There's no point to it at all. The trick is its own reward."

Jerry turned his crinkled face to me. "You mean they do it just for the fun of it?"

"Right."

"*What* fun?" He turned back to Bob. "Did this guy stick around to see what happened?"

"No," Bob said, "he just left."

I put in my oar again. "Practical jokers don't have to actually be present when their trick springs itself," I said. "In fact, most of them prefer not to be. They just set up their little time bombs and go away."

"Like the stink bombs," Phil said. More disgusted.

"Right," I said, and Billy cracked his knuckles. I really wished he wouldn't do that.

"You know," Max said, "we got one of those birds right here in this prison."

Jerry turned to him. "Yeah? Who?"

"I wish I knew," Max said. "The son of a bitch put Saran Wrap on one of the toilets in C Block."

Billy cracked his knuckles.

"It wouldn't have been so bad," Max said, "if I was just taking a leak."

I closed my eyes. I listened to Billy's knuckles cracking. They sounded like boulders knocking together at the very beginning of an avalanche. And guess who's at the bottom of the mountain.

Speaking thoughtfully, Joe said, "You know, one of my cigarettes blew up on me a couple weeks ago. I figured it was something wrong with the tobacco. Could that be the same guy?"

I opened my eyes. I must not draw attention to myself, I thought. I stared at the retired shirt of 4611502. Be like him, I told myself. Be intrepid. Be unflinching. Be ready to run a four-minute mile.

Phil was saying to Joe, "You, too? One of *my* cigarettes went up, too. Scared the crap out of me."

"I'm telling you," Max said, "we got one of those practical joker birds right here inside this very prison."

I have to take part, I thought. I have to divert suspicion. I have to do it right now, right this second, because if I do it later I'll just *attract* suspicion. I opened my mouth. What am I going to say? Nothing about blood types, all right? I said, "You know, he got me too."

They all looked at me. Billy cracked his knuckles. Joe said, "How, Harry?"

"In the mess hall," I said. "The sugar and salt had been switched. I put sugar all over my mashed potatoes."

Jerry, his eyes alight with discovery, said, "So *that's* what happened to my coffee that time!"

"And my eggs," Bob said.

"And my cornflakes," Eddie said.

Max said, "I'd like to get hands on that bastard."

"The one *I* want," Phil said, "is the one in town, with his fucking stink bombs."

"That was probably a kid," Max said. "Stink bombs, you know, that's the sort of thing a kid does."

"I get my hands on him," Phil said, "he'll never grow up."

Billy cracked his knuckles.

25

The following Friday I met Marian James, and I almost met Fred Stoon.

It happened at a party Max invited me to. He had a whole social life going on the outside, much more than any of the others, most of whom contented themselves in the outer world with their little felonies, an occasional movie, a meal in a good restaurant, every once in a while a session with one of the few local whores; they were like Navy men taking shore leave. Max, on the other hand, had integrated himself into the local community as much as possible for someone who could never invite anybody over to his place. He had a whole circle of friends and acquaintances, and was even involved in a regular Thursday night bowling league.

He was also thinking of taking an apartment somewhere in town, though the ramifications of that could get a little tricky. He talked with me about it as we walked to the party Friday night, strolling through a light fall of snow, the first of the year. After a while he asked me if I'd like to come into the deal with him. "Two of us would be better," he said. "We could share the rent and the phone bill and everything, and there'd be somebody actually there more often. People get suspicious when there's nobody around a place. You interested?"

"It sounds pretty good," I said.

"Think it over," he said.

I promised I would, but I didn't know how much brain I was going to have left over from my main worries, which were (A) the robbery coming up two weeks from now, and (B) my fellow conspirators' having tipped to the presence of a practical joker among them. I didn't see anything I could do about (A) for the moment but worry, and maybe hope the world would come to an end before December 30th, but about (B) there were things I could do, at least in a negative sense. To begin with, I was performing absolutely no practical jokes. None, not in the prison and not in town. If I was caught just once, that would be the end of me. The only reason Max and Phil and the others thought there were two practical jokers was because it hadn't occurred to them yet there might be just one practical joker who had the ability to be both inside and outside the prison. One of us eight, in fact. Guess which one.

Well, I had been hoping prison would cure me, and apparently it had. For the last three days I hadn't even been tempted. No more. Never again.

Including the next scheduled robbery date. God knows I still didn't want to be involved in that, but I couldn't very well set off stink bombs in the bank every last time the gang decided to knock it over. One coincidence they might accept, but two never. And if I couldn't stop the robbery with one of my tricks, I couldn't stop it at all. So it would happen.

I was almost beginning to look forward to it, just to get the damn thing done and out of the way.

I wished I didn't have these things hanging over my head. In so many other ways life was really rather pleasant. I was in a position that was rare among prisoners in American penitentiaries—perhaps unique. There was much to enjoy in life, with the security of prison on one side and the freedom of town on the other.

Take this night, for instance. The snow drifted lazily, fat wet flakes falling straight down through the windless air, disappearing when they hit the ground. The air was crisp and cold and clear, the snow was gentle and delicate, the night was beautiful, and we were on our way to a party. A pre-Christmas party. Why couldn't I just relax and enjoy it?

I determined to try.

The house, when we got to it, was large and white, on a corner lot, its windows flooded with light upstairs and down. Christmas music and the sound of many conversations surrounded the place like a halo. Max and I went up on the porch together, and he simply pushed the door open and walked in. I followed, and we entered a fairly large square foyer. Directly ahead was a flight of uncarpeted stairs leading up for half a flight and then turning left. On the right was a wooden bench mostly hidden beneath coats. A wide arch on the left led to a living room full of people, with a Christmas tree in a far corner. Max and I were taking off our coats, adding them to the pile on the bench, when a woman came over to us from the living room, smiling, her hand out to Max.

It was our hostess, a slender good-looking woman in her early thirties. Her dark brown hair was tied back, tightly controlled, and her clothing de-emphasized her figure. Max introduced her as Janet Kelleher, and me as Harry Kent; I smiled at her, and at the sound of my new name, and she said, "Glad to meet you, Harry." The hand she offered was slender and pale and full of delicate bones. Max had already told me something about her, on the walk over; that she was divorced, had young twin daughters, was teaching at a local high school, and was going to bed with Max from time to time. I later learned that this kind of slightly complex thirtyish woman was his normal style, that he filled in with the Dotty Fleisches only because the Janet Kellehers were a relative rarity in this part of the world. I didn't know Max that well then, so I was surprised at the apparent bloodlessness of this girlfriend, as opposed to the raw galumphing meatiness of Dotty Fleisch.

The next hour was a strange time for me. Max and my hostess left me to my own devices, so I mostly just wandered through the crowded rooms. I was pleased to be at a happy party full of smiling faces, but on the other hand I didn't know any of these people and very much felt my aloneness. I spent most of my time concentrating on the house instead.

It was a good house, large, with a lot of wood showing. It was slightly underfurnished, with obvious blank spots in all the rooms and with here and there a dusty rectangle on the wall to show where a painting had been. I assumed the house was left over from the marriage, and that when the husband moved out he'd taken some of the furnishings with him.

Being on a corner lot, there was much opportunity for glass. An enclosed sun porch full of plants ran along the side of the house, and a big-windowed breakfast room was off the kitchen at the back. Also off the kitchen was a large open back porch; because of the crowd in the house, and because it wasn't all that cold outside, the kitchen door to the back porch was left open, and there were always several people out there, getting some air.

Upstairs were four bedrooms, three of them open. The door of the fourth was locked, and since I hadn't seen Max or Janet at all since I'd gotten here I guessed they were saying hello to one another in there. That such a pale girl should be so passionate as to abandon her own party for an hour in bed amazed me. And cheered me, too. Now that I'm Harry Kent, I thought, paraphrasing Bobby Fischer, I'll be spending more time with girls.

One of the other bedrooms was full of children; the two little girls in identical pale blue dresses stood out at once from the crowd. Toys were being played with in here, a full mini-party was going on. The parents of these children were all downstairs, mixed with a very conglomerate crowd; Janet

Kelleher seemed to have invited everybody she knew, including several of her high school students. The youngest guest upstairs seemed to be about three, and the oldest downstairs were a white-haired cheery couple who had to be in their sixties.

Food and drink were all downstairs, and all serve yourself. The food was spread on a sideboard in the dining room, and the liquor bottles were lined up on the kitchen table. I made occasional visits to both places, and was in the dining room, standing next to the cake, when a girl I'd noticed before came over and said, "You don't seem to be having a great time."

I looked at her. She was medium height, a trifle overweight, with a round-cheeked elfin face and long curling ash-blonde hair. She was wearing no bra, a fact that the pockets of her white blouse failed to conceal. I said, "I don't?"

"You're just standing around," she said, and nodded at the glass in my hand. "With that drink."

"Everybody's just standing around," I said. "With drinks." I was a bit irritated, and also embarrassed that somebody had noticed I was alone.

"If you come talk to me," she said, still good-humored despite my manner, "I won't eat that cake."

I frowned at the cake, of which I'd already had two slices. "What's wrong with it?"

"Carbohydrates," she said, and puffed out her cheeks.

"You're big-boned," I said, gallantly.

She laughed. "Come take me away," she said, "before my bones get any bigger."

So that's how I met Marian James. We walked into the sun porch, sat down amid the philodendra, and she told me who she was while I told her who I wasn't. Her name was Marian James, she was twenty-nine, childless, separated from her husband, and also a teacher at Amalgamated High. "History," she said, and when I asked her what specialty in history she said, "American. That's all the poor little bastards get in high school. We're surrounded by people who think mathematics, gunpowder, public street-lighting and drama are all Wasp inventions." Her husband she described as a "freak" who found domestic life too confining and who was now making a small living as a photographer and marijuana smuggler in Mexico. "Turn off, tune out, drop dead, that's my advice to Sonny," she said. "And my advice to *you* is, never trust a grown man called Sonny."

My own self-description could have been equally as colorful, but I very carefully avoided the temptation. I felt uncomfortable telling Max's lie about being a civilian employee out at Camp Quattatunk, though now that I'd been there I could at least refer to the place with some familiarity. And I assured her that Max and I were thinking of taking an apartment together in town. "For the convenience," I said.

"You had some excitement out at the camp the other night," she said.

Honey, I *was* some excitement out at the camp the other night, I thought, but what I said was, "Yeah, I read about it in the papers. I didn't know anything about it at the time."

"They blew up a fence or something?"

"One of the gates," I said. "Not the main gate, one out by the storage compound."

"The paper said they were Weathermen disguised as Army officers." The skin crinkling around her eyes, she frowned a bit and shook her head. "Doesn't sound right to me," she said.

"I wouldn't know," I said. And I was thinking that lies were supposed to be *more* colorful than the truth, not less. I was managing to lie myself into contention as bore of the year.

We went on like that. The Army hadn't released details of

what had been stolen, and she asked me about it, and I said I didn't know either. She asked me if I personally knew the sentry who'd been attacked, and I said no. Oh, I was in top form, I had her on the edge of her chair. Ready to fall off asleep.

God, I needed a drink. "Refill your glass?" I said.

"I'll go with you."

So we went to the kitchen, where I was pouring bourbon when she said to somebody facing the other way, "Oh, Fred. I'd like you to meet a friend of mine, Harry Kent, from out at the Army base. Harry, this is Fred Stoon, he works at the—"

Stoon! I slapped the bottle down, staring in horror. The man was turning around, but I didn't need to see his face to know who it was. And I didn't need Marian to tell me where he worked. It was Stoon the prison guard! It was the one who escorted me to the warden's office every time, the one who shifted his weight skeptically from foot to foot.

"Ulp," I said. I slapped my hand over my mouth, turned, bowled my way through the crowd and out the kitchen door.

"—peniten—Harry?"

Maintain the fiction. There were four people on the back porch; I shoved through them, hand still clenched over my mouth, and flung myself like an old mattress across the rail. I hung there, draped, head down, and sensed the four people all drifting inexorably but somewhat urgently back into the house.

I was alone. I stared at the grass below me, noticing distractedly that the snow was starting to stick. It was coming down more heavily, too.

I'm doomed. It's all over. I'm dead, I'm doomed.

A tread on the porch. My shoulders hunched, awaiting the ax.

"Harry?" It was Marian's voice.

Slowly I raised myself, slowly I turned, step by step. Marian was alone, looking at me in some concern, saying, "You okay, Harry?"

The doorway behind her was empty, though the kitchen was full. I said, "I guess I'm okay now. I'm sorry, all of a sudden I really thought I was going to throw up."

"Boy, you sure took off," she said, and Stoon appeared in the kitchen doorway, looking out.

So the first time I kissed Marian James was to hide my face.

26

"I can't meet Fred Stoon," I whispered forcefully through the kiss. Our teeth clacked together painfully.

"Why?" She had a hell of a time pronouncing the 'w.'

"Tell you later."

She broke the clinch. Stoon had discreetly removed himself from the doorway again. Marian said, "You'll tell me now. Come on, we'll go to my place."

"I can't go through that kitchen. Once he sees me, it's all over."

She gave me a frank appraisal. "You're weird, Harry," she decided. "Come on."

So we left the porch, walked around the outside of the house through the snow, went back in through the front door, found our coats in the welter on the bench, and left.

She had a car, a blue Volkswagen beetle. On the trip I said, "I sure hope you have something to drink at your place."

"I do," she said. "And you better have an awful good story to tell by the time we get there."

I didn't. I didn't have any story at all. A great weariness and emptiness had overtaken me, and though God knows I tried to think up some sort of lie that would cover the circumstances, it was just impossible, and when we got to Marian's place, a small snug three-room apartment in an elderly brick apartment building, I simply sat down and told her the truth.

The whole truth. My entire life story, from the dog crap in the pencil to the stink bombs in the bank. Everything, including my real name. "With an umlaut," I said hopelessly.

I don't think she ever entirely disbelieved me, though on the other hand she found it very very hard to believe me. "You're a *prisoner*?" she kept saying. "A *convict*? At the *penitentiary*?"

"Yes," I said, and went on with my story.

Well, it took a while to tell, and Marian kept both of our glasses full the whole time, and by the time I was finished I was utterly weary and in despair. "Poor baby," she said, and cuddled my head against her bosom for consolation, and shortly after that we went to bed.

I woke up and it was still dark. But what time was it? I sat bolt upright and said, "Hey!"

"Mmf?" A sleepy form moved obscurely in the darkness next to me. "What?"

I remembered everything, I knew I had told the whole thing to this woman I didn't even know. But I didn't care about that now, I had a much more urgent problem. I said, "What time is it?"

"Um. Oom." Rustling and rattling. "Twenty after five."

"Holy Christ!" I shouted, and jumped out of bed. "I've got to get back to prison!"

She sat up and switched on the bedside lamp. Squinting at me, she said, "I've known some weird guys, Harry, but you're the winner. I've had them wake up and say, 'I've got to get back to my wife,' 'I've got to catch a plane,' 'I've got to go to Mass.' But I never in my *life* heard anybody say they had to go back to prison."

I was rushing into my clothes. I kissed her, hastily, sloppily, and ran from the room, crying over my shoulder, "I'll see you! I'll call you!" And as I left I could see her in the light of the beside lamp, sitting up, shaking her head.

I ran. I ran through ankle-deep snow, with more snow still coming down, all the way back to the Dombey house.

27

Eight-fifteen in the morning. The snow had stopped, and I was on my way across the yard from breakfast toward my cell-block, hoping to catch a few more hours sleep, when a voice called me. "Kunt!"

"Künt," I said wearily, turning. "With an um—"

It was Stoon. I stopped, paralyzed. He'd recognized me last night after all, the dream was over, it was all over, it was all coming to an end. And just when I'd met Marian, whom I realized in this first instant of loss that I needed terrifically, I needed her the way I needed lungs. How can you come right out and say you're in love with a woman you've known for seven hours? By having her taken away from you in the eighth, that's how.

"Warden wants to see you, Kunt," Stoon said. He made a thumb waggle over his shoulder. "Let's go."

I went. Despair, doom. And how could I keep from implicating the others? Phil and Jerry and Billy and Bob and Max and Eddie and Joe. Once I admitted how I was getting out of the prison, they would be in as much trouble as I was, no matter how much I tried to protect them.

So I wouldn't tell, that's all. I would clam up, I would button my lip, I would keep my trap shut. You ain't gettin nuttin outa me, copper.

Stoon, about to enter the administration building ahead of me, turned his head and said, "What?"

Had I said that aloud? Good God. "Frog in my throat," I explained.

"Tell him to shut up," Stoon said, and entered the building.

We walked down the corridor together, and at a given point I turned left and walked into Stoon's elbow. "Oof," I said, and he said, "Watch it, Kunt. What's the matter with you?"

I pointed down the side corridor toward the warden's office. "Aren't we—?"

"Just come with me," he said.

So I went with him, on down the main corridor to a staircase, and then up two flights. I had no idea what was going on. All I could think about was that Stoon had recognized me at the party last night, that I had lost Marian just as soon as I had found her, and that I must keep silent about the tunnel and the others. I *must.*

The administration building was three stories high, so once we'd climbed the second flight we were on the top floor. Nevertheless we went up one more flight, narrower and darker than the first two, and bewilderment was beginning to take precedence in my mind over terror and despair when Stoon pushed a metal fire door open at the top of the stairs and the two of us stepped out onto the roof.

Warden Gadmore was there, with his topcoat on, his hands jammed down into his coat pockets. There was a cold damp wind up here, but it wasn't the only reason I was shivering.

The warden gave me a discontented look, saying to Stoon, "Well, you found him all right."

"Yes, sir."

The warden considered me for a moment, while I tried to figure out why we were going to talk about my unauthorized absence from the prison on the administration building's roof. I noticed that his hair looked thinner and skimpier in the wind, that frills of it whisked around his circular bald spot, and that he was looking decidedly less sympathetic than when I'd first seen him.

"Well, Kunt," the warden said, sans umlaut, "what do you have to say for yourself?"

"Nothing sir," I said.

He looked out over the roof. "Are you proud of yourself, Kunt?"

"Proud of myself?" It seemed a strange phrase under the circumstances. Also looking out over the flat roof, trying to work out exactly what the man meant when he asked that question, I noticed for the first time that lines seemed to have been drawn in the snow. Scuffed in the snow, someone moving back and forth, creating lines and angles by dragging his feet through the inch or so of snow on the roof. Lines and angles making some sort of design, like letters, like…

"Oh, for God's sake," I said.

The warden looked back at me. "Did you really think," he asked me, "you could get away with it?" The lines nearest me, in the snow on the roof, said PRISONER. The next row of lines, out there across the roof, black lines in the white snow, said, BEING HELD. And the farthest row of lines said, HELP I AM.

"I," I said, and shook my head.

"You aren't going to deny this, are you?"

In imagination I suddenly visualized the way this must look from the air, to anybody in an airplane passing by. Giant letters in the roof of the building, requesting help of the passing world because, after all, the writer was being held prisoner.

It was *not* because of the party! Stoon had *not* recognized me! I had *not* lost Marian!

I was grinning from ear to ear.

"You find this amusing, Kunt?"

Relief made me reckless. "Yes, sir," I said. "I think it's pretty funny. Can you imagine somebody going by in an airplane, he looks down—"

"That's enough," the warden said. He was beginning to be angry.

"Whoever did that," I said, still smiling broadly, "has a sense of humor I really like."

"*You* did it, Kunt," he said. "Don't waste my time with denials."

I didn't care about anything. I hadn't been found out, that was all that mattered. "I'll tell you two things, warden," I said, "and they're both true. One, I didn't do that sign there *or* the one in the license plates. And two, my name isn't Kunt. It's Künt, with an umlaut, and it always has been."

"We're not talking about your name, we're—"

"Well, we goddam well ought to," I said. He stared at me in astonishment, Stoon shifted from foot to foot behind me in outrage and disapproval, and I roared on. "My name is *Künt*," I said. "It's not that hard to pronounce, if you'd just make the effort. How would you like it if I called you Warden Gadabout?"

"*What?*"

"I may be a prisoner, but I still have my name, and a man's name is—"

"You certainly are a prisoner," the warden snapped. "I'd begun to think you'd forgotten that. Stoon, you will place Mister Koont in a cell in the restricted area."

Solitary. A little late, I closed my mouth.

"Yes, sir," said Stoon. "Come along, Kunt." He pronounced it wrong.

28

There's a difference between *solitude* and *solitary*. I had solitude in my one-man cell in the regular cell-block, and I was
happy for it. But now I was solitary in a different one-man cell,
and it didn't make me happy at all. I had nothing to read,
nothing to look at but the concrete block walls, nothing to do
but sit on the hard metal bunk and think about the errors of my
past life. Particularly my recent past life. Particularly on that
goddam roof.

What would they do to me now? Warden Gadmore had said,
in our initial meeting, that he was going out of his way to give me
privileges rarely extended to a newcomer. Would those privileges
be taken away, now that I had yelled at the man on the roof of
his own administration building? Would I no longer have a job
at the gym? Had my stupidity, my big mouth, taken the gym
and the tunnel and Marian and all the rest of it away forever?

I was kept in solitary over the weekend, and when I was
taken out on Monday it was only long enough for a meeting
with the prison psychiatrist, Dr. Jules O. Steiner, a seedily
dressed man with five o'clock shadow and shoulders covered
with dandruff. He didn't seem particularly competent or intel-
ligent or sympathetic, but he was the only contact I had with
the world of authority, so I opened up to him completely about
my name and the practical jokes, the connection between the
two, and their regrettable conclusion in my outburst on the
roof. He listened, asked a few questions, made a few notes,
gave very little reaction, and at the end of the hour I was taken
back to solitary for two more days.

On Wednesday afternoon I was again taken out—I was like a pie being constantly pulled out of the oven by a nervous cook—this time by Stoon, who once more marched me to the administration building. But not to the roof; we went directly to the warden's office, where I found Warden Gadmore himself in his usual place behind his desk, reading a dossier on me that had grown noticeably thicker since the first time I'd seen it.

"Warden," I said, before he said anything at all. "I want to apologize for my—"

"That's all right, Künt," he said. He pronounced it right! Without irony, without malice, without prompting, he pronounced it right. With the umlaut. And when he looked up at me I saw that he was sympathetic once again. "I've just been reading Doctor Steiner's report," he said. "I think I understand you better now, Künt." Twice!

"Yes, sir," I said. Did I dare to hope?

He lowered his head, showed me his pancake, studied the report. "I see here," he said, "you still deny you had anything to do with that business on the roof."

"The message? That's right, sir, I didn't do that."

"I also have a report," he said, tapping another sheet of paper, "that says you were locked in the gymnasium all that night."

"Yes, sir," I said eagerly. Stoon was an awful presence behind me, but I surged forward anyway. "I was in there all night long," I said.

"At least we can't prove otherwise." Bunk bunk; he was thinking again, drumming his fingertips on my dossier. "I notice," he said, "you do admit several other antisocial actions since arriving here."

"I've stopped all those now, sir," I said. "It—it took a while to quit. But I'm through with it now."

"Yes. Hmmm." Bunk bunk.

Was I off? Was I scot free? I found I was leaning toward the warden so precipitously I was about to fall forward onto his desk. No, no; that would never do. I leaned back, shifted my feet, waited.

Bunk bunk.

He sighed. He did his squinting act up at me, reading my face. "I wish I knew," he said, "why you persist in denying this one thing."

"Because I really didn't do it, sir," I said. "I really didn't do it. I'd tell you if I did."

"It may be," he said, "against all the evidence, it just may be that you are telling the truth."

Hope, a wide-winged bird, soared up within me, over the mountain peaks of doubt and despair.

"But—"

The bird faltered. A few feathers fluttered away earthward. Is that anti-aircraft fire up ahead?

"—I'm still not entirely convinced," the warden said. "There's also the matter of your outburst the other morning."

"Sir, I am truly—"

"Yes, I'm sure you are. And I do have more understanding on that score, now that you've had your little chat with Doctor Steiner."

"Yes, sir."

"However, it did happen." Bunk bunk. "I'll tell you what I'm going to do, Künt."

I hardly notice the proper pronunciation. I was leaning forward again. "Sir?"

"I see you don't have a cellmate," he said. "I'm going to put a man in there with you that I hope will be a good example to you. His name is Butler, and—"

I said, "Andy Butler, sir?" I gestured toward the garden outside his window, now sleeping beneath its white blanket of snow. "The gardener?"

"That's right," he said. "You know him?"

"My former cellmate," I said, "Peter Corse, introduced me."

"Fine," he said. "Andy Butler has been in this institution a good long time. He knows the ins and outs of life around here better than just about any other man in the place. You listen to him, *watch* him, emulate him, and you'll be a lot better off, Künt, believe me."

"Yes, sir," I said. "Thank you, sir." A cellmate, that wasn't so bad. Andy Butler, he was a nice old guy, he wouldn't be any trouble at all.

"In order," the warden went on, and I knew at once that the bird of hope had flown too soon, that a new cellmate wasn't the worst news of the day after all, "for you to begin right away to get the advantage of Butler's companionship, I've decided to take you off privileges for the next two weeks. That means you won't be working in the gymnasium, nor will you have the unlimited yard privileges that accompany a work assignment."

Two weeks. Christmas and New Year's. (It was only later that it occurred to me even this cloud had a silver lining: the two weeks would take me safely past the rescheduled bank robbery.) Two weeks away from Marian, away from the entire outside world.

All right, so what? Two weeks wasn't forever. I could survive. "Yes, sir," I said. Then, struck by an awful thought, I said, "Sir, when the two weeks are up, will I be going back to the gym?"

"We'll decide that at the time," he said.

The bird dropped down dead, and when it landed in the pit of my stomach it was heavy and cold. "Yes, sir," I said.

"All right, Künt," the warden said. "That's all." He started to toss the dossier in his out-basket.

"Sir!" I said, feeling sudden urgency.

He paused, the dossier in his hand, and looked at me with faint irritation. "Yes?"

"Sir, I—" I tried to organize the words to get this point across. "There's some people in this prison," I said, "that I pulled tricks on, when I first came here, that if they found out it was me, sir, I don't know what they'd do."

"You should have thought of that at the time," he said. No sympathy on this point at all.

"I was still under the compulsion then, sir," I said. "I'm not anymore, I'm cured, as you'll definitely see. But if those other convicts, sir, if they find out about me, about what I did, there's some of them that might even go so far as to kill me."

I'd caught his attention. He put the dossier down, not in the out-basket. "Hmmmm," he said.

I said, "Sir, if we could not mention what I'm being punished for, I mean the message on the roof, I promise you won't regret it."

He squinted at me. "What are you suggesting?"

"The reason for the punishment, sir," I said. "If we just made it insubordination, without the other thing, that I anyway didn't even do, but if we could leave it out, and…" I ran down, my argument exhausted.

"I see." He thought about it, so deeply that he didn't even go bunk-bunk. Then, decisively, he nodded. "It's a valid request," he said. "*If* you've stopped the practical jokes."

"Oh, I have, sir!"

"Then we won't mention any of that," he said. "At least for the next two weeks."

"Thank you, sir," I said. "Uh—"

"Yes? What else?"

I wasn't sure how much he knew about the trusty subculture.

I said, "Sir, that would also mean the trusties, any prisoners working in your office, or—"

"I understood that, Künt," he said, and gave me a surprisingly flinty smile. "I really do know what goes on in my prison," he said.

Well, yes and no, I thought. "Thank you, sir," I said.

29

Andy Butler was sympathetic, but in order for him to be sympathetic I had to tell him an awful lot of the truth: the practical jokes I'd pulled here in the prison, mainly, so he'd understand why Warden Gadmore was so convinced I was the one leaving the help-i-am-being-held-prisoner messages. "I had no idea you were doing that sort of thing," he said. His kindly face was full of a combination of sympathy and humor. He did see the funny side of it, thank God, which was a bit more than I could do at the moment.

I said, "But you've got to keep it to yourself, Andy. *Please*. If some of those guys find out—"

"I won't say a word," Andy said. "Guaranteed."

"Thanks, Andy. Thanks a lot." But it seemed to me things were getting too tangled. There were too many secrets, with too many people knowing too many fractions. One wrong conversation, in or out of the prison, would blow the whole thing sky-high.

My friends at the gym were properly sympathetic. "Tough titty, pal," Phil commented.

I asked Max if he'd get word to Marian James that I wouldn't be seeing her for two weeks, and he said he would. Of course, in making the request I did have to admit that Marian knew the truth about us—another secret, another fraction, another person I had to trust to keep things to himself. Max, obviously, shouldn't let Phil and the others know I'd told an outsider about being a prisoner. Good *God*, the complexity of it all!

Anyway, Max was a little disgruntled at first to learn I'd

given *his* secret to Marian, but when I explained about Stoon being at the party he agreed I hadn't had much choice. He himself had managed to miss Stoon by missing most of the party; when he and Janet had finally come downstairs most of the guests had already departed.

So. One way and another, I now had secrets and portions of secrets being held for me by my mother, the seven tunnel insiders (with an extra parcel just for Max), Andy Butler, Warden Gadmore, Fred Stoon and Marian James. Let just one of them say one indiscreet word and the whole tottering structure would come collapsing onto my head, like the bricks falling one by one onto Oliver Hardy's head as he sits in gloomy fatalism in the fireplace.

I spent the rest of Wednesday, after making my deals with the warden and Andy Butler and Max, fretting about the house of cards I had built, trying to think of some way to shore it up a bit here and there, and Wednesday night was full of dreams about floors, lawns, chairs, platforms and airplane bottoms giving way beneath me. After a night of sudden drops, I was so twitchy by morning I was almost ready to say the indiscreet word myself and get it over with.

Then Andy stepped in, with a distraction that more or less saved my life. He was traditionally Stonevelt's Santa Claus in the Christmas Eve pageant put on every year by the prison amateur theater group, known rather wistfully as the Stonevelt Touring Company. STC, generally called Stick by its members, assayed high in Joy Boys, and put on five or six plays a year, tending mostly toward comedy. Their version of *Stalag 17* had a great echoing vibrancy to it unavailable in other circumstances, and the production they did of *The Women* had to be seen to be believed.

Anyway, Christmas Eve was coming up next day, Friday, and

Andy asked me to help him with his costume and props. Grateful
for anything at all to take my mind off the shrinking ice floe I
was standing on, I threw myself into the production, becoming
a kind of extra stagehand, which startled the Stick people and
made them very happy. They never, they explained to me, had
enough backstage people; if I would like to make 'grip' my in-
prison career, they would be delighted to have me. Some of
them, I think, meant that in more ways than one. In any event,
I thanked them all and told them I'd think it over.

What I was actually thinking over was my own life. Warden
Gadmore had either been very shrewd or very lucky in rubbing
me up against Andy Butler; in listening to him, talking with
him, watching the way he interacted with the people around
him I became truly aware for the first time of the possibility of
a life passed in cooperation and amicability with other human
beings, rather than a life passed as a sort of running gun battle
or ongoing guerrilla operation.

He was so *nice*. Niceness always sounds bland, but by golly it
was a pleasure to be around. In books and movies the devil
always gets the best lines, and in truth Andy didn't have anything memorably witty to say, but whenever he spoke the
people around him smiled, and how can you do better than
that? He made people cheerful by his presence, and he didn't
try to sell them anything once he had them softened up.

And he was a perfect Santa Claus. He *looked* the part, from
the round cheeks to the round belly, from the white hair to the
red nose, and when he delivered his lines, in a deeper resonant
voice than his usual speaking style, 'ho ho ho' seemed to ripple
through every sound.

We talked a bit on Friday afternoon, during the pauses and
delays of the dress rehearsal, and I told him I felt maybe I'd
been doing things somewhat inaccurately all my life. "I used to

be like that," he said, nodding, grinning at some memory. "My right hand never knew what my left hand was doing. The first time I ever planted a little garden I pulled everything up again before it was half-grown."

"Why?"

He shrugged, and gave me a broad sunny smile. "That was my sense of humor around that time," he said.

I didn't get it, but on the other hand my own sense of humor would probably baffle a lot of people, so I didn't push the point.

This was my first experience with the world of the theater, and I found it interesting and bewildering. An incredible amount of running, screaming, arguing, weeping, jumping, chaos and frenzy seemed to be required in the backstage area before one small quiet moment could be presented out front. And even when the show was on, with the wise men in procession, for instance, there was still whispering, rustling, rushing about, finger-pointing and hair-tearing taking place just out of sight of the audience—to such an extent that a returning wise man lifted his own voice once he'd exited to ask how anybody expected him to maintain a *performance* out there with all of this *clatter* going on. I didn't hear him get a useful answer.

The show itself was a series of tableaux on The Meanings of Christmas with here and there a nod to Chanukah for the benefit of Jewish prisoners, plus an occasional bewildering reference to Islam for the sake of any Black Muslims so frivolous as to have attended. Actually they weren't really tableaux, as one of the shepherds that watched by night explained to me when his stint was over. "In a tableau," he said, "you just stand there and don't move." He demonstrated, with a pose that seemed more pin-up than shepherd. "Sort of like a living painting," he said. "And usually there's a narrator or somebody to read something out loud that tells the audience what it's all about. What we're doing is sort of moving tableaux; we walk on and off, and go through our little movements, like when I pointed at the star in the east—did you see that part?—but we don't say anything. Except for Santa Claus, of course."

Of course. To fill in the silence otherwise there was a traditional narrator, reading a commentary on The Meanings of Christmas that had been jointly written by three staff members of the prison newspaper, the Stonevelt *Ripple*. The narrator was a onetime Mafia bigwig who had a beautiful operatic baritone. When he rolled out with, "And they come from out of Egypt," you could *see* it. Besides seeing it in the tableau, I mean.

The show was actually pretty interesting, at least from backstage. A lot of work had been put into the costumes and the sets, and everybody took it all very seriously. I thought the fellow doing Mary was an absolute knockout, if maybe just a little too flouncy, and Joseph had just the right nebbishy feeling I've always thought appropriate to that exemplar of passive inactivity.

But the highlight of the show was Andy Butler, who came romping on in his Santa Claus suit and reeled off a list of gifts he said he'd be leaving in people's stockings later on tonight. They were all local gags, referring to well-known prison personalities, both convict and administrative. The assistant warden charged with unearthing plots and conspiracies among the inmates, for instance, was given a canary, and one of the more notorious Joy Boys was given a subscription to *Family Circle*. A convicted murderer who'd spent the last ten or twelve years going on death row every time the death penalty was put back on the books and coming off death row every time the death penalty was abolished again was given a lifetime ballpoint pen guaranteed to skip. The audience ate it all up, howling with laughter, and only once did Andy come up with something too obscure for the crowd to appreciate. "And for Peter Corse," he said that time, "a new set of teeth." There couldn't have been more than three of us in the auditorium who knew what that one was all about, and none of us would have thought it funny. In fact, I thought it was touching, Andy in this happy moment remembering his unfortunate friend. I remembered having hidden Peter's lower plate on him, and winced in misery at the memory. How bad I'd been!

30

The next day was Christmas. I started it feeling such gloom and self-abasement that I just about had to reach up to tie my shoelaces.

And things did not get better. Christmas is a gloomy day in a prison anyway, so apart from having nothing to do and apart from feeling sorry for myself whenever I could pause in disliking myself, everywhere I turned I saw faces looking just as drawn and morose as I felt. Wonderful.

Then Bob Dombey came around in the afternoon with two Christmas presents for me. His wife Alice, the reader, whom I had not as yet met, was making Christmas dinner for the boys, which of course I wasn't going to be able to attend, so Bob had smuggled in a piece of fruitcake for me. That made me feel both better and worse. Bob also had a present for me from Alice, and it turned out to be a copy of Mailer's *Armies of the Night*. Holy Christ, the woman really was a reader!

So I spent a part of the day immersed in a writing style that combines the tortuousness of Henry James with the colloquialness of Rocky Graziano, until Max showed up with a message and a present, both from Marian. The message was that she'd be waiting for me when I got out of prison, which I suppose was a pretty funny line under the circumstances, and the present was another book, *The Prison Diary of Ho Chi Minh*. That was very funny, under the circumstances, and more fun to read than the other. But too short.

And the best was yet to come. As I was on my way to Christmas dinner in the mess hall—I'd already eaten Alice Dombey's fruitcake, and was thus grimly aware of what I was missing—Phil joined me, walked along with, me, and said, "You're not getting off restriction until January fifth."

"I know."

"Listen, Harry, I hope you don't mind, but we're going ahead without you."

All I could think about was Alice Dombey's dinner. "Well, sure," I said.

"We'll still give you your piece," he said, "just as though you were there."

They were going to smuggle a whole dinner in? "You don't have to do that," I said.

"Don't turn down a good deal, pal," Phil said. "Nobody can afford to say no to maybe fifty, sixty grand."

Fifty, sixty... The robbery! "Oh!" I said. "The bank!"

"Jesus Christ, keep your voice down!"

I ducked my head, and looked around the yard. "I thought you meant dinner," I said.

"You what?"

"It doesn't matter. You'll hit the bank without me, huh?"

"Next Thursday. Too bad you can't be with us, but we don't want to hold it off any more."

"Gee, that's tough," I said. "I really wanted to be there."

"I know you did. But you'll get your piece just the same, so don't worry about it."

"That's really nice of you guys, Phil," I said.

"Ah, what the hell. See you around, Harry."

"See you around, Phil."

Christmas dinner in the mess hall stunk. I smiled through every mouthful.

31

Thursday I was in a complete state of nerves. This afternoon the boys were going to pull the bank job, and now that I was excused from attendance I felt guilty. Can you imagine? Feeling guilty about robbing a bank.

But what if they were caught? I would always feel that my absence had made that tiny little bit of difference, that one more gun, one more hand, two more eyes, would have added up to success instead of failure. I had lied to those people, conned them, played practical jokes on them, and now I was letting them down when it really mattered. And they were even going to give me my share of the proceeds, just as though I'd come through.

They're a swell bunch of fellows, I kept telling myself all day, completely forgetting the many times I'd felt I was one tiny revelation from violent death at their hands. Forgetting, in fact, that I still *was* only one tiny revelation from violent death at their hands. A swell bunch of fellows, I kept repeating in my head. Gee, I hope they don't get caught.

They didn't. Phil came around to my cell about eight o'clock that night, and he looked disgusted again, as though he'd been smelling more stink bombs. Andy was present sitting on the other bunk, and Phil nodded meaningfully toward him, saying to me, "Hey, Harry, come for a walk."

Being now a man without privileges, the extent of the walk I could take was up and down the corridor outside my cell, so that's what the two of us did. From the look on Phil's face I knew the news was going to be bad, and the only question was just *how* bad. Had there been gunfire? Were some of the boys dead? Had they gotten away, but with no money? On the other hand, was the bad news more personal than that; which is to say, had Phil tipped to any of the things about me that I didn't want him to know.

I felt very nervous, therefore, when I stepped out into the corridor with him, and the two of us began to stroll up and down. Phil didn't say anything, and when I sneaked a look at his profile he was looking extremely disgusted. So finally I was the one who broke the silence, saying, "Everything go okay?"

"No."

"Trouble in the bank?" Some sort of lump was in my throat; maybe it was my heart.

"You could call it trouble," he said. He stopped and gave me a flat look and said, "They were having a party."

"A what?"

"They can't have a Christmas party like everybody else," he said. "*Last* week, like everybody else. They have to have a New Year's party instead."

"A party," I said. "In the bank?"

"All over the fucking bank." he said. "Three o'clock comes around, they throw the customers out, they lock the door, they break out the booze and the record player and they proceed to have a blast."

"Good Christ," I said. "It's as bad as the stink bombs."

"It's worse than the fucking stink bombs," Phil said. "When Joe got there in the typewriter truck, he didn't notice what was going on. We're all in the luncheonette waiting for our coffee, we can see what's happening, but he's right there on the sidewalk in front of the fucking place and he doesn't notice anything going on. So he gets the typewriter out of the truck and goes over and knocks on the bank door, and it isn't till some secretary opens the door wearing the guard's hat that Joe notices there's maybe some activity taking place inside the fucking bank."

Phil had a really remarkable capacity for expressing disgust. While marveling at that, I said, "So what did he do?"

"What *could* he do, the dipshit? He gave her the typewriter. So now we got to cop another fucking typewriter for the *next* time we try the job."

The next time. "Ah," I said.

"One good thing," he said, "you'll be able to come back into it by then."

"Right," I said. I tried to sound enthusiastic.

"Anyway," he said, "I thought you'd like to know." He looked at his watch. "Listen, I gotta take off, I'm bowling with Max tonight. I'm maybe joining that league of his."

"That's nice," I said. Next time. They're going to try again. I'll be able to come back into it.

Phil looked back. He still looked disgusted. "Sometimes," he said, "I think God doesn't *want* us to rob that fucking bank."

32

On Wednesday, the fifth of January, Fred Stoon came for me in my cell just after eleven in the morning and escorted me once again to Warden Gadmore's office. The warden was genial, and declared himself pleased at my development. "You've done very well, Künt," he said. Pronouncing my name right had become an absolute habit with him.

"Thank you, sir," I said. "I want you to know I appreciate everything you've done for me."

"You're an interesting case," he said. "I'll be frank about that. You're getting along with Andy Butler?"

"He's a great man, sir," I said.

"In the spring, if you want," he told me, "I'll transfer you out of the gym, make you Andy's assistant in the garden out here."

My stomach closed up like a day-blooming flower, but I knew better than to sound anything but delighted. "Thanks a lot, sir," I said. "I'm sure that would be wonderful."

"It's almost like being outside the prison," he said, turning to smile fondly at the garden, which was now, as the saying goes, covered with a mantle of white. A mantle of pale gray, actually, since the prison incinerator had not as yet been upgraded to match pollution-emission standards.

"I'm sure it's—nice, sir," I said. Damn that hesitation; I could only hope he hadn't noticed it.

Apparently he hadn't. Turning back to me, still with the genial smile on his face, he said, "But that's for the spring. If you continue as well as you're doing now, and I'm sure you will."

"Thank you, sir."

"For now, you're back on your regular assignment at the gym."

"Thank *you*, sir."

"That's all, Künt," he said. "Good luck."

"*Thank* you, sir," I said, and turned for the door. Behind me, the warden said, gently, "And there won't be any more of those notes, will there?"

Ung. Turning back, I said, "Warden, *honest*, that isn't me."

"But there won't be any more," he suggested.

Sincerely, but with terror, I said, "I hope not, sir."

"We both hope not, Künt," he said, and his smile—if this isn't an absurd statement—had teeth in it.

"Yes, sir," I said, and left. And walking back across the yard toward the gym, I chewed over these two new worries that I could add to the growing pile of them on my forehead. A promotion from the gym to the garden would just about finish me, wouldn't it? If I wasn't finished first by the appearance of another of those goddammed 'help' messages. If they weren't my doing, and they weren't, then I couldn't control their appearance or non-appearance. I had no way of knowing if or when another of the damn things would strike.

Biter bit. The practical joker is placed in a position where he can learn the trepidation and apprehension of the victim. Goody.

Ho, in one of the poems of his prison diary, says, "So life, you see, is never a very smooth business, and now the present bristles with difficulties."

But it's impossible to fret over difficulties forever, particularly when things are, at least for the moment, going right. I had completely forgotten my cares and woes by the time, four hours later, I entered Marian's apartment, Marian's bed and Marian, in that order; I wasn't worried at all.

"I thought you might forget me," Marian said, smirking.

"Ha ha," I said.

33

Alice Dombey needed culture the way the John Birch Society needs Godless Communism; it defined her existence and furnished her with purpose. Plump and matronly and as neat as a zeppelin, she was not at all what I'd expected from the wife of weasely Bob Dombey, not even after the fruitcake and the book. She managed to let me know within an hour of our meeting that she belonged to a dozen book clubs, subscribed to a dozen of the more cultured magazines, saved old copies of the Arts and Leisure section of the Sunday *New York Times*, had bought the imitation paintings all over her walls at different visits to the Greenwich Village Art Show, drove to places like Albany and Buffalo to browse in their museums, and had ferreted out a Monday Club of like-minded local ladies to join. "It helps us 'keep up' with current events," she told me, smiling in her bubbly way, and the quotation marks fairly hummed in her voice.

Marian loved her. The two women got along beautifully from the outset, Marian humoring Alice and Alice "allowing for" Marian, as she would undoubtedly herself have phrased it. Each permitted the other to feel superior, and what more could anybody hope for than that? The dinner party we had been invited to, at which I met Alice and at which Marian was introduced to the rest of the tunnel insiders, turned out to be a successful affair all the way around, though I did personally spend a lot of the evening twitching with leftover apprehension. I couldn't seem to get used to the idea that the boys knew that Marian knew and that it was all right.

My second day back in the gym I'd learned that one of my fears, about Phil and the others finding out I'd told a girl in town the truth about myself, had already happened, and I'd been wasting my time chewing my nails over that particular indiscretion. Max, immediately on my telling him and swearing him to secrecy, had gone straight to Phil and told him the whole story. He had also given Phil my side of it, the presence of Stoon and the absence of a sensible alternative, and finally he had given Phil an encouraging report about Marian herself. So the group had met and discussed the situation and eventually had decided it wouldn't be necessary to murder Marian and me after all. "You got a majority in the vote," Max told me. I said, "It wasn't unanimous?" and he said, "Don't worry about the past, Harry."

So Marian was now an insider, and I was the only one present with a date at the Dombey dinner party at which I finally met Alice, and which was given mostly in my honor, to celebrate my return to full privileges.

The dinner party itself was a bit unreal. Alice Dombey, wife of a convicted professional forger, produced an incredibly complex and tasty dinner (*Gourmet* was one of the magazines she subscribed to) for eight AWOL cons who sat around making polite conversation with one another. Alice beamed genteelly at everybody, used her knife and fork as though it were an intricate skill she'd learned from a correspondence course, and actually extended her pinky when lifting her coffee cup.

At the other end of the scale, and the table, there was Billy Glinn, absentmindedly snapping chicken bones and crunching through his food as though he'd wind up by eating the plates. Jerry Bogentrodder became silly and giddy in Marian's presence, coming on with her in the style of a collegian who has drunk too much at his first beer party. Max also came on with her, though both more subtly and more seriously; I was beginning to feel a bit ambivalent about that fellow.

As to the others, Phil and Joe spent most of the evening talking shop with one another: guns, alarms, lawyers, stolen goods. And Eddie Troyn kept popping in and out of his Captain Robinson persona—never in quite far enough to call me Lieutenant, but in enough for me to recognize the genial authoritarian style. And Bob Dombey, our host, was so clearly madly in love with his wife and his home, so patently proud of both, that the great warmth of his feeling filled the room with a kind of amber Dickensian glow.

Afterwards, Marian and I rode to her place in her Volkswagen, and she said, "I keep thinking it has to be a put-on. I know you're a practical joker, and this is a whole elaborate rib. No way on *Earth* those people are crooks."

"Oh, they're crooks, all right," I said. I hadn't mentioned the bank robbery, or the stings by which the others supported themselves, and though I was tempted now I once more refrained. Even with Marian I didn't feel that trust could be one hundred percent.

"Some of them I can believe," she said. "Like that monster Billy Whatsisname."

"Glinn."

"Right. And Eddie Troyn, your Army friend. He seems crazy enough to commit anything. And Max Nolan; I knew a long time ago *he* couldn't be trusted."

That made me feel better. "There," I said. "That's half of them already."

"Bob Dombey," she said. "That's no more a criminal than Santa Claus."

"You ought to meet Andy Butler," I said. "You can't tell a book by its cover, honey."

"That's catchy," she said.

"Don't be a smartass."

"And Jerry Whatsisname," she said. "What did *he* do, cheat in an exam?"

"He's a burglar and an armed robber," I said, "and a general strongarm man." I considered telling her that between one and three of the men at that dinner party had recently voted to murder the both of us, but that too I thought was best kept to myself. And I wondered which of them it had been, and just how close a margin I was alive by.

Conversation flagged after that. We arrived at Marian's, and in the bedroom I said, "Be sure to set the alarm for four-thirty. I have to get back to the prison."

She shook her head. "Sometimes," she said, "I think I would have been better off going to Mexico with Sonny."

"No you don't," I said, and a while later she said, "All right, I don't."

34

Friday, January 14th, five days after the Dombey dinner party. Five o'clock in the afternoon. Once again I sat in the window booth at the luncheonette, staring in dulled terror toward the bank past Billy Glinn's profile. Once again we were assembled here. Phil and Jerry and Billy and I, to rob that bank over there and that other bank over *there*, and this time so far as I could see we were going to do it. I kept praying for a miracle, such as that both banks would suddenly become swallowed by a hole in the ground, but no miracles were occurring. In half an hour the typewriter truck would arrive, with Joe and Eddie and the second typewriter Max had stolen for this operation, and we four would leave this table and walk across the street with our hands on the guns in our coat pockets, and we would rob those two banks.

Oh, God.

I had wanted to do something, I would have been willing to do something, but what was there to do? Another round of stink bombs would be a coincidence just too strong for somebody with the quick exasperated intelligence of a Phil Giffin to accept, and I did not want him thinking any more about practical jokers.

But what else was there? My mind seemed to work exclusively in the well-worn groove of practical jokes, and whenever I tried to come up with a scheme for thwarting the bank robbery it turned out to be no more than another practical joke. I was in the position of a man forbidden to operate within his specialty.

In fact, I had reached the stage now where my mind was teeming with nothing but practical jokes: jokes I'd done, jokes I'd heard of, tricks I'd pulled as a teenager and before. All sorts of foolish things. Phone somebody and ask if they're on the bus line: "Yes, we are." "Well, you better get off, there's a bus coming." Hang up and giggle. Phone a tobacconist and ask, "Do you have Prince Albert in a can?" "Yes, we do." "Well, let him out, he'll suffocate." Hang up and giggle. Call six cab companies and have them all send cabs to the same address, usually a disliked teacher. Hang up and giggle. Call—

It came to me. My head lifted, it was almost as though I'd heard the sudden faint *ting* of a bell. I looked at the luncheonette clock, and it was ten past five. Was there time? It had to happen before the truck got here, or we'd be worse off than ever.

I had to chance it. "I think I've got a nervous bladder," I said. I had to say that because I'd already been to the men's room twice in the past hour. Getting to my feet, I said, "I'll be right back."

"Right," Phil said.

The rest rooms were at the back, through a door and down a corridor to the left. At the end of the same corridor were the two pay phones. I fumbled a dime out of my pocket, dropped it in one of the phones, and then realized I didn't know the number.

I hung up, got the dime back, found the phone book on a shelf underneath the phone, and looked up the Fiduciary Federal Trust. Got it.

"*Douch*eeary Fedrul."

"The manager, please."

"Who's calling please?"

"The man who planted the bombs in your bank," I said. I looked over my shoulder, but the corridor was empty.

There was a tiny silence, and the female voice at the other end said, very quietly, "Would you say that again, sir?"

"You Establishment pigs are about to go up in smoke," I said. "I'm calling from the Twelfth of July Movement, we're the ones that made the raid on Camp Quattatunk, and we planted a couple bombs in that bank of yours this afternoon. They're going off at five-thirty. We don't kill people, just money and pig Establishment banks. So this is a friendly warning. Get your asses out of there before five-thirty."

"One, uh, one moment, please." She believed me; I could hear the jittering nervousness in her voice. "I'll put you on hold," she said.

A sudden vision came to me of the call being traced. "No, you won't," I said. "I gave you the word, so just heed what I said. Up the Revolution!" And I hung up.

I *did* have a nervous bladder. After a visit to the men's room, I returned to the table and sat down and looked out at a perfectly quiet normal street scene. It was eighteen minutes past five. There was no one visible inside the bank except the guard, who was standing by the front door with his usual calm.

What the hell had happened to that girl? Maybe she *hadn't* believed me, after all. But how could she take such a chance?

Twenty after. Twenty-three after. Why wasn't something *happening*?

"By God," Phil said, "I believe it's gonna work this time."

"Me, too," I said.

Twenty-five after. Twenty-six after.

Jerry said, "Here comes the truck."

"He's early!" I said, and I just couldn't keep the protest out of my voice.

"Just as well," Phil said. "We'll go in and get the fucking thing over with before something *else* goes wrong."

The red truck stopped in front of the bank. Joe, moving with such studied casualness, such elaborate calm, that I would have mistrusted him from half a mile away, got out of the truck, slammed the door, and walked around to the back to get the typewriter.

"Get ready," Phil said, and a siren sounded in the distance.

Joe froze, his head and arms in the back of the truck.

Jerry said, "Oh, no."

Oh, yes. Joe was in motion again, slowly removing the typewriter, but then the police car slowed to a stop directly behind the truck, its front grill practically kissing the seat of Joe's pants, and both cops jumped out of the car and ran over to the bank entrance. The guard opened for them, as Joe with the same slow elaborate unconcern put the typewriter back inside the truck, closed the rear door, sauntered around to the driver's door, climbed in, and drove slowly and safely away.

A crowd was forming in front of the bank. The flasher light was revolving atop the police car. The other employees had now come running from the rear of the bank, and a great deal of conversation was taking place between them and the cops in the doorway.

And more sirens were sounding, coming this way.

Phil put his right elbow on the table and rested his jaw in the palm of his right hand. I have never seen anybody look so disgusted in my life, and I've seen people drink salted coffee, put their feet into shoes half-full of strawberry jam, and enter beds in which the sheets have been liberally treated with lard. But Phil topped them all.

A fire engine arrived. Another police car arrived. Another fire engine arrived.

Phil said, "Jerry—"

"I know," Jerry said. He got up and left the luncheonette and went across the street, mingling with the crowd around the bank.

"What a mess," I said.

Billy Glinn was frowning like a Parker House roll. "I don't get it," he said. "I just don't get it."

A bomb squad vehicle arrived; on a truck bed stood the world's largest wicker basket, painted red. "Holy Jesus," Billy said.

Jerry came back across the street. He came in and sat down and said, "Bomb scare."

Phil looked at him. "Bomb scare," he said.

"Some revolution group planted bombs in the bank," Jerry said.

Phil took a deep breath. I thought he controlled himself very well. "I don't piss off all that easy," he announced, "but I'm getting there."

"One thing," Jerry said, hopefully, trying to make Phil feel better. "At least Joe kept the typewriter this time."

35

The following Monday, Max and I took an apartment together in town.

He had mentioned the idea before, but we hadn't done anything about it, and when he brought it up again on Saturday, the day after the third abortive attempt to rob the bank, I spoke with him frankly about my feelings of ambivalence toward him. He had, after all, broken a promise to me to keep a secret of mine, and he had also come on a bit heavily toward my girlfriend during the Dombey dinner party.

He said, "Yeah, I've been meaning to talk to you about that. Why I talked to Phil is, we got a very delicate arrangement here, and I think it's a bad idea if we start keeping secrets from one another. You'd explained the situation to me in a way that I had to go along with, and I figured I could pass it on to the others and they'd go along with it, too. And they did."

"Why didn't you tell me you'd do that?"

"Argue with you? You were *terrified*, man, you figured if the boys found out it was all up. So I kept you calm, and I carried your message, and it worked out."

It all made sense, and I believe it was all basically true, but I also remembered that the vote to keep Marian and me alive had not been unanimous. On the other hand, I also remembered that it was Max who'd told me that. And it had, after all, worked out. "But what about Marian?" I said.

"I come on to all the girls, man," he said. "They expect it. But I'm not gonna steal your chick. Ask her yourself."

All right, he wasn't. I knew Marian, and I knew Max wouldn't steal her even if he wanted to. So that was also okay.

If you wait to make friends exclusively with people that you don't have to feel ambivalent about at all, you won't have many friends. "So we'll take an apartment," I said, and on Monday we did, using the previous day's local newspaper.

The first place we looked at was a pleasant enough apartment, but the landlady was a compulsive talker, and her talk was limited almost exclusively to questions—"You boys born around here?" "Do you know Annie Tyrrell, works at the Officer's Club out to the Camp?" and so on—and both Max and I agreed at once that she'd drive us crazy within a week. There weren't enough lies in the world to satisfy her craving for answers, and God knows we didn't have any truths to tell her.

At the second place, an attic apartment in a private home with a tacked-on outside staircase to give the place a separate entrance, the landlady didn't talk too much at all. In fact, she very nearly talked too little; we were on the verge of taking the place when she let it drop that her husband was a guard over at the prison. "Sorry, lady," Max said, as we left her attic with orderly haste, "but heights give me nosebleed."

The third one was it. The block was neat, quiet, residential—very like the one around the Dombeys' house, but without that giant prison wall across the street. The house had an enclosed front porch full of mohair furniture, and the woman who responded to our ring, a frail faded skinny lady in her fifties, told us her name was Mrs. Tutt. She spoke in a failing voice, her brow was furrowed with anxiety, she constantly washed her hands together or clutched her bony elbows, and she seemed ever to be on the edge of telling us the reason for her despair. When I mentioned the ad for the furnished apartment, she said, "Oh, yes," speaking so mournfully I fully expected her next to say that unfortunately it had just burned to the ground.

But she didn't. Instead she said, "I'll show it to you," and came out of the house to lead the way around to the driveway and back toward a simple white clapboard one-car garage. "We don't have a car any more," she said mournfully, "since Roderick had the accident."

I felt I didn't want to ask any questions.

The garage was the apartment. It stood at the rear of the property, flanked by a nicely green back yard, and it had been converted to living quarters, but not very much. It still, for instance, had its original overhead door; basically, one entered the place by lifting the living-room wall.

Inside, a plywood platform had been built over the original concrete flooring, with plumbing and electric wiring in the underneath space. Green-flecked indoor-outdoor wall-to-wall carpeting covered the living-room plywood, which bounced gently beneath our feet, like a discreet trampoline.

"Elwood's quite a handyman," Mrs. Tutt said, and washed her hands in despair.

The living-room walls were cheap maple paneling. With the door up, nothing showed of the front wall but a length of rope dangling from one corner of the cardboard-like dropped ceiling. Max pulled this rope and the wall door descended, revealing a paneled interior.

Mrs. Tutt said, "In the summer, you could leave that open and have a nice breeze."

The furniture in the room seemed to have come from some motel's bankruptcy sale: sofa, chairs, end tables, coffee table, all repeating the maple-tone motif of the paneling. Washed-out prints of Caribbean-scene watercolors were spotted around the walls, including two fastened to the wall door.

Max and I explored deeper. The one bedroom was seven feet long and six feet wide. Grayish paneling, blue-flecked indoor-outdoor carpet, one window in the side wall. A double bed, a maple dresser, a maple chair. Behind a line of louvered doors in the end wall were closets.

The bathroom. Three feet by four. One window. Toilet, sink and shower, all basically built on top of one another. Lavender tile.

The kitchen. Avocado sink, avocado stove, avocado refrigerator. Yellow formica counter, the size of a pizza box. A wallpaper of avocados on a yellow background. Yellow metal cabinets. An extremely narrow window over the extremely narrow sink. Floorspace the size of an airmail stamp, covered in yellow vinyl tile.

"Elwood laid it all out himself," Mrs. Tutt told us, and through her despair a note of pride could be heard in Elwood's accomplishment. "He didn't have no architect to help him or nothing."

"Mm hm," I said, and Max said, "Is that right?"

Mrs. Tutt became silent. She had shown us everything, she had regaled us with her store of anecdotes—Roderick, Elwood—and now there was nothing left but our decision. Clutching her elbows, hunching her shoulders, she gazed dismally at us.

Max glanced at me. "What do you think?" he said.

I looked around. It was amazing; here in this small upstate New York town, far from the world, thirty years of family-handymanism, of do-it-yourselfitis, had reached its apotheosis in this one-car garage. "It's," I said, "the ugliest thing I ever saw in my life."

"Right," he said.

"So we'll take it," I said.

"Right," he said. He turned to Mrs. Tutt, "We'll take it."

36

Life, like the Army, is a case of hurry-up-and-wait. After all the frantic chaos of December and much of January, life suddenly settled down into something that could almost be described as placid; though a life composed of four or five jail-breaks a week can never truly be described as placid, I suppose.

Nevertheless, calmness had settled, and God knows I was grateful for it. The apartment was a boon, a base, a lovely refuge from the world, though in fact I used it less often than I did Marian's place. But just knowing it was there, it was mine, gave me a feeling of stability and safety.

Then there was Marian. I think what I loved about her most was her inability to take me seriously. She thought it was *funny* that I was an escaped con, that I had been spending months walking a tightrope between various horrible contingencies. Whenever we talked, and particularly when I spoke miserably and grimly about all the problems facing me, the end result was always that Marian would become helpless with mirth. How she loved to laugh!

She also gave me a book called *The Trickster* by Paul Radin, which was all about a cycle of myths among American Indians concerning a trickster figure, a prankster or practical joker, whose symbolic meaning was much more than that. He was both creator and destroyer, both good and evil, both helpful and harmful, and by the end of the cycle he had outgrown his pranks and had gone to work to make the Earth a useful place for mankind. "The trickster is the undifferentiated form," Marian told me, after I'd read the book. "He doesn't know who or what he is or what his purpose is. He gets into a fight with his arm because he doesn't realize it's part of him. He wanders and gets into trouble because he doesn't have any goal. At the end he matures into self-awareness, and finds out he's supposed to help human beings, that's why he was sent to Earth. I think maybe you were like that, all practical jokers are like that. They don't know who they are yet, it's a case of arrested development."

"Seems like a roundabout way," I said, "to tell me I'm childish." Which also made her laugh.

As to the robbing of the banks, that had temporarily ceased to be a problem. Not that Phil or the others had given up their ideas of committing the robberies, not at all. Quite the reverse; Phil, battered by fate and failure, simply became more and more dogged, hunching his shoulders and setting his teeth and looking increasingly disgusted. And the others followed his lead; none of them wanted to quit.

Well, they might as well quit. All at once I was full of ploys. Within three days of the bomb scare phone call, I had two more stunts to pull, and the sudden conviction that I'd *never* run out of ideas. How silly I'd been to go into despair; my mind had come through in the clutch, hadn't it?

The next scheduled bank robbery was for Friday, January 28th, two weeks after the bomb scare attempt. I was ready well in advance, and this time I wouldn't stop it by doing anything to the bank. Instead, I took a walk late Thursday night, went over to where the typewriter repairman kept his truck, and did everything to that poor truck that I'd ever done to *any* vehicle. All at once.

I felt rather bad about that, though. Not only because it was a kind of backsliding, a return to a renounced former self, but also because of the trouble I was making the typewriter repairman.

But I had no choice; it was either inconvenience for him or utter destruction for me.

So that truck got the business. Sand in the gas tank was merely the garnish. Wiring was ripped out, radiator hoses were punctured, the gas pedal spring was removed…I don't want to repeat the whole catalog. Suffice it to say that when I was finished the only way that truck was going to leave that parking space was behind a towtruck. Which gave me my last bit of vandalism: I removed the lug nuts from the rear wheels. The truck would be towed less than a block before the rear wheels would fall off.

The following afternoon, when Joe and Eddie didn't show up at five-thirty, Phil began to get very grim-looking. Jerry, who told me later that he'd been afraid Phil might go berserk, might leap to his feet, pull out a pistol and start shooting everybody in sight out of simple frustration, began to try to placate Phil with reassurances and hearty little pep talks that sounded as hollow as a snare drum. He was still being desperately cheerful, in fact, at ten minutes to six, when a cab pulled up in front of the luncheonette and Joe and Eddie climbed out, Joe carrying the typewriter and Eddie wearing his guard uniform beneath his overcoat. Phil just looked at them through the window, and nodded. He didn't say a word.

"The truck wasn't there," Joe said, and though much discussion followed—everybody talking except Phil, who was dangerously quiet—there was really nothing else that anybody could add to that. So far as I know, none of the gang ever did find out why the truck hadn't been in its proper place that day.

The next robbery attempt was on Monday the fourteenth of February, and I'd been ready with my counterattack to that one for nearly a month, but when the time came I didn't have to do anything at all. God stepped in and gave me a hand, for which I was grateful; the northeast got one of those record snowfalls without at least one of which no northern winter is complete. *Everything* was closed that day, including both banks. And all the schools; instead of robbing a bank, I spent that day tobogganning with Marian. That was the day I discovered it actually is possible to have sex outdoors during a snowstorm. With a toboggan beneath you and a blanket above you, body heat will do the rest. And there ain't nothing like sex to produce body heat.

It was just around this same time that Andy Butler got the word that he was being thrown out of prison. *Clemency* it was called, but it was the same inclement thing that had been done to Peter Corse: throw the old men out of jail. In Andy's case, he was literally being thrown out into the snow.

Everybody felt bad about it, even the guards and the warden. The prisoners got up a petition, asking the Governor of the state to permit Andy to stay, but nothing came of it. We did have a speech from the warden in the mess hall one noontime that I happened to be present for—I was the only tunnel insider there—in which he tried to explain that it was impossible to get the message across to administrators or Civil Service people or public officials that there were men who wanted to be in prison, who were better off in prison, and who should be permitted to stay in prison. "Ideas like that contradict everything such officials believe," he said. "They're trying to *punish* you men. Telling them some of you *want* to be here could only confuse them at the best, or actively annoy them at the worst."

Most of the prisoners were more direct individuals than that, and rather than try to work out the intricacies of the warden's thought most of them merely decided the son of a bitch didn't care and was only protecting himself and was the enemy anyway, so what can you expect?

Andy had been given a month's warning, meaning he had to

leave on Saturday, March 12th. He himself told me, though, in one of the few evenings we shared together in the cell, that he had known of this for a long time. "I knew it was coming when old Peter got it," he said. "I was given private word from one of the trusties that my name was going to be on the next list."

"I'm really sorry, Andy," I said.

He gave me a smile that wasn't quite as sunny as usual. "You take the good with the bad," he said. "It won't be so rough on the outside. Maybe I'll get a gardening job somewhere."

"You won't see your garden here come up."

His smile shifted a bit more, but he said, "That's all right, Harry. I know how I planted it in the fall. I can see it in my mind's eye. I'll know when it's growing, and what it looks like."

"I'll get somebody to take a picture of it," I said, "and send it to you."

"Thanks, Harry," he said.

My harping on the garden like that was, I must admit, only partly caused by my sympathy for Andy. His removal also, of course, meant that I wouldn't be transferred from the gym in the spring to be his gardening assistant; the eviction of Andy Butler had saved for me the life I'd been constructing for myself, and though I truly did feel very badly for him, I must admit I also wallowed somewhat in my own sense of relief.

Then there was the ongoing bank job. The next date for its launching was Friday, the twenty-fifth of February. This was the sixth try at robbing those two banks, and in my conversations with the others it seemed to me the general consensus of opinion had divided itself into two camps: those who were dogged and fatalistic, and those who were ready to forget it and go think about something else. Phil was the captain of the dogged ones, and Max was the most outspoken of the defeatists, with the rest of us more or less raggedly lined up behind one or the other.

Eddie Troyn was strongly on Phil's side, of course, he being a man who had already expressed his belief that one never aborts the mission. Billy Glinn was also with Phil, but in his case I think it was because his attention span was so short that he wasn't truly aware of the grinding frustration of all this to the same degree that the rest of us were.

On the other side, Jerry was almost as big a quitter as Max, and I also permitted myself a statement from time to time doubting the wisdom of persisting in the teeth of all these indications of a jinx on the job. Neither Bob Dombey nor Joe Maslocki would ever allow themselves to be pinned down to an opinion on the subject, but public opinion believed that Joe leaned toward Phil's point of view and that Bob leaned toward Max.

Which left us split down the middle, four and four. But even if it had been lopsided, if it had been seven against one, with Phil the only one wanting to go on, I believe that his determination, his bulldog refusal to let go, would have carried the day just the same. Phil was going to rob those banks, he'd decided to rob them, and he was damned if *anything* was going to stop him.

I must admit I did do some idle thinking from time to time about providing Phil Giffin with the kind of accident he'd once considered for me. But I'm not a violent man by nature, particularly against somebody as all-around frightening as Phil Giffin, so I did nothing.

And February 25th arrived. That was all right; I was prepared. Earlier in the day I had made my visit to Western National, the *other* bank, and left my two little packages in wastebaskets there.

More bombs, yes, but not stink, not this time.

Smoke.

When, at five past five, the billows, the clouds, the profusions of thick black smoke began dribbling from every nook and cranny of that pseudo-Greek temple, when the ten-foot-high gold-painted metal front door was thrown open by a coughing wheezing guard, followed by an unrolling sail of cloud that came beating out of that bank like the ghost of one of those tanks out at Camp Quattatunk, and when, in addition, the distant sound of sirens was heard yet again, coming this way, Phil did not lose his temper. No, he did not.

What he did, he got to his feet, slowly, deliberately. He stood next to the table, looking straight out through the luncheonette window at the shimmying wall of smoke now obliterating the entire other side of the street, and in a quiet, calm—yet grim— voice he said, "I am going to get those banks. I'm telling you, and I'm telling those banks, and I'm telling God and all the saints, and I'm telling anybody who wants to hear it. I'm not giving up. I'm going to be here twice a month, every month, for the rest of my life if it takes that long, and you fucking people are going to be here with me, and those fucking banks are going to be waiting over there, and one of these times, I'm going to rob those two banks. I'm going to do it."

Saying which, he left, and went straight back to jail, and stayed in his bed for the next three days. But we all knew that on Monday, the fourteenth of March, we would be back in that luncheonette.

And, apart from my growing terror of Phil, I had run out of tricks again.

37

And besides that, another of those damn 'help' messages showed up.

With the advent of Marian and the apartment, I had been choosing mostly to spend nights off the reservation, covering for other members of the group who were away during the day. So I was in the mess hall for lunch that day, and it was at lunch that it happened. Since the call went out immediately, and rather urgently, for me to get my ass over to the warden's office, it's just as well I was present in prison at the time.

Warden Gadmore, when Stoon escorted me into his office, was looking very annoyed, though it was impossible immediately to tell whether he was annoyed at me or at the large plastic shampoo bottle dribbling vegetable beef soup down its sides onto the surface of his desk. I knew it was vegetable beef soup because I'd just had some for lunch, ladled out to me from one of the big vats they used on the serving line in the mess hall.

It turned out the warden was annoyed at us both. Glaring at me, he said, "Do you know what day this is, Künt?" Annoyed or not, by God, he pronounced my name right.

It was Monday, the seventh of March, and after a brief hesitation I told him so. He nodded, and through his annoyance he affected sadness; but I knew he was really just annoyed. The sadness was rhetorical. "It is just two months and two days," he said, "since I gave you your privileges back."

I had been worried when Stoon arrived to bring me to the warden's office, but I had tried to thrust fear away; after all, I hadn't done anything the warden could know about.

But someone else could have. I had deliberately avoided thought of the 'help' messages on the walk over, but now I knew the worst had happened. Feeling a cold inevitability, I said, "There's been another message."

"Very funny, Künt," he said, and gestured at the shampoo bottle. "It really does have its comical side, I must admit."

"I don't know what you mean, sir," I said.

"I mean the bottle found floating in the vat of vegetable beef soup," he said. He thrust a tattered piece of brown paper at me. "With this message in it!"

The same old message, scrawled this time with pencil on a wrinkled torn-off piece of a brown paper bag. I said, "The message was in the bottle?"

"By God, Künt," he said, "you are either a consummate liar or you have an imitator somewhere in this prison. I wish to *God* I could read your mind."

"So do I, sir," I said, thinking only of my innocence in connection with the message in the bottle. But almost immediately I thought of what else the warden would find in my head if he happened to look there, and I felt an incipient twitch in my cheek.

No no! If I started blinking and twitching and scratching he'd *never* believe me! To distract myself, not caring whether I was protesting too much or not, because the important thing was to regain self-control, I said, "Sir, if you could see inside my head you would find that I haven't performed one single practical joke since last December, since before you took away my privileges."

I said that in all sincerity, too, and I meant it, regardless of the things I'd done to the typewriter repairman's truck, and regardless of the smoke bombs in the Western National Bank's wastebaskets, and regardless of the bomb threat phone call to Fiduciary Federal Trust. Those had not been practical jokes.

They had been practical, in the sense of useful, but they hadn't been jokes. No, they had been deadly serious.

"I have only one question, Künt," the warden said. "If you aren't doing these damn things, who is?"

"I have no idea, sir," I said. "I wish I knew."

"Haven't you *thought* about it?"

"Yes, sir, I have. But I don't even have any suspects to mention. I just can't think of *anybody* who might be doing this stuff."

"Is there anybody here who knows about *your* practical jokes?"

"Good God, no! Not among the prisoners, sir."

He gave a somewhat grim smile. "I think I have to believe a response that forceful," he said. "But you realize, Künt, that not every prisoner in this institution could have performed these little tricks."

"Sir?"

"It requires a man with privileges," he said. "A man like you, with access to various parts of the prison closed to many of the inmates."

"Yes, sir, I see that."

He shook his head. "It just keeps coming back to you," he said. "I want to believe you, I want to believe that I'm capable of making an accurate estimate of a man, but goddammit Künt it just keeps pointing at nobody else but you."

"I realize that, sir," I said. "And I just don't have anything to say, except it isn't me."

He ticked it off on his fingers. "You have a record in this area," he said. "You have the kind of access needed by whoever is doing these things. And neither one of us can think of anybody else likely to be doing them."

It did sound damning, I had to admit it. "If I couldn't read my own mind," I said, "I'd be inclined to think I was guilty myself. I really can't argue with that."

"There's another point," he said. "Small, but significant.

None of these events occurred before you arrived here. And none of them occurred during the two weeks that I took away your privileges."

I thought I knew what was coming, and never has anyone awaited a sentencing with such mixed feelings. I was sure I was about to be relieved from attendance at the next bank robbery, which was beautiful with me since I had as yet no way to counter the thing, but of course simultaneous with that I would also be relieved from attendance at my sessions with Marian. That part wouldn't be so much fun. I waited, and said nothing.

Nor did the warden. He'd seemed about to go on, but instead he sat there, frowning at me, studying me, thinking about me, and once again his fingers began to go bunk-bunk. Except that this time they more nearly went blup-blup, because he had inadvertently drummed his fingers into the little pool of vegetable beef soup at the base of the shampoo bottle.

He gave a little start, looked at his fingertips with a glare of disgust that reminded me strongly of Phil, and pulled a handkerchief from his breast pocket to deal with the matter. While doing that, he turned his glower on me and said, "I don't believe in coming at a man from his blind side, Künt, so I'm going to give you fair warning. If this sort of thing happens again, and you don't have a rock-solid alibi, and there is no absolutely convincing alternate explanation, I will take you off privileges of any kind. And I will *keep* you off privileges until it happens *again*. If it happens while you're off privileges, in a way that could only be done by a man with access to privileged areas, I'll accept that as proof of your innocence."

"Yes, sir," I said. So I was reprieved once more, both for Marian and the bank.

If only once I could greet an event in my life without ambivalence.

"In the meantime," he said, "assuming you really are inno-cent, it might pay you to do some detective work on your own."

Be an informer, he meant, and I was more than willing to do so. "Yes, sir," I said. "I'll be trying to find him, I promise."

"That's good," he said. He considered me, seemed to think of various other things he might say, and in the end merely shook his head slightly and said to Stoon, "Very well."

Outside, as Stoon and I walked down the corridor together, he said, "If it was me, I'd lock you in over in the restricted cells and throw the key away."

I was glad it wasn't him.

38

That Saturday Andy Butler left. The day before was a very emotional experience for everybody, and especially for Andy. The cooks prepared a special meal for him, and the mess hall that evening turned into a kind of testimonial dinner on Andy's behalf. It was a mark of his universal esteem that all eight of the tunnel insiders stayed in prison to attend that dinner.

Although silence—or at the most a kind of semi-whispered conversation—was the order of the day in the mess hall under normal circumstances, the rules were abrogated this time sufficiently to allow particular inmates to stand up and make acclamatory speeches, which tended to make up in enthusiasm what they may have generally lacked in polish.

Then I abruptly found that I too was making a speech. I had been sitting near Andy, watching him smile, watching him blink back tears and swallow down the emotions welling up within him, and at a moment when a speaker had finished and the applause had died down without anyone immediately leaping to his feet damned if *I* didn't leap to my feet. "Gentlemen," I said, and as the faces turned eagerly, happily toward me, I stopped dead.

What the hell was I doing? I'd been ready to Confess All. I'd been just about to tell them the entire truth about my past as a practical joker, and how Andy's good example, his ability to get along with all the people around him, had cured me. Good Christ, talk about sealing your own death warrant!

They were all watching me, hundreds of faces staring up, waiting. I had to say something, I realized that, but it wasn't going to be the thing that had driven me to my feet, not by a long shot. "Uhh," I said, "I don't really have much to say." Well, that's beautiful, I thought. "It's just, uh, that Andy and I have been cellmates for almost three months now, and I want to say he's the finest man I ever lived with."

Christ. The whole place cracked up; gales of laughter bounced off the gray walls. I stood there for a few seconds, but they weren't going to quiet down so I could say anything more, and in any event I couldn't think of anything rational that I could add. So finally I just sat down again, and after a while somebody else got up, and then somebody else, and gradually I began to feel that my contribution was maybe going to be forgotten after all.

At the end Andy got to his feet. He thanked everybody, he told us he was choked up with emotion, and he said he'd never forget us. "I can only hope the people on the outside are as good as you fellows," he said.

He glanced my way just once, and I saw a twinkle in his eye, and I thought, Don't do it, Andy, don't make a joke, I don't think I could stand it. I winced, bracing myself for it, but the moment passed, he said nothing, and at the finish he was given a standing ovation and a round of "For He's A Jolly Good Fellow."

The next day, just before he left, he told me he'd thought of one or two comments he might make at that juncture, but that when he'd seen my stricken expression he'd decided to let it ride. "A joke wouldn't have been worth it," he said. "Not the way you were going to feel. And I didn't want them razzing you for a couple months later on."

Another lesson for me. "Thanks, Andy," I said. "You really are a prince."

He laughed, and we shook hands. "Don't let problems worry

you, Harry," he said. "They'll work themselves out pretty soon. Just hang in there."

Hang in there. Two days from now, I thought, I'm going to rob a bank. "I'll do my best, Andy," I said. "Good luck."

"Good luck to you, too, Harry."

39

But it was going to take more than luck.

With my mind so completely distracted by the problem of the authorship of the "help" messages, plus the further distraction of Andy Butler's departure, I still hadn't come up with a bank robbery stopper by Monday afternoon. So once again, for the fifth time, here I was in the luncheonette with Phil and Jerry and Billy, waiting for the red typewriter truck to arrive at five-thirty.

(It was the fifth time I was here, and the sixth time the others were here, but it was actually the seventh robbery attempt. The time of the great snowstorm, a month ago, we hadn't bothered to come to the luncheonette at all.)

My mind will not fail me, I thought. Four o'clock, four-fifteen, four-thirty. My mind will not fail me. I've come up with last-minute solutions before this, and I'll do it again.

But not the same solutions. I didn't dare repeat any of those earlier ploys, for fear the repetition would click something in Phil Giffin's mind. I was straining coincidence to the breaking point as it was, though in fact two of those instances, the bank party and the snowstorm, were simply natural occurrences that nobody could have set up in advance. But three of the remaining four had involved bombs of one sort or another—stink, smoke and scare—and that was permitting the ice to get a trifle thin.

That's all right, I told myself, as five o'clock came by, you'll think of something. You'll think of something, Harry. You always think of something.

Not a bomb. Nothing to the truck. Not a phone call.

Tip the police? Tell them a robbery was about to happen?

No. They wouldn't rush to the scene with sirens blaring, they'd sneak up and capture us the instant we made our move.

I'll think of something. I'll think of something.

Five-fifteen. Five-twenty-five.

If I pretended a heart attack? No, they'd go on anyway, and I couldn't afford to be taken away in an ambulance to some hospital's emergency ward, where they'd request identification.

Five-thirty.

I'll think of something.

The typewriter repair truck arrived. It was a new truck, also a red Ford Econoline van just like the old one; I must have really done a good job on that earlier truck.

So I can do a good job now. I'll think of something in just a second.

Joe got out of the truck, walked to the back door, opened it.

Maybe the Third World War will start. Or we'll get a visitor from outer space.

Joe took out the typewriter, carried it over to the Fiduciary Federal door. Eddie, overcoat on over his guard uniform, climbed out of the truck and walked over to stand with Joe.

"I don't believe it," Phil said. I looked at him, and his expression was awed, as though he were seeing a vision of the Virgin Mary, who was telling him how to attain Peace on Earth.

The bank door opened. Joe and Eddie walked in.

"Let's go," Phil said.

I'll think of something, I thought. I got to my feet with the others, and we trooped out of the luncheonette and across the street.

I'll think of something. Wait a second now.

40

Eddie Troyn opened the door to us. He'd taken off his over-coat, revealing his guard uniform, and I had to admit he looked perfect in the part. "Everything's fine," he assured us, and it took me a second to realize he'd said that exactly the way a bank guard would. He was calm, quiet, a bit hushed.

There was just something about Eddie and a uniform. Whenever he put one on, he assumed the personality that went with it.

I'll think of something, I told myself, and the four of us stepped into the bank, and Eddie closed and locked the door behind us. And over to the right Joe Maslocki had put down the typewriter and had taken out a gun—one of the automatics Eddie and I had stolen from Camp Quattatunk—and was holding it aimed at the real guard, who was standing without moving.

It's too late, I thought. I couldn't believe it. We're robbing the bank, I thought.

41

I stood and pointed a gun at the woman in the tweed skirt and the man with the red tie while the man with the sideburns phoned his wife. Phil was pointing a gun at the man with the sideburns. Joe was pointing a gun at the bank guard, who had been relieved of his own gun, which Jerry now had in his pocket. Eddie, in his guard uniform, was standing by the front door, acting precisely like a bank guard; I was sure he thought he was a bank guard, and I hoped he wouldn't blow the whistle on us. Jerry and Billy, who would be operating the laser which Joe had brought in from the typewriter repairman's truck, were standing around waiting for the phone calls to be made before either of them could get started.

When the man with the sideburns finished telling his wife about the sudden unexpected audit that might keep him at work in the bank all night—he'd had to keep assuring her that there was no suspicion that he himself was an embezzler—he came over and took the place of the woman in the tweed skirt. That is, he became one of the two people I was pointing a gun at, and the woman in the tweed skirt became the person Phil was pointing a gun at, in the course of which she made a phone call to her husband explaining the business about the audit. In her case, the suspicion evinced at the other end seemed to have nothing to do with embezzlement: "You can call me right here at the bank any time you want," she said, with some asperity, "all night long." She seemed quite annoyed when she hung up and came back to be gun-pointed at by me again, while the man with the red tie took her place in front of Phil and at the phone.

None of the employees seemed more than annoyed or perhaps slightly worried by our presence, in fact, except the bank guard, who had been just about petrified with fear until he'd been disarmed, after which he calmed down considerably. But he still did twitch from time to time, and lick his lips, and look around nervously for somebody to appease.

Once we had all entered the bank and moved behind the partition to the area which held the private offices and the vault, we had immediately put on the black masks from the five-and-ten that Phil had bought back in December. They were ordinary domino masks, of the type the Lone Ranger wears. I don't know what I looked like, but the others looked like characters from nineteen-thirties comic strips rather than the Lone Ranger. Rough clothing, masks. Only the fact that we were all clean-shaven and had no speech balloons over our heads saved us from out-and-out obsolescence.

The man with the red tie, on the phone with his wife, had to follow up the story of the audit with a rather weary defense of his choice of banking as an occupation. "You knew I worked in a bank when you married me," he said at one point. Some sort of dinner party involving members of his wife's family had apparently been scheduled for this evening, and his wife was clearly of a mind that he was using the audit as an excuse for non-attendance. He denied this consistently, and ultimately with some vehemence, but I noticed that when he finished the call and came back over to be gun-pointed at by me again he did seem to have a faint smile hovering in the general vicinity of his lips.

Finally the guard, a somewhat pudgy elderly man with a red roll of fat around his neck, was escorted by Joe over to the telephone, and therefore made his phone call under the watchful guns of two tough guys with masks on. It did seem a bit excessive.

That is, he made his phone *calls*. First he had to call his wife and tell her not to hold dinner because of the audit, etc., etc. Then he had to call his daughter-in-law and tell her he couldn't babysit for her and her husband that evening because of the audit, etc., etc. Then he had to call somebody named Jim and tell him not to come over for checkers at his, the guard's, daughter-in-law's house this evening because he, the guard, would not be present because of the audit, etc., etc. It seemed a complicated social life for such an old man.

Finally, though, the bank guard's arrangements for the evening had been thoroughly rearranged and he left the phone and came over to stand with the woman in the tweed skirt and the man with the red tie and the man with the sideburns, all of whom had guns pointed at them by Joe and me, while Phil sat near the phone in case of problems, Eddie stayed up front doing his bank guard imitation, and Jerry and Billy took the laser into the vault to go to work.

All of this was what was happening on the surface. What was happening inside me was:

EEEEEE!!!

42

For those who have never tried it, let me say right now that bank robbery is a very boring occupation. So boring, in fact, that by six-thirty, a scant hour into the job, I had been bored completely out of terror, moral qualms and legal considerations, and dulled down into a torpid state of acceptability. So we were robbing a bank; what else was new?

The phone calling and other pre-arrangements had taken about half an hour, so it was just after six when Billy and Jerry started to work with the laser. Phil remained seated at the desk by the phone, the gun lying handy to his hand. Joe and I sat in swivel chairs, our guns resting in our laps as we continued to watch our four prisoners, who were sitting on the floor against a side wall. Eddie stayed up front, moving around like any bank guard.

Whenever any of our prisoners had to go to the toilet, it was my job to escort them, and to wait outside the door, once it had been established that neither bathroom had any windows large enough to permit an escape. And whenever one of them had to go, it was usually the guard. That man had kidneys every bit as bad as his nerves. Up and down, up and down; he punctuated my boredom with intervals of irritation.

Still, I suppose it would have been even worse just to sit there hour after hour, with no excuse at all for getting to my feet. What I really minded about all those trips to the men's room, I must admit, was the weight of the gun. I was toting one of the Colt .45 automatics Eddie and I had stolen from the Army, and it was amazing just how much that gun weighed. Or maybe it wasn't; the thing was, after all, made out of solid metal. Still, in movies people ran around with guns in their hands as though the things weigh no more than a soft drink straw. This automatic was the first handgun it had ever been my misfortune to hold, and it was *heavy*. Particularly because I didn't feel it was psychologically proper to let it hang straight down from the end of my arm, not with the prisoners watching. So whenever I walked around at all, following the bank guard or whoever on a potty run, I always made sure to keep the gun pointing fiercely at the person I was guarding. The strain on my wrist and thumb was really grinding after a while.

Then there was the mask. I don't mean it itched or anything as specific as that, but it was foreign, it was not a natural part of me. It pressed on the bridge of my nose, the eye-holes weren't absolutely aligned with my eyes, and every time I fussed with it the elastic band around the back of my head shifted around and started pulling hairs out. That can hurt.

All in all it was a very discomforting business, robbing banks, and I was looking forward to it being over just as rapidly as possible.

Which wasn't going to be all that rapid. Billy and Jerry were taking turns with the laser, spending five minutes on and five off, and they were evidently having slow going. They'd started at six, and by six-thirty they'd both stripped down to their jockey shorts. It was apparently getting very hot in there, in a fairly confined and mostly metal space, running a laser which was in essence melting a hole through the metal.

Through a lot of metal. A line of locked storage boxes, all containing stock certificates, covered the rear wall of the vault. First the doors of several of these had to be burned off and the smoking metal remnants carried out to cool in the anteroom. Then the partitions had to be burned away in further smoking chunks—enough partitions to make it possible for a man to move through there. After that the wall itself had to be burned through, leading to the wall of the Western National vault, plus God alone knew what further cabinets or other obstructions we'd find on the other side of that second wall.

Originally the idea had been to cut completely through into the second vault before assembling any of the money, but when the storage box doors were all burned away the leading edges of the exposed partitions were all too hot to touch. The air-conditioning system in the vault was working full blast, but not making much headway, and it was impossible for either Billy or Jerry to reach in among the partitions to do the work with the laser. So, while waiting for the metal to cool off, they began to fill the empty liquor store cartons that Joe and I brought in from the typewriter truck. Jerry and Billy, standing there in their masks and underpants, sweating like a metal bucket on a hot day and beginning to look a bit red, not unlike lobsters, held our guns pointed at the man in the red tie and the man with the sideburns and the bank guard with the kidneys and the woman in the tweed suit while Joe and I went out to the truck and got the cartons. Six of them that first time, three apiece. Eddie held the door for us, exactly like a real bank guard.

This happened a little after seven. Jerry and Billy loaded stacks of bills into the cartons until seven-thirty, and then went back to work with the laser again, cutting away the partitions.

That took until nearly eleven. Before that, around nine o'clock, the man with the sideburns said to me, "May I speak?" Until then, except for murmured conversation among themselves, the prisoners had all been very quiet, none of them talking to us at all. Not even to tell us we wouldn't get away with it, or any of the stock lines in this situation that they all surely must have heard enough times on television to be letter perfect in them.

But now one of them had spoken to one of us—the man in

the sideburns to me, requesting permission to speak. "Sure," I said, though I did glance sidelong at Joe, sitting near me. I thought of myself as merely an apprentice in this operation after all, maybe an auxiliary; the real pros should do any of the talking required.

But it was me the man in the sideburns had chosen to talk to; perhaps the portions of my face not covered by the mask looked less intimidating than the portions of Joe's face not covered by his mask. "As you know," he said to me, "none of us has been permitted to go home for dinner. I don't know about my companions, but I'm getting hungry. Would it be all right for us to have something to eat?"

How the hell did I know? I said, "Do you have any food here?"

"No, but we could send out," he said.

Send out? In the middle of a bank robbery? Helplessly, I said, "I don't think—"

"It's a fairly common practice," he assured me. "I suppose you've cased the joint—that is what you say, isn't it?"

I'd never said any such thing in my life. "That's what we say," I agreed.

"Then you know," he said, "that whenever we're going to be working here, we do order out for food." Then Joe said, "I'm getting a little hungry myself." He turned to Phil. "What about you?"

"Good idea," Phil said. "We'll order from the luncheonette."

The man with the sideburns said, "The place across the street? That's terrible. Durkey's is better, around the corner on Massena Street."

"Okay," Phil said. "You got the number?"

"I believe it's on the Rolodex on that desk there," the man with the sideburns said.

"Right." Phil found the Rolodex, twirled it, and apparently

found the number. "Right," he said again, and pointed at me. (We weren't using names with one another.) "Take everybody's order," he said.

So I took everybody's order. The man with the sideburns recommended the roast beef plate, which Joe and I both took, and the woman in the tweed skirt said the turkey diet plate was first-rate for anyone concerned with calories; Jerry took that. For the rest, it was a standard run of hamburgers, BLTs, and so on. Plus the usual run of coffees, with two teas; Jerry, and the man in the red tie.

I turned the list over to Phil, who looked at it, picked up the phone, turned to the Rolodex, stopped, looked at the list again, hung up the phone, and said, "I'm not gonna order out for ten people. There's only three, four people here at night. They'll know something's going on."

"Excuse me," the man with the sideburns said. "You could certainly go out and get the food yourselves, but in fact we occasionally do have up to a dozen people here through the dinner hour, in connection with audit or internal inventory or other procedures."

I knew I'd be the one sent out, I just knew it. So I said, "What do they care at the luncheonette? They'll just bring the order over, that's all."

"Not the luncheonette," the man with the sideburns said. "Durkey's, around the corner on Massena Street."

"I know," I said. "Durkey's."

Joe also came over to the desk where Phil was sitting. We three were clustered together now, with the four prisoners way the heck over on the other side of the room. Joe said, "You know, we better send out. We've seen them in the evening, you and me we both have, and they really do send out. And if we don't tonight, with the lights on in the bank and all, maybe somebody'll notice something and get a cop to check into it."

"The last thing we want," the man with the sideburns said, "is a shoot-out, or a hostage-type situation."

That was the last thing I wanted, too. I said, "I tell you what. Order for five, and I'll go out and get for the other five."

"Don't go to the luncheonette," the man with the sideburns advised me. "Go to Dur—"

"I know, I know. Durkey's, around the corner on Massena Street."

I thought he was slightly offended—not used to being interrupted, from the look of him. "That's right" he said stiffly.

Meanwhile, Phil was thinking over my proposition. "Fine," he said at last. "You get five, I'll call for five."

"Right."

So then we sat down and split the list into two parts, so that Phil would phone for all the larger items like roast beef plates, and I'd be getting the hamburgers. "I won't call for five minutes," Phil said. "Give you a little lead time."

"Fine." I put the list in my pocket and glanced at the man with the sideburns, but he didn't tell me to go to Durkey's around the corner on Massena Street. In that silence I walked up front again where I explained to Eddie—he was one of the hamburgers and regular coffees—that I was going out to collect a partial order, but that the rest would be delivered. He said, "Where do I get the money to pay for it?"

"Ask Phil." I had cash on me, and planned to be reimbursed.

"Okay," he said, and unlocked the door to let me out. As I was going through he said, "Take your mask off."

"Oh! Right."

So I went around the corner to Durkey's and put in my order. People were sitting around, eating, waiting for food. I'm in the middle of committing two bank robberies, I thought; what do you people think of that? They didn't think much of it.

I considered calling Marian, telling her to pack a bag and gas up the VW, and then the two of us would make a run for the border. Into Canada, get a job, establish a new name, make a new life. Never return, never be a party to this bank robbery again.

My package was handed to me. I paid for it, and went back to the bank. As I was sorting it out on one of the desks, and figuring out who owed me what, the other half was delivered, and Eddie came back to get the cash to pay for it. So Phil walked into the vault and came out with two twenty dollar bills. "Don't give him too big a tip," he warned Eddie, and handed me the other twenty. "Here. You paid out of your pocket, right?"

"This is too big a tip," I said.

He laughed. "Take it, take it," he said. So I took it, and he said, "See? You get nervous ahead of time, but not during the job. Am I right?"

"Absolutely," I said.

"I got you figured out pretty well, Harry," he said.

"You sure do," I said. Then we all sat down and ate, and as I said to the man with the sideburns later, he was absolutely right: there was no comparison between Durkey's and the luncheonette. "This roast beef plate is delicious," I told him, as I was finishing it. "Thanks for recommending it."

"My pleasure," he said. "We may have differences of opinion on some financial matters, but that doesn't mean we can't treat one another like human beings."

It's really encouraging to hear a banker talk like that.

43

By two in the morning, it had become obvious we weren't going to get into the Western National vault but Phil and Joe kept refusing to give up, no matter what reports Jerry and Billy staggered out with, and so another hour went by and it was after three before we finally gave up.

Before that we'd had our visit from the police. That was around eleven-thirty. Eddie had just previously come back to report that a patrol car had gone by three times in the last twenty minutes, and that he had seen the two occupants looking curiously at the lit-up interior of Fiduciary Federal. "Don't worry," Phil told him. "We're covered."

"I'm not worried," Eddie said.

I didn't entirely believe him when he said it, but I must admit he carried off the police visit with assurance and calmness. They stopped just in front of the typewriter truck out front, and both of them got out of their car. They walked over to the door, which Eddie unlocked and opened in order to greet them. They asked where Duffy was, and Eddie said Duffy was home with the flu, which was going around again at that time. They asked what was happening to keep people at the bank so late, and Eddie told them it was some kind of audit. Then they just hung around, chatting, and it was obvious that while they weren't exactly suspicious they weren't exactly satisfied either.

In the back, Jerry and Billy had suspended operations with the laser, and were panting together near the vault anteroom doorway, where they reminded me of a team of stagecoach horses who have just outrun the band of Indians. At the partition, Phil and Joe and I listened to everything that was happening up front So, I presume, did our four prisoners.

Finally, Phil muttered, "We got to take care of this." He went over to the man with the sideburns and, speaking quietly, said, "You know the cops on this beat, don't you?"

"Yes, of course."

"And they know you."

"I assume so."

"I'll tell you what you're going to do," Phil said. "You're going out where they can see you. Just walk across where they can see you, pick up a piece of paper off a desk or something, turn around and walk back here. On the way over, nod at them. You'd nod at them, wouldn't you?"

"Yes, I would."

"Fine. Nod at them."

"Very well," he said, and nodded. "Now?"

"Sure now."

The man with the sideburns got to his feet, brushed the wrinkles out of his suit, adjusted his tie and glasses, cleared his throat, and took a step.

Phil said, "I didn't threaten you."

The man with the sideburns stopped, and looked back at Phil.

Phil gave him a grin, from under his mask. It scared even me, and I was on the guy's side. "I don't have to threaten you," he said.

The man with the sideburns was a very calm type. "No, you don't," he said, and went out and did exactly what Phil had told him to. He picked up a piece of paper from a desk over there, nodded at the cops, and walked back. "Fine," Phil said. "Sit down again."

He gestured with the piece of paper. "I'll want to put this

back again if I may. I don't want any more disruption of files than absolutely necessary."

"Sure thing," Phil said. "Only wait a minute, okay?"

"Of course."

And by the end of that exchange the cops had left. Seeing a face they knew, in calm circumstances, had convinced them. They went away, the man with the sideburns put the piece of paper back on the desk where it belonged, and we settled down to inactivity and boredom again.

And the beginning of bad news from the vault. A total of ten cartons full of money had been packed from the Fiduciary Federal vault, which was all the cash Jerry and Billy found in there, but progress toward the Western National vault was slower than expected, and very difficult. The removal of the partitions had been a long slow process, requiring frequent intervals of no activity while metal was cooling, and the vault wall when they reached it turned out to be solid concrete, full of metal rods, heavy mesh and cable. Concrete was harder to laser than metal. They couldn't slice away great pieces of it the way they'd done with the partitions; instead, they had to more or less melt every bit of it, turning it from concrete into lava, boring an ever-widening circle and trying for tiny advantages.

The advantages were few, the disadvantages many. The concrete, in its molten form, ran down over other concrete yet to be melted, where it cooled and hardened again into something glasslike, much tougher than it had been before as concrete. Sometimes this glasslike skin wound up on top of concrete that itself had to be melted, so first the hardened lava had to be re-melted again.

Also, the lava was dangerous to be around; it occasionally splashed, sometimes popped, and constantly ran. Jerry and Billy were both pretty well covered with burns before very long, and neither of them was happy about it. They were also getting redder and redder from all the heat in the vault, and sweat was literally running down them like cataracts. They were drinking water by the gallon, but it wasn't enough; they were both losing moisture, and Jerry in particular could actually be seen losing weight. His red skin hung more and more loosely on his frame, and his face was drooping as though it were made of wax. Even Billy was wearing down, and I wouldn't have believed that possible.

But failure didn't enter anybody's conversation until shortly after midnight, when Jerry came out of one of his five-minute sessions in the vault, handed the laser to Billy, and came plodding moistly over to say to Phil, "I don't think we're going to make it."

"What?" Phil brushed it away at once. "Sure we'll make it," he said. "You're tired, sit down a while."

It was over an hour later, after one o'clock, when Billy for the first time said that it wasn't going to happen. "We didn't hit that other wall yet," he said to Phil.

"We'll hit it any minute," Phil assured him.

Billy shook his head. "We won't hit it at all," he said. "We'll never get through this first wall." Then he turned and went back inside and took his five minutes.

Between one and two, Phil and Joe gave Billy and Jerry frequent pep talks, which had no effect that I could see, and Eddie drifted back every once in a while to comment to the world at large that he didn't believe in aborting missions.

As for me, I kept quiet for some time, but eventually it seemed to me I had to start taking some sort of stand, so at the end of one of the pep talks I said to Phil, "You know, it's almost two o'clock now, and we still aren't out of this vault, much less into the other one. And we agreed we couldn't stay after five."

"They'll make it," Phil told me.

I didn't say anything that time, but twenty minutes later when we had essentially the same conversation I said, "They won't make it, Phil. We're just wasting time here, and making those two guys work harder than they have to."

"We won't quit," Phil said.

But we did. Jerry came out at three o'clock, gasping and weaving back and forth, and though Billy held his hand out for the laser Jerry walked right on by him, carried it over to where Phil was sitting at the desk, and dropped the laser onto the desk in front of him. "You do it," he said.

Phil just looked at him. It was hard to tell with the mask, but I think he was just bewildered, couldn't think of a thing to say.

"I'm not doing any more," Jerry said. "And neither is my buddy here. *You* do it."

"If there's a problem—"

"There's a problem," Jerry told him. "Go on in and take a look."

So Phil went in and took a look, and when he came out he seemed very shaken. "All right," he said. "So it didn't work out. We got half the dough."

We'd had possession of half the dough by six o'clock, nine hours ago, which neither I nor anybody else pointed out. Maybe because we were all too tired.

So. Jerry and Billy wearily dressed themselves, while Joe tied and gagged the four prisoners under the watchful gun of Phil. I began carrying liquor store cartons of money up to the front, where I got to be the one to inform Eddie that we were aborting the mission. "I knew we should have held onto those hand grenades," he said. "Always prepare for the unforeseen, that's the way to run a successful operation."

By three-fifteen we were out of the bank. The cartons were in the typewriter truck, which Joe and Phil and I traveled in to the Dombey house. We unloaded the cartons into the basement, the Vasacapa corridor, and as we were finishing Jerry and Billy and Eddie showed up in a car they'd just stolen for the purpose. Joe took the typewriter truck away to return it, Phil took the stolen car away to dump it, and the rest of us crawled through to the gym in the prison, leaving the cartons in the Dombey basement.

And that's how I helped to rob a bank.

44

The two months following the robbery were completely un-eventful, which I found startling. I was now a bona fide graduate bank robber, a hardened criminal, no stranger to guns and vio-lence; and yet I was completely the same. And so was the world around me, the pattern of prison and tunnel and apartment and Marian, all exactly as it was before.

Except that my financial problems had been relieved. I'd been eating into the three thousand my mother had sent me, pretending to commit stings now and again to explain where my cash was coming from, but that money couldn't last forever. Particularly once I had an apartment of my own, and a girl-friend. Now, with an additional nine thousand in the kitty, I might even make it through the two years till parole.

Yes, nine thousand. We'd been hoping for a top of a hundred fifty thousand from the two banks, but of course we'd only managed to rob the one. Luckily, our half-accomplishment had been at the high end of our estimates. Just under seventy-three thousand dollars had been carried out of Fiduciary Federal in those liquor store cartons; divided equally among eight men it came to nine thousand one hundred twelve dollars apiece.

Not bad for one night's work. That's one way to look at that number, as my fellow conspirators did. Pretty goddam small pickings to risk a life sentence for, that's the way *I* looked at it. I just didn't have the proper criminal attitude.

Nevertheless we'd done it, and apparently we'd gotten away with it. Marian had no idea I'd been involved in the big bank robbery—the most exciting crime in Stonevelt's history—and I saw no reason to burden her with the knowledge. As to Joe and Billy and the rest, now that the robbery had actually been performed they were all as calm and gentle and easygoing as well-fed horses. And lazy. Despite their sudden wealth, most of them hardly took a turn outside the prison at all for a while, meaning much more opportunity for me to be out; having to return every damn day for breakfast and dinner was becoming an annoyance, in fact.

So March went out like a lamb, with April gamboling after. The weather improved, Marian and I took some outings in her Volkswagen, and Max developed a pleasant new girlfriend named Della; the four of us double-dated sometimes. I was happy and content, playing no practical jokes, putting on a little weight, wallowing in my happy life. Then, on Wednesday, the twenty-seventh of April, the Mad Message Maker struck again.

45

By now, I had become resigned to the fact that whenever the warden sent for me it was going to be another of those damn notes, and all I hoped as I followed Stoon across the yard and through the administration building to Warden Gadmore's office was that *this* time I would have a good solid in-prison alibi. This thing hanging over my head was the only serpent left in my paradise, and I wanted to be rid of it.

But when we walked in the Catholic chaplain was also present in the office, standing to one side, hands folded together in front of his chalk-stained black robe, and I got confused. What did *he* have to do with anything? Father Michael J. P. Flynn his name was, and though I'd never had any direct dealings with him, I had seen him around the prison and I knew who he was. But I wasn't Catholic, so why was he here? And why was he glowering at me in that disapproving way?

The warden was also glowering, giving me his had-enough look, his no-more-Mister-Nice-Guy-look. He was also giving me something small and white and crumpled. "Here," he said. "Take this and read."

"Read?" So I'd been right. "Another prisoner message," I said.

Warden Gadmore turned and nodded at Father Flynn, saying to him, "You see what I mean? Isn't he convincing?"

"Not particularly," Father Flynn said. A heavyset middle-aged man with a round white face and black hair emerging wildly from his head, eyebrows, ears and nostrils, Father Flynn was known to be short-tempered, and at the moment he seemed more than moderately angry at me. Glaring in my direction he said, "Be careful how you treat that. It's the Body of Our Lord and Savior Jesus Christ."

"The what?" I bowed my head to look more closely at the thing the warden had handed me. It was like an underdone Ritz cracker, round and white, slightly soft, folded in the middle. "It looks like an uncooked fortune cookie," I said.

"Very funny," the warden said. "Open it, and read your fortune."

"Open it," I echoed, and I didn't like this at all. "Be careful with it," Father Flynn warned me. "I consecrated the entire batch before I noticed anything wrong, so that is now a Holy Wafer. It is the Body of Our Lord and Savior Jesus Christ."

This time I understood him. What I was holding was a small round of unleavened bread, the wafer used by Catholics in Holy Communion. Once I'd unfolded it to its normal flat circle I could see exactly what it was.

I could also see the note in it; a narrow strip of paper, just like those in fortune cookies. I didn't have to open it to read what it said, but I did anyway.

Printed. Tiny letters, black ballpoint ink. I refuse to repeat the words.

"The thing that gets me, Künt," the warden said, when at last I looked up from the sacrilege in my hands, "is the timing."

"Timing, sir?"

He pointed at the wafer and note in my hand. "That was done," he said, "three days after the episode of the bottle in the vegetable soup."

"What?"

"The note in the bottle," he said, "occurred on March seventh, just one month ago tomorrow. The Communion hosts used by Father Flynn are dated when they arrive here, to assure freshness, and the carton containing that particular host was dated March tenth. On that date, the carton arrived at the chapel, and spent the first night in a side room. The following morning Father Flynn locked the carton in his storage area in the chapel, and never took it out again until this morning. The *only* time those twelve hosts could have—"

"*Twelve?*"

"Yes, twelve," the warden said.

Father Flynn said, "Don't deny it, man. Guilt is written all over your face."

"Father— Warden—" But what was there to say? So the warden went on without further interruption: "The only time the hosts could have been tampered with," he said, "was the day and night of March tenth. Just three days after you gave me your solemn word this sort of thing would never happen again."

"No, sir," I said. "I never promised you it wouldn't happen again. I *couldn't* make a promise like that, because *I'm not the one doing these things*."

"Künt," the warden said, and his manner was more grieved than angry, "do you remember what I told you back in March, three days before these hosts were treated this way?"

"Yes, sir," I said.

"I told you at that time," the warden said, "that if such a thing ever happened again, and you failed to have a solid alibi or a provable alternate explanation, that I would take you off all privileges, and I would keep you off all privileges until such a thing happened yet again. Because that's the only way to prove your innocence."

"Yes, sir," I said, and I could practically feel myself grow shorter as I stood there, slumping down into myself.

Off privileges. I'd always known it was a possibility, but I'd done my best to ignore the knowledge. I'd made no real effort to find out who was actually leaving these notes around, and now it was too late. Off privileges. Indefinitely.

That was the worst of it, of course. The gym, the tunnel, Marian—the whole outside world—were being taken away from me, and there was no way to tell for how long. Would it be a week before another message, or a month, or a year? There was no pattern in the damn man's actions, no real guarantee that he'd ever strike again at all.

Oh, no; he *had* to do it again. He couldn't stop now.

A year and a half before I was eligible for parole: eternity. A year and a half without Marian, without going through the tunnel even once?

I was going to be a *prisoner*.

Help, I thought.

"I'm sorry, Künt," the warden said, possibly because my despair was showing in my face, "but I see no alternative."

"No, sir," I said.

"That's all," he said. "You may go."

Father Flynn said, "That's *all*?" He, I'm sure, would have preferred to see me burned at the stake.

But the warden told him, "Until we have proof one way or the other, there's nothing else to do." He nodded to me to leave.

"Yes, sir," I said. But as I started out Father Flynn called me, saying, "You. Whatever your name is."

"Künt, Father," I said. "With an umlaut."

"I'm not going to forget you, Künt," he said. "Nor I should think will several of the good God-fearing Catholic boys in this institution."

"I didn't do it," I said, but he'd turned his back on me.

And so I left the warden's office to go spend my season in Hell.

46

The month between Wednesday, April 27 and Friday, May 27 was the most horrible month of my life. In the first place, I was in prison.

Well, I hadn't been before. I'd been a visitor, a roomer, hardly a prisoner. But starting the twenty-seventh of April I was a *prisoner*, and no mistake.

What does a prisoner do? He gets up at seven-thirty in the morning and cleans his area. He eats breakfast. He exercises for an hour on the yard and spends the rest of the morning in his cell. He eats lunch. He exercises for an hour on the yard and spends the rest of the afternoon in his cell. He eats dinner. He spends the evening in his cell. He goes to bed. Much later, he goes to sleep.

What else does a prisoner do? Once a week he gets permission to go to the library and get three books. If he has full privileges he works at a job somewhere in the prison, but if he only has partial privileges he at least gets to wander around much of the prison area during the day and he gets to see a movie once a week and he gets to *sit down* in the library and read a magazine. But if he has *no* privileges he sits in his cell and tries to read his three books a week very, very slowly. No movies, no wandering around, no job, no nothing.

It is all extremely boring. Boredom is a horrible punishment, just about the grimmest long-term thing you can do to somebody. Boredom is very boring. It's very bad. I don't know how to establish this point without becoming boring, and God knows I don't want to do that.

The only respites I had from boredom were the occasional attacks made on my person by good God-fearing friends of Father Flynn. They were potentially dangerous, since they usually came after me in bunches of ten or twelve, but I quickly learned that whenever a tightly massed group of mesomorphs moved toward me I should move toward a guard, so they never managed to do much damage. However, it was the one time that my belonging to the gymnasium tough guy group didn't protect me from the violence endemic to a prison situation, and it helped to make me feel even more remote from my former existence.

I had little opportunity for practical joking, and in any event no desire. I was too depressed. I lived for the occasional verbal message from Marian passed on to me by Max—a written note would have been too dangerous to carry around—and every morning I woke up hoping that today another note would be found: today, today, today.

But it never was. The bastard had stopped again. Day after day went by, and no messages, and every day without a message was another day for the warden to become more convinced that I was the guilty party after all.

Until, on Friday, the twenty-seventh of May, Guard Stoon came to my cell to escort me once more to the warden's office. Feeling suddenly alive again, I said, "Did something happen? Another message? Is that why he wants me?"

"No," Stoon said. "Nothing's happened, no more messages, and it's been a month today. *That's* why he wants you." And there was a grim satisfaction in the way he said it.

47

We were crossing the yard, me in the lead and Stoon behind me, when we met some new fish coming the other way, still in their free-world clothing. I was passing them, head down, brooding about my own troubles, when I suddenly noticed that one of them was Peter Corse! "Peter!" I cried, and stopped so suddenly that Stoon walked into me.

Peter gave a great toothless smile and boomed out, "Harry, how are you! I told you I'd be back!"

"Move along," Stoon told me, and gave me a small shove.

I moved, but shouted back over my shoulder to Peter, "How did you do it?"

He too was being forced to move along. He cupped his hands and yelled, "I crapped in a graveyard!"

There's hope, I thought, there's hope for us all. If Peter Corse can get back in here, I too can surmount my difficulties. After all, I have all my teeth.

Yes, and half of his.

48

The warden was behind his desk, and Father Flynn was once again standing to one side. Stoon remained back by the door in his usual position, where he could comment on the proceedings by shifting his weight from foot to foot.

Warden Gadmore said, "Künt, I'm sorry to have to say that absolutely nothing has happened since I took you off privileges."

"I know that, Warden," I said.

"This business with the communion hosts," he said, "goes beyond a prank or a practical joke, you know. To a Roman Catholic, it's a very serious thing."

"I know that, sir," I said. "Some of Father Flynn's boys have been trying to impress that on me."

"I hope you listened to them," Father Flynn said.

"It's hard to listen to fists," I said.

The warden raised a hand. "Let's not get off the subject," he said. "The point is, this business of mocking religion is very serious, and Father Flynn wanted more action than a simple loss of privileges."

"Yes, sir," I said.

"Father Flynn," the warden said, "wrote to his Monsignor, who telephoned the Governor, who telephoned me."

"Yes, sir," I said. For the first time I was getting hints that maybe Warden Gadmore didn't like Father Flynn all that much, but his personal feelings toward the priest weren't going to do me any good at all. It had gone beyond that, I could see it already.

"I wanted you to know," the warden said, "that indictments are being drawn up against you. You'll be appearing before the Monequois County grand jury sometime in the next month. The Governor's feeling is that a trial will produce a definitive truth and end all this uncertainty."

"Yes, sir," I said.

"Unfortunately," the warden said, "that means the *whole* truth will have to come out, Künt."

"Sir?"

"Your former activities against your fellow inmates," he said.

My practical jokes. "They'll find out?"

"There's no way to avoid it."

Father Flynn, eyes flashing, said, "Find out what?"

"All in good time, Father," the warden said, and to me he said, "I wanted you to be forewarned. If you can possibly mend your fences, I think you should get to it."

"Yes, sir," I said. In despair, I looked past him, out at the garden, now a flashing panorama of spring colors. If only Andy could see that, I thought, trying to distract myself from contemplation of the mess I was in. All those flowers out there, sheets and trails and—

"Hee hee," I said.

They both looked at me. Father Flynn frowned very heavily. Warden Gadmore said, "What was that Künt?"

"Hee hee," I said again. "Ho ho. Ha ha ha ha ha ha—"

"What's the matter with you, man?" The warden was rising out of his chair, Father Flynn was staring at me in astonished disapproval, and Stoon was moving up from the rear. "Have you gone—"

"Look!" I shouted. "Look out there!" And I pointed at the garden. "Butler did it!" I yelled. "Butler did it!"

Oh, that garden! Oh, my, oh, *my*, that garden!

HELP spelled out in lavender-blue Sweet William amid banks of white pansies.

I in a line of white English daisies, and AM in pink azaleas, both surrounded by a swath of golden alyssum.

BEING in yellow tulips set off by white rock-cress.

HELD in orange cowslip on a sheet of mountain pinks.

PRISONER in a riot of blue pansies, Virginia bluebells, blue iris and blue forget-me-nots on a mat of white dusty-miller.

"He *knew*!" I yelled. "When you threw Peter Corse out he *knew* he was next, he told me so himself!"

They were all over by the window, staring out—even Stoon. I shouted at their uncomprehending backs, too relieved to do anything but go on yelling. "It was the style of the man!" I yelled. "The irony, the reversal! He wanted help because he *wasn't* being held prisoner, and he knew there wasn't any help, and this is what he did!"

They turned slowly to face me. The warden looked stunned. "It wasn't you, Künt," he said. "It wasn't you all along."

49

Much had changed in the month I'd been away. Eddie Troyn had received an abrupt and unexpected parole, and had become a paying boarder in the Dombey house. He'd gotten a job as a tollbooth attendant at the big bridge just north of town, and I must say he looked well in his uniform; but he missed the prison, and would occasionally sneak in on his day off from the toll-booth to spend an afternoon in his old haunts.

The new insider, taking Eddie's place, was a jolly, stout check-kiter from Buffalo named Red Hendershot. Max told me that when Hendershot had turned over his twenty-three hundred dollar entrance fee he'd said, "Here you go, the first good check I wrote in seven years," and they wouldn't let him through the tunnel until the check cleared.

There were other changes. Phil Giffin, Jerry Bogentrodder and Billy Glinn had pooled their nine thousand dollar bank profit, had rented a big loft downtown, and had opened a sort of school devoted to the martial arts; judo, kung fu, all that stuff. Max had grown very serious about Della, so much so that they were making plans to both return to college—she was also a dropout—once he got out of prison; in the meantime, Max wanted me to move out of our apartment because Della, in my absence, had moved in. So I wound up living with Marian, which wasn't at all unpleasant.

A few days after I got back, they gave me a surprise welcome-home party, in the Dombey house. All the insiders were there, plus Marian and Alice Dombey and Della. Toasts were drunk and I became maudlin. There had been questions during the past month about the reason for my removal from privileges, but

I'd evaded them all—until tonight. Tonight, when Jerry asked me just what had gone wrong to get me in trouble, I put my hand on his massive shoulder and I said, "Jerry, it's a long story." And I told him about the notes; the ones in the license plates, the one in snow on the roof, the one in the bottle in the soup, the one in the communion wafer, and finally the one made of flowers. By the time I'd finished my audience had grown, and several people wanted to hear it from the beginning, so I told it all over again. And then Alice Dombey, of all people, said, "But Harry, why did they think it was you?"

I knew now I'd gone too far to turn back; plus I was a bit drunk; plus I was maudlin. I was in a confessional mood, as when Andy'd had his farewell dinner. "Well," I said, drawing it out, "it's because I used to be a practical joker."

That one settled slowly. Phil got it first and Billy Glinn got it last, but they all did get it. The eyes looking at me became increasingly speculative, and then increasingly flat. Marian, standing beside me, put both hands on my arm, and I could feel that she was trembling slightly.

Joe Maslocki was the one who finally broke the silence, saying, "Maybe you better tell us about that Harry."

So I told them. "My parents were German refugees," I said, and I went right on through. It took them a long while to like it but when Della started laughing Max followed suit and a while after that Jerry began to grin, and then Billy chuckled some, and one after the other they found things to amuse them in my past depredations.

Phil was last and the least amused, and when I got to the bank robbery attempts the best he could show was a strained smile while the rest of them hooted with laughter. But it was far enough in the past now, and the robbery *had* at last been successfully pulled off, so nobody got really angry. In fact Joe Maslocki told me, "You're fucking ingenious, Harry. If you'd applied yourself to crime, you could have got rich." And a little later Max said, "Harry, I understand the smoke bombs, and I understand sabotaging the truck. But what I don't understand is, how did you do that storm?"

So I was finally out in the open, and it was all right. They knew my past, they knew what I'd done, they knew I wasn't really a crook in their league, but they accepted me anyway. The party ended late and cheerful, with expressions of eternal friendship in all directions, and over the next several weeks every single one of the tunnel insiders came around to ask my recipe for stink bombs, or how to do some other one of my former outrages. I had become a kind of professor emeritus of the practical joke—retired, but still sought out for my expertise.

Marian, of course, had been hearing about the bank robbery for the first time during that party, and she wasn't sure for a while whether or not she was going to forgive me for not trusting her completely. But I explained that rather than a question of trust it had been a case of me not wanting her to have to worry about me, so that too sorted itself out, and life at last did settle down to comfort and joy.

One afternoon in August, as Marian and I picnicked by a stream very near the Canadian border, I said, "You know, I keep thinking about Andy Butler."

"They never found him, did they?"

"I don't think they tried very hard. What could they charge him with? All he did was plant flowers."

"Yes, and all you did was park your car beside the Long Island Expressway."

I smiled, looking at the wild flowers along the stream bank. "Remember the book you gave me about the trickster?"

"It was about you."

"No, it was Andy. I was just an amateur, but he's the real thing. Knock knock."

She stared at me. "What?"

"Knock knock," I said.

"Okay," she said, laughing in bewilderment. "Who's there?"

"Amos."

"Amos who?"

"A mosquito just bit me. Knock knock."

"Did it really?"

"No, that's just the joke. The first half. Here's the second half. Knock knock."

"Who's there?"

"Andy."

"Andy? Andy who?"

"And he did it again." I grinned at her. "The butler always does it," I said.

"You don't do it any more?"

I spread my hands out on the grass; the black dirt was cool beneath the green leaves. "I feel as though Andy drew that whole thing right out of me," I said. "When I saw those flowers through the warden's window, it was like nectar, it was warmth running through me. I was my own sun, shining on those flowers."

"That was just relief."

"No, it was more than that. I was changed, like dough turning into bread."

"You won't change back?"

"Into dough? Can't be done." Nodding, tossing pebbles into the stream, watching the sun-glints scatter, I said, "What I'm going to do, when my sentence is up I'm going to stick around this area. Get a job, settle down, be Harry Kent forever."

Marian laughed at me. "Do you know, Harry," she said, "prison has rehabilitated you!"

And so it had.